THE SWISS FAMILY ROBINSON

by Johann David Wyss

Abridged by Nora Kramer

SCHOLASTIC BOOK SERVICES
New York Toronto London Auckland Sydney Tokyo

ISBN 0-590-03121-X

Published by Scholastic Book Services, a division of Scholastic Inc.

17 16 15 14 13 12 11 10 9 8 2 3 4 5 6 7/8

Printed in the U.S.A. 01

CONTENTS

1. SHIPWRECK AND DELIVERANCE

ALREADY the tempest had continued six days. On the seventh its fury seemed still increasing; and the morning dawned upon us without a prospect of hope. For we had wandered so far from the right track that none on board knew where we were. The ship's company were exhausted by labor and watching, and the courage which had sustained them was now sinking. The shivered masts had been cast into the sea. Several leaks appeared, and the ship began to fill. Many sailors were at prayer on their knees, offering miracles of future piety and goodness, as the condition of their release from danger. "My beloved children," said I to my four boys, who clung to me in their fright, "God can save us, for nothing is impossible to Him. We must hold ourselves resigned, and rely on what He sees fit to do."

My excellent wife wiped her tears and became more tranquil. She encouraged the youngest children, while I, who owed them an example of firmness, was scarcely able to hide my grief at what would most likely be the fate of beings so tenderly beloved. We all fell on our knees and prayed the God of Mercy to protect us. The boys arose in a state of mind so improved that they seemed forgetful of the impending danger and I myself began to feel my hopes increase, as I beheld this. Heaven will surely have pity on them, thought I, and will save their parents to guard their tender years!

At this moment a cry of "Land, land!" was heard through the roaring of the waves, and instantly the vessel struck against a rock. A tremendous cracking succeeded. The sea rushed in, in all directions. The vessel had grounded, and could not long hold together. "Lower the boats!" the captain shouted. "All is lost!" The sounds fell on my heart like a thrust from a dagger. "We are lost!" I exclaimed, and the children broke out into piercing cries. Recollecting myself, I addressed them again, exhorted them to courage, observing that the water had not yet reached us, that the ship was near land, and that Providence would assist the brave. "Keep where you are," added I, "while I go and examine what is best to be done."

On deck a scene of terrific and complete disaster met my eyes. The ship was shattered in all directions, but on one side there was a complete breach. The ship's company crowded into the boats till they could contain not one man more, and the last who entered were now cutting the ropes to move off. I called to them with frantic entreaties to stop for us also, but in vain. The roaring of the sea prevented my being heard, and the waves, which rose to the height of mountains, would have made it impossible to return. As I spoke, the boats, and all they contained, were driving out of sight.

My best consolation now was that the slanting position of the ship would afford us present protection from the water. The stern, where was enclosed all that was dear to me on earth, had been driven upwards between two rocks, and seemed immovably fixed. At the same time, to the southward, I descried through mist and rain, several points of land, which offered the only hope I could form in this distressing moment.

Sunk and desolate as I felt, it was yet my duty to appear serene before my family.

"Courage, dear ones," cried I on entering their cabin, "take heart! The ship is aground; but we are in greater safety than if she were beating upon the rocks; our cabin is above water and when the sea is calmer, we may yet find means to reach the land safely."

My family trusted my word, and now began to feel the advantage of the ship's remaining still. My wife, however, accustomed to read my inmost thoughts, perceived my anxiety. I made her a sign to convey the hopelessness of our situation, and I saw that she was resigned. "Let us take some nourishment," said she. "We shall need this comfort to support a long night."

Night set in. The fury of the tempest had not abated. The planks and beams of the vessel separated in many parts with a horrible crashing. We thought of the boats, and feared that all were lost.

My wife had prepared a slender meal, and the four boys ate with an appetite which their parents lacked. They went to bed, and soon were sound asleep. Fritz, the eldest, sat up with us, "I have been thinking," said he, after a long silence, "how it may be possible to save ourselves. If we had some bladders or cork jackets for my mother and my brothers, you and I, Father, would soon contrive to swim to land."

"That is a good thought," said I. We looked about for some small empty firkins; these we tied two and two together with handkerchiefs or towels, leaving about a foot distance between them, and fastened them as swimming jackets under the arms of each child, while my wife prepared one for herself. We provided ourselves with knives, some string, and other necessaries which could be put into the pocket in the hope that if the ship went to pieces in the night, we should either be able to swim to land, or be driven thither by the waves.

Fritz now lay down near his brothers, and was soon asleep. But their mother and I, too anxious to close our eyes, kept watch, listening to every sound that seemed to threaten a further change in our situation. We passed this awful night in prayer, in agonizing apprehensions, and in forming various resolutions as to what we should next attempt. We hailed the first gleam of light. The raging of the winds had begun to abate, the sky was serene, and hope came with the sun tingeing the horizon.

Thus revived, I summoned my wife and the

boys to the deck. The youngest children asked with surprise why we were there alone, and what had become of the ship's company? I reminded them and then added, "Dearest children, a Being more powerful than man has helped us, and will continue to help us, if we do not lose hope. Our companions, in whom we had so much confidence, have deserted us, but Divine Providence, in its goodness, has given us protection! Let us show ourselves willing in our exertions, and thus deserve support from Heaven!"

Fritz advised that when the sea was calm, we swim to land. "Ah! That may be well enough for you," said Ernest, "for you can swim, but we others should soon be drowned. Would it not be better to make a float of rafts, and get to land all together upon it?"

"Vastly well," answered I, "if we could contrive such a float. But come, my boys, look each of you about the ship, and see what can be done to enable us to reach the land."

They all sprang to do as I desired. I determined what we had to depend upon as to provisions and fresh water. My wife and the youngest boys visited the animals, whom they found in a pitiable condition from hunger and thirst. Fritz repaired to the ammunition room; Ernest to the carpenter's cabin; and Jack to the apartment of the captain. But scarcely had he opened the door, when two large dogs sprang upon him, and saluted him with such rude affection that he roared for assistance. Hunger, however, had rendered the poor creatures so gentle that they licked his hands and face. At last he began to understand, and gently taking the largest dog by the ears, sprang upon his back, and presented himself before me, as I came out of the ship's hold. I praised him, but exhorted him to be cautious, as hungry animals might be dangerous.

By and by my little company were assembled with what each had to contribute. Fritz had two fowling pieces, some powder and small shot contained in horn flasks, and some bullets in bags.

Ernest produced his hat filled with nails, and held in his hands a hatchet and a hammer. A pair of pincers, a pair of large scissors, and an auger peeped out of his pocket.

Even little Francis carried under his arm a large box from which he produced some little sharp-pointed hooks. His brothers smiled scornfully. "Vastly well, gentlemen," said I; "but let me tell you that the youngest has brought the most valuable prize. These little sharp-pointed hooks are fishing hooks and will probably be of more use in preserving our lives than all else we may find in the ship. However, what Fritz and Ernest have contributed will also be valuable to us."

"I," said my wife, "have some tidings which I hope will be welcome. I have found on board a cow and an ass, two goats, six sheep, and a sow big with young. I have just supplied them with food and water, and I hope to be able to preserve their lives."

"All this is admirable," said I to my young laborers, "and there is only Master Jack, who, instead of something useful, has brought us these dogs who will eat more than we shall have to give them."

"Ah!" replied Jack. "But if we can once get to land, you will see that they will assist us in hunting and shooting."

"True enough," said I, "but please tell us how we are to get to land, and whether you have found the means?"

"I am sure it cannot be very difficult," said Jack. "Look here at these large tubs. Why cannot each of us get into one of them, and float to the land?"

"That is worth a trial," I cried. "Quick, then,

boy! give me the saw, the auger, and some nails; we will see what is to be done." I recollected having seen some empty casks in the ship's hold. We went down, and found them floating in the water which had got into the vessel. We hoisted them up, and placed them on the lower deck, which was at this time scarcely above water. They were all sound, well guarded by iron hoops, and in every respect in good condition. They were exactly suited for the object, and, with the assistance of my sons, I instantly began to saw them in two.

In a short time I had produced eight tubs of equal size, and of the proper height. We now took some refreshment of wine and biscuit. I viewed with delight my eight little tubs, ranged in a line. I was surprised to see that my wife sighed deeply as she looked at them. "Never, never," cried she, "can I venture to get into one of these."

"Do not decide so hastily, my dear," said I, "and you will see presently that it is better than this shattered vessel, which cannot move from its place."

I then found a large pliant plank, and placed my eight tubs upon it, leaving a piece at each end reaching beyond the tubs, which, bent upward, would present an outline like the keel of a vessel. We next nailed all the tubs to the plank, and then the tubs to each other, as they stood, side by side, to make them the firmer. And two other planks, of the same length as the first, were nailed on each side of the tubs. When all this was finished, we found we had produced a kind of narrow boat, divided into eight compartments, which I had no doubt would be able to perform a short course in calm water.

But now we discovered that our contrivance was so heavy, that all united were not able to move it an inch. I bade Fritz fetch me a crow. In the meanwhile I sawed a thick round pole into several pieces, to make some rollers. I then, with the crow, easily raised the foremost part of my machine, while Fritz placed one of the rollers under it.

"How astonishing," cried Ernest, "that this engine, which is smaller than any of us, can do more than our united strength was able to effect!"

I explained to him as well as I could the power of Archimedes' lever, with which he said he could move the world, if you would give him a point upon which to stand. And I promised to explain the nature of the operation when we should be safe on land.

One of the points of my system of education for my sons was to awaken their curiosity by interesting observations. I explained that God compensated the natural weakness of man by gift of reason, of invention, and of adroit hands; and that human thought and skill had produced a science, called mechanics, to teach us how to make our own natural strength act to an incredible distance, and with extraordinary force, by the use of instruments.

Jack here remarked that the action of the crow was very slow.

"The purpose of the crow, Jack," I replied, "is to raise what is exceedingly heavy. And the heavier the thing we would move, the slower is the mechanical operation. But what compensates for this slowness?"

"Turning the handle quicker!"

"Wrong. The true answer, my boy, is patience and reason. With these I am in hopes of setting my machine afloat." As I said this, I tied a long cord to its stern, and the other end to one of the firm timbers of the ship, so that the cord would serve to guide and restrain it when launched. We now put a second and a third roller under, and applying the crow, to our great joy our machine descended into the water with such velocity that, but for the rope it would have gone far out to sea.

But now a new difficulty presented itself. The boat leaned so much on one side that none could venture into it. It suddenly occurred to me that ballast was needed to set it straight. I drew it near, and threw all the useless things I could find into the tubs, so as to make weight on the light side. By degrees the machine became quite straight and firm in the water, seeming to invite us to take refuge in it. All now would get into the tubs but I recollected that savage nations make use of a paddle for preventing their canoes from upsetting. I set to work to make one of these.

I took two poles of equal length and fixed one of them at the head, and the other at the stern, to enable us to turn them to right or left for the purpose of guiding and putting out to sea. I stuck the end of each paddle into the bunghole of an empty brandy keg, which served to keep the paddles steady.

There remained nothing more to do, but to find a way to clear out from the incumbrance of the wreck. I got into the first tub, and steered the head of the machine so as to make it enter the cleft in the ship's side, where it could remain quiet. I then remounted the vessel, and sometimes with the saw, and sometimes with the hatchet, cleared away, to right and left, everything that could obstruct our passage. That being done, we next secured some oars for the voyage we planned.

It was already late and we were obliged to pass a second night in the wrecked vessel, which at every instant threatened to fall to pieces. We now refreshed ourselves by a regular meal, for during the day's work, we had scarcely allowed ourselves a biscuit or a glass of wine. Now in a more tranquil state of mind than the day before, we all prepared to sleep. I had taken the precaution to tie the swimming apparatus round my three youngest boys and my wife, in case the storm should again come on. But first I had advised my wife to dress herself for convenience in the clothes of one of the sailors, and she left us to look for some that might best suit her size. In a quarter of an hour she returned, dressed in sailor's clothing, and joined in the merriment her costume occasioned.

Then one and all crept into our separate hammocks, and welcomed sleep.

2. WE LAND ON A BARREN SHORE

BY THE break of day we were all awake and alert. When we had finished our morning prayer, I said, "Now, my best beloved, we must enter upon the work of our deliverance. First give to each animal on board a hearty meal. Put food enough before them for several days. If our voyage succeeds, we will return for them. Bring together what is absolutely necessary for our wants. Our first cargo should consist of a barrel of gunpowder, three fowling pieces, and three carbines, with as much small shot and lead, and as many bullets as our boat will carry; two pairs of pocket pistols, and one of large ones, a mold to cast balls in. Each of the boys, and their mother also, should have a bag to carry game in; you will find plenty of these in the cabins of the officers." We added a chest containing cakes of potable soup, another of hard biscuits, an iron pot, a fishing rod, a chest of nails, and one of hammers, saws, pincers, hatchets, augers, etc., and lastly, some sailcloth to make a tent. I exchanged the worthless ballasts for articles for use in our subsistence.

When all was ready we each stepped bravely into a tub. At the moment of our departure the cocks and hens began to cluck. This suggested to me the idea of taking the geese, ducks, fowls, and pigeons with us. If we could not find means to feed them, at least they would feed us.

We accordingly put ten hens and an old and a young cock into one of the tubs, and covered it with planks; we set the rest at liberty, to find their way home.

My wife, who had the care of this last part of our embarkation, joined us loaded with a large bag, which she threw into the tub that contained her youngest son. I imagined that she intended it for him to sit upon and asked no questions concerning it. The order of our departure was as follows:

In the first tub, at the boat's head was my dear wife, and in the second, our Francis, a lovely boy, six years old, of the sweetest and happiest temper. In the third, Fritz, our eldest boy, between fourteen and fifteen years of age, a handsome youth, full of intelligence and vivacity. In the fourth was the barrel of gunpowder, the cocks and hens, and the sailcloth. In the fifth, the provisions of every kind. In the sixth, our third son, Jack, a lighthearted, enterprising lad, about ten years old. In the seventh, our second son, Ernest, a boy of twelve, rational, reflective, well informed for his age, but somewhat indolent. In the eighth, a father, whose task was to guide the machine for the safety of his beloved family. Each of us held an oar, and near each was a swimming apparatus, in readiness for whatever might happen. The tide was already at half its height when we left the ship, and I had counted on this to help. We held the two paddles longways, and thus we passed without accident through the cleft of the vessel into the sea. To our good fortune our boat steered in a straight line.

The two dogs plunged into the sea and swam to the boat. They were so large, I dreaded lest they jump in and upset us. Turk was an English dog, and Flora, of a Danish breed, and I feared it would not be possible for them to swim so far. The dogs, however, managed the affair with perfect intelligence. When fatigued, they rested their forepaws on one of the paddles, and thus succeeded.

Our voyage proceeded securely, though slowly; but the nearer we approached the land, the more unpromising it appeared. The coast was clothed with barren rocks, but the sea was calm. The waves gently washed the shore, and the sky was serene in every direction.

Casks, bales, chests, and other vestiges of shipwreck floated round us. In the hope of obtaining some good provisions, I bade Fritz have a rope, a hammer, and some nails ready, and to try to seize the casks as we passed. He succeeded in laying hold of two and drew them after us to the shore.

Close on land, the rocks no longer appeared one undivided chain and Fritz, with his hawk's eye, already descried some palm trees. I regretted that I had not thought to bring a telescope from the captain's cabin, when Jack drew a small one from his pocket, and with a look of triumph presented it to me.

Now I remarked that the shore before us had a desert and savage aspect, but by and by we perceived a little opening between the rocks, near the mouth of a creek toward which all our geese and ducks betook themselves. Relying on their sagacity, we followed. This opening formed a little bay; the water was tranquil, and deep enough to receive our boat. Entering it, I cautiously put on shore to a spot where the coast was about the same height above the water as our tubs, and where there was a quantity sufficient to keep us afloat.

All that had life in the boat jumped eagerly on land. The dogs, who had swum on shore, received us, jumping round us with every demonstration of joy. The geese kept up a loud cackling, to which the ducks contributed a perpetual bass. The cocks and hens, which we had already set at liberty, clucked, and the boys chattered all at once, producing an overpowering confusion. To this was added the disagreeable scream of some penguins and flamingos, the flamingos flying over our heads, the others sitting on the points of the rocks at the entrance to the bay.

On finding ourselves safe on land, we first fell on our knees, and returned thanks to the Supreme Being for our deliverance.

We next employed our whole attention in unloading the boat. We looked about for a convenient place to set up a tent under the shade of the rocks, and having agreed upon a place, we set to work. We drove one of our poles firmly into a fissure of the rock; this rested upon another pole, which was driven perpendicularly into the ground, and formed the ridge of our tent and a frame for our dwelling. We next threw some sailcloth over the ridge, and stretching it to a convenient distance on each side, fastened its extremities to the ground with stakes. Lastly, I fixed some tenterhooks along the edge of one side of the sailcloth in front to enclose the entrance during night by hooking on the opposite edge. The chests of provisions, and other heavy matters, we had left on the shore.

Next I desired my sons to look about for grass and moss, to be spread and dried in the sun, to serve us for beds, while I erected near the tent a kind of little kitchen. A few flat stones I found in the bed of a fresh-water river, served for a hearth. I got a quantity of dry branches, and with some of our turf, made a brisk cheering fire. We put some of the soup cakes, with water, into our iron pot and placed it over the flame; and my wife, with little Francis as helper, prepared the dinner.

Fritz, after reloading the guns, wandered along the side of the river. Ernest took to the seashore; Jack toward a chain of rocks which jutted out into the sea, intent on gathering some of the mussels which grew upon them.

Now I endeavored, in vain, to draw the two floating casks on shore, for our place of landing, though convenient enough for our machine, was too steep for the casks. While I was looking about to find a more favorable spot, I heard loud cries and recognized the voice of my son Jack. I snatched my hatchet, and ran anxiously to his assistance. He was up to his knees in water in a shallow, and a large lobster had fastened its claws in his leg, while the poor boy struggled to free himself. I jumped instantly into the water, took the lobster up by the body, and carried him off, followed by Jack, shouting our triumph all the way.

Ernest bawled out that the lobster had better be put into the soup, which would give it an excellent flavor; but this his mother opposed. The lobster itself would furnish a dinner for the whole family. I left them and examined the shallow, in which I fixed my two casks securely on their bottoms.

On my return, I complimented Jack on his being the first to procure an animal that might serve for subsistence.

"Ah, but I have seen something too, that is good to eat," said Ernest; "and I should have got it but that I would have wetted my feet—"

"Fortunate enough, my dainty gentleman," I interrupted, "since you are acquainted with the place where such food can be found, you will be so obliging as to return and procure us some, so trifling an inconvenience as wet feet, notwithstanding."

"I will do my best to bring the oysters,"

answered Ernest; "and also some salt, which I have seen in immense quantities in the holes of the rocks, dried by the sun. I tasted some of it, and it was excellent."

What he brought had the appearance of sea salt, but was mixed with earth and sand. However, my wife dissolved and afterwards filtered it through muslin and we found it admirably fit for use.

"Why could we not have used some sea water," asked Jack, "instead of having all this trouble?"

"So we might," answered I, "if it had not a sickly taste." While I was speaking, my wife tasted the soup with a little stick with which she had been stirring it, and pronounced that it was all the better for the salt, and now quite ready. "But," said she, "Fritz is not come in. And then, how shall we manage to eat our soup without spoons or dishes? Why did we not remember to bring some from the ship?"

"Because, my dear, one cannot think of everything at once."

"But, indeed," said she, "this is a matter which cannot easily be set to rights. How will it be possible for each of us to raise this large boiling pot to his lips?"

My wife was right. We all cast our eyes

upon the pot with a sort of stupid perplexity. Silence was at length broken by all bursting into a hearty laugh at the thought of our own folly in not recollecting that spoons and forks were things of absolute necessity.

Ernest observed, "We can use some oyster shells for spoons."

"Why, Ernest," said I, "this is a useful thought. Run then quickly for some of them."

Fritz was not yet returned, but soon we heard him shouting to us from a small distance. In a few minutes he was among us, proudly displaying his prize, which I immediately perceived, from the description I had read in different books of travels, was an agouti, a piglike animal common in that country.

Fritz related that he had passed over to the other side of the river where the shore is low, and a quantity of casks, chests, and planks, and different sorts of things are washed there by the sea. "Ought we not to obtain some of these treasures?"

"We will consider it soon," answered I, "but first we have to make our voyage to the vessel, and fetch away the animals."

"I must tell you too," continued Fritz, "that over on the other side there is as much grass for pasturage as we can desire; and besides, a wood, in the shade of which we could repose. Why then should we remain on this barren desert side?"

"Patience," I replied; "there is a time for everything, friend Fritz. But I am eager to know if you discovered, in your excursion, any traces of our ship companions?"

"Not the smallest trace of man, dead or alive, on land or water," replied Fritz.

Soon after we had taken our meal, the sun began to sink into the west. My wife produced the bag she had so mysteriously huddled into the tub. It contained various sorts of grain for feeding poultry—barley, peas, oats, etc., and also different kinds of seeds and roots of vegetables for the table. She scattered several handfuls upon the ground, which the fowls began eagerly to seize. Our pigeons sought a roosting place among the rocks; the hens, with the two cocks at their head, ranged themselves in a line along the ridge of the tent; and the geese and ducks betook themselves in a body to a marshy bit of ground near the sea.

A little later, we began our preparations for repose. First, we loaded our guns and pistols, and laid them carefully in the tent. Next, we assembled together and joined in offering up our thanks to the Almighty. With the last ray of the sun we entered our tent, and after drawing the sailcloth over the hooks to close the entrance, we laid ourselves down close to each other on the grass and moss we had collected in the morning.

3. WE EXPLORE OUR LAND — RETURN TO THE TENT

WE WERE roused at dawn by the crowing of the cocks, and consulted together as to the day's occupations. We agreed that Fritz and I should seek traces of our late ship companions, and at the same time examine the nature of the soil on the other side of the river, before we determined on a fixed place of abode.

The children were soon roused; even Ernest submitted to the hard fate of rising so early in the morning.

We prepared for departure. Each took a bag for game, and a hatchet. Fritz and I each carried a gun, a pair of pistols in a leather band round the waist, with a stock of biscuit and a flask of fresh river water.

In about an hour we had completed the preparations for our journey. I had loaded the guns we left behind, and I now enjoined my wife to keep by day as near the boat as possible, which in case of danger was the best and most speedy means of escape.

My next concern was to shorten the sad moment of separation, for neither knew what new misfortune might occur on either side during the interval. We all melted into tears. I drew Fritz away, and in a few moments the sobs and adieus of those we left behind died away in the noise of the waves which we now approached and turned our thoughts upon ourselves and the immediate object of our journey.

The banks of the river were everywhere steep and difficult, excepting at one narrow slip near the mouth on our side, where we had drawn our fresh water. We followed the course of the river till we arrived at a cluster of rocks. By stepping upon large fragments of rock in the river, we contrived to reach the other side. We proceeded a short way along the rock we ascended in landing, forcing ourselves a passage through tall grass.

When we had walked about a hundred paces, we heard a loud noise behind us, and a rustling in the tall grass. However, not an enemy, but our faithful Turk, rushed out. Our anxious relatives had sent him on to us!

We pursued our way. On our left the sea and on our right the continuation of the ridge of rocks which began at the place of our landing, and ran along the shore. We proceeded as near the shore as possible, casting our eyes alternately upon its smooth expanse and upon the land in all directions to discover our ship companions, or the boats which had conveyed them from us. But in vain.

Soon we entered a wood situated a little farther from the sea. Here under the shade of a tree, by the side of a clear running stream, we took out our provisions to refresh ourselves. Fritz caught a glimpse of some apelike animals among the bushes, stole softly about to be sure, and presently stumbled on a small round body which lay on the ground. He brought it to me, observing that it must be the nest of some bird. "What makes you of that opinion?" said I. "It is, I think, much more like a coconut. Let us break the shell, and you will see the nut inside."

We ate the coconut for our dinner, by which means we were enabled to save the provisions we had brought. We made a hearty meal, and then continued our route.

At length we reached a plain, which afforded a more extensive view and a path easier to follow.

To the right of the plain we entered a forest where some of the trees were of a singular kind. Fritz went up to examine them closely. "Oh heavens! Father, what odd trees, with wens growing all about their trunks!" I assured him that they were bottle gourds, the trunks of which bear fruit. "Is the fruit a sponge or a wen?" asked Fritz. "We will see," I replied. "Try to get down one of them, and we will examine it minutely."

"Here is one," said Fritz, "and it is exactly like a gourd, only the rind is thicker and harder."

"It can be used for making various utensils," I observed, "plates, dishes, basins, flasks. We will give it the name of the gourd tree."

"How happy my mother will be!" Fritz cried. "She will no longer think, when she makes soup, that we shall scald our fingers."

I taught my son how to divide the gourd with a bit of string, which would cut more equally than a knife; I tied the string round the middle of the gourd as tight as possible, striking it pretty hard with the handle of my knife, and I drew it tighter and tighter till the gourd fell apart, forming two regular-shaped bowls or vessels. While Fritz, who had used a knife for the same operation, had entirely spoiled his gourd by the irregular pressure of his instrument. I recommended his making some spoons with the spoiled rind, while I completed two dishes of convenient size, and some smaller ones to serve as plates.

Fritz was astonished. "I cannot imagine, Father," said he, "how this way of cutting the gourd could occur to you!"

"I have read of this process," I replied, "in books of travels, and also of savages who have no knives, and who make a sort of twine from the bark of trees; they are accustomed to use it for this purpose."

"And the flasks, Father?"

"For this they make preparation a long time beforehand. If a Negro wishes to have a flask, or a bottle with a neck, he binds a piece of string, linen, or bark of a tree, round the part nearest the stalk of a very young gourd; he draws this bandage so tight that the part at liberty soon forms itself to a round shape, while the part which is confined contracts, and remains ever after narrow. By this method they obtain flasks or bottles of a perfect form."

Fritz now proudly showed his completed plates. "How delighted my mother will be to eat upon them!" cried he. "But how shall we convey them to her?"

"We must leave them here on the sand for the sun to dry them thoroughly. We shall return this way, and can then carry them with us. But we shall fill them with sand, that they may not shrink or warp in the heat." Our sumptuous service of porcelain was accordingly spread upon the ground to await our return.

After a walk of about four leagues, we arrived at a spot where a slip of land reached far out into the sea, on which we observed a rising piece of ground or hill. We ascended to obtain a clear view of adjacent parts to save us the fatigue of further rambles.

At the top of the hill we beheld a scene of wild and solitary beauty, a vast extent of land and water. The shore was rounded by a bay of some extent, the bank of which ended in a promontory on either side. The blue sea, its shimmering waves reflecting the rays of the sun and the variegated hues and verdure of the woods was magnificent. But the recollection of our unfortunate companions, engulfed perhaps in this very ocean, saddened our hearts.

We, however, became all the more sensible of the goodness of the Divine Being, in the special protection afforded to ourselves, in conducting us to a home where there was no present cause for fear of danger from without, where we had not wanted for food, and where lay future safety for us all.

We descended the hill, and made our way to a wood of palms. We advanced slowly and cautiously, fearing at every step a mortal bite from some serpent that might be concealed among them. We made Turk go before, to give us timely notice of danger. I also cut a reed stalk of uncommon length and thickness, for my defense against any enemy. With surprise I perceived a glutinous sap proceed from the divided end of the stalk. Curious, I tasted this liquid, and found it sweet and pleasant so that not a doubt remained that we were passing through a plantation of sugar canes. I again sucked the cane for some moments, and felt singularly refreshed and strengthened.

As Fritz was at some distance before me, I called out to him to cut a reed for his defense. This he did, and soon cried out, "Father, Father, I have found some sugar! Some syrup! I have a sugar cane in my hand! Run quickly, Father!" We were soon together, jointly partaking of the pleasure we had in store for his dear mother and the younger brothers.

Fritz cut at least a dozen of the largest

canes, tied them together, and dragged them to the end of the plantation. We regained the wood of palms, stretched out in the shade, and finished our repast.

A great number of large monkeys, terrified by the sight of us and the barking of Turk, stole nimbly, yet quietly up the trees, till they had reached the topmost parts. From this height they saluted us with hostile screams. Being now satisfied that the trees were palms, bearing coconuts, I hoped to obtain some of this fruit through the monkeys. With difficulty I prevented Fritz from firing on them, and we now began to throw stones instead.

Furiously they tore off, nut by nut, all that grew near them, to hurl them down upon us. With difficulty we avoided the blows, but in a short time a great number of coconuts lay on the ground round us. Collecting them, we chose a place where we could feast on this rich harvest. We opened the shells with a hatchet after sucking some of the milk through the three small holes pierced by the point of a knife. The milk of the coconut has not a pleasant flavor, but is excellent for quenching thirst. A kind of solid cream which adheres to the shell, and which we scraped off with our spoons and mixed with it a little of the sugar-cane sap, made a delicious repast.

Our meal over, I tied together all the coconuts with stalks, and threw them across my shoulder. Fritz resumed his bundle of sugar canes. We divided the rest of the things between us, and continued our way toward home.

My poor boy now began to complain of fatigue and of the sugar canes galling his shoulders. "Yet how glad I shall be when my mother and Ernest are tasting them!" he said.

"The juice of the sugar canes is apt to turn sour soon after cutting and leave us with but a few sticks for firewood," said I. "We may suck them, therefore, without fear of lessening their numbers."

We found our gourd utensils perfectly dry, as hard as bone, and not the least misshapen. Putting them into our gamebags, we continued on our way. As we passed through the little wood in which we breakfasted, Turk sprang upon a troop of monkeys, who were skipping about and amusing themselves. Taken by surprise, before we could get to the spot, our ferocious Turk had already seized one of them, a female with a young one in her arms. The poor creature was killed, and the young one hid himself in the grass. Fritz flew like lightning to make Turk let go his hold, but he was too late to prevent the death of the mother.

Now the young monkey sprang nimbly on Fritz's shoulders, and fastened his feet in the stiff curls of his hair; nor could the squalls of Fritz, nor all the shaking he gave him make him let go his hold. With a little gentleness and management I succeeded in taking the creature in my arms as one would an infant. He was not larger than a kitten, and quite as unable to help himself.

"Oh, Father," cried Fritz, "do let me have this little animal to myself. I will take the greatest care of him; I will give him all my share of the milk of the coconuts."

"I have not the least objection," I answered. "It is only just that the little protégé be given up to your management."

We now resumed our journey. The little monkey jumped again on the shoulders of his protector, while I relieved my boy of the bundle of canes. Scarcely had we proceeded when Turk overtook us full gallop. Fritz tied the monkey on Turk's back and said, "Now, Mr. Turk, since you had the cruelty to destroy the mother, it is for you to take care of her child."

At first the dog was restive, and resisted. But by degrees we succeeded in gaining his good will, and he quietly consented to carry the little burden. Fritz put another string round Turk's neck, by which to lead him.

We soon found ourselves on the bank of the river, and near our family. Flora from the other side announced our approach by a violent barking, and Turk replied heartily and ran off to meet his companion. Shortly after, our much-loved family appeared in sight, with joyful demonstrations at our safe return.

Not one of our new acquisitions afforded my wife more pleasure than the plates and dishes. We now observed with pleasure the preparations for an excellent repast. On one side of the fire was a turnspit, which my wife had contrived by driving two forked pieces of wood into the ground, and placing a long even stick, sharpened at one end, across them. By this invention she was enabled to roast fish or other food, with little Francis to turn it round from time to time. She had prepared for us a goose, the fat of which ran down into some oyster shells placed there as a dripping pan. There was, besides, a dish of fish, which the little ones had caught, and the iron pot upon the fire provided a good soup, the odor of which increased our appetite. By the side of these most exhilarating preparations stood one of the casks which we had recovered from the sea.

My wife had knocked out the head and exposed a cargo of the finest sort of Dutch cheeses, contained in round tins.

We seated ourselves on the ground, and my wife placed each article of the repast in one of our neat new dishes. Unable to wait, my sons had broken the coconuts, and already convinced themselves of their delicious flavor. They fell to making spoons with the fragments of the shells.

The thought struck me, that by dividing the nuts carefully with a saw, the two halves, when scooped, would remain in the form of teacups or basins already made to our hands. Jack, the most active, brought the instrument, and in a short time each of us was provided with a convenient receptacle for food.

By the time we had finished our meal, the sun was setting, and recollecting how quickly the night would fall upon us, we were in great haste to regain our place of rest. My wife had considerately collected a tenfold quantity of dry grass, which she had spread in the tent, so that we anticipated with joy the prospect of stretching our limbs on a substance somewhat approaching the quality of mattresses. We said our prayers, and lay down in the tent, taking with us the young monkey who had become the little favorite of all, myself remaining last to fasten the sailcloth in front of the tent. Heartily fatigued by the exertions of the day, we soon fell into a profound and refreshing sleep.

But I had not long enjoyed this pleasing state, when I was awakened by the motion of the fowls on the ridge of the tent, and by a violent barking of our vigilant dogs. I was instantly on my feet. My wife and Fritz rose also, we each took a gun, and sallied forth.

The dogs continued their violent barking. We had not proceeded many steps when we perceived by the light of the moon a terrible combat. At least a dozen jackals had surrounded our brave dogs, who defended themselves with the stoutest courage. Already three or four of their adversaries lay on the ground.

I had feared something worse than jackals.

"Let us fire both together, my boy," said I, "but aim with care. Fire so that you may not miss, and I shall do the same." We fired, and two of the intruders fell instantly dead upon the sands. The others made their escape. Turk and Flora pursued them, and put the finishing stroke to what we had begun. And thus the battle ended.

The body of one of the jackals was left on the rock, by the side of the tent in which the little ones still slept undisturbed. We lay down by their side until the cocks awoke us both at daybreak, and we consulted together respecting the plan for the ensuing day.

4. RETURN TO THE WRECK

I CONFESSED to my wife my alarm over the many cares and exertions to be made. "First, a journey to the vessel is of absolute necessity, if we are to save the cattle and other useful things which we risk losing by the first heavy sea. Yet should not our first endeavor be a better habitation, secure from wild beasts, and a separate place for our provisions?"

"All will fall into the right order by degrees," observed my wife. "I shudder at the thought of this voyage to the vessel. But if it be of absolute necessity, it cannot be undertaken too soon. Let us not be overanxious about tomorrow. 'Sufficient unto the day is the evil thereof.' These words of the true Friend of mankind are wise counsel for our own benefits."

"I will follow your advice," said I. "You shall stay here with the three youngest boys; and Fritz, being so much stronger and more intelligent than the others, shall accompany me."

I started from my bed, crying out loudly and briskly, "Get up, children, get up; it is almost light, and we have some important projects for today."

At these words Fritz sprang nimbly out of the tent, while the young ones began to gape and rub their eyes. Fritz ran to his jackal, which during the night had become cold and perfectly stiff. He fixed him upon his legs, and placed him like a sentinel at the entrance of the tent, joyously anticipating the effect on his brothers. But no sooner had the dogs caught sight of him, than they began to howl, and Fritz barely restrained them from falling upon him, instantly, thinking he was alive.

The younger boys ran out of the tent, much surprised at the sight of a yellow-colored animal standing motionless at the entrance.

"Oh, heavens!" exclaimed Francis, stepping back a few paces for fear. "It is a wolf!"

"No, no," said Jack, going near the jackal, and taking one of his paws, "it is a yellow dog, and he is dead; he does not move at all."

"It is neither a dog nor a wolf," interrupted

Ernest in a consequential tone. "Do you not see that it is the golden fox?"

"Best of all, most learned professor!" now exclaimed Fritz. "A jackal is the creature you see before you, and I killed him myself in the night."

Ernest said, "In the night, you say, Fritz? In your sleep, I suppose—"

Fritz answered, "No, Mr. Ernest, not in my sleep but broad awake, and on the watch to protect you from wild beasts! But I cannot wonder at this mistake in one who does not know the difference between a jackal and a golden fox!"

Ernest said, "You would not have known it either, if Papa had not told you—"

"Come, come, my lads, I will have no disputes," I interrupted. "You are both to blame, and all are at once right and wrong. The jackal partakes at once of the nature of the dog, the wolf, and the fox."

Then followed questions and answers in abundance. "And now, my boys," said I, "he who begins the day without first addressing the Almighty ought to expect neither success nor safety in his undertakings."

Having finished our prayers, the thought was of breakfast. Today their mother had nothing to give them for their morning meal but some biscuit, which was so hard and dry that we swallowed it with difficulty. Fritz asked for a piece of cheese to eat with it, while Ernest examined the second cask we had drawn out of the sea. In a minute he came up to us, joy sparkling in his eyes. "Father," said he, "if we had but a little butter spread upon our biscuit, do you not think it would improve it?"

"That indeed it would; but—if—if—these never-ending ifs. I had rather eat a bit of cheese with my biscuit at once, than think of ifs!"

Ernest said, "Perhaps, though, the ifs may be worth something, if we were to knock out the head of this cask which is filled with excellent salt butter. I made a little opening in it with a knife; and see, I got out enough to spread nicely upon this piece of biscuit."

"That glutton instinct of yours for once is of some general use," I answered. "But now let us profit by it."

The boys surrounded the cask in a moment, while I made a hole in the bottom of the cask, sufficiently large to take out a small quantity of butter at a time, and leaving the rest protected from the heat.

We sat down to breakfast, some biscuits and a coconut shell full of salt butter being placed upon the ground, round which we all assembled. We toasted our biscuit, and while it was hot, applied the butter and made a hearty breakfast.

"One of the things we must not forget to look for in the vessel," said Fritz, "is a spiked collar or two for our dogs, as a protection to them should they again need to defend themselves from wild beasts."

"Oh!" says Jack, "I can make spiked collars, if my mother will give me a little help."

"That I will, my boy; I should like to see what new fancy has come into your head," cried she.

"Yes, yes," pursued I, "as many new inventions as you please; but now for work. You, Mr. Fritz, with your superior age and discretion will undertake with me our voyage to the vessel, to bring away whatever may be possible. You younger boys will remain here with your kind mother. I rely on your perfect obedience to her will, and general good behavior."

While Fritz was getting the boat ready, I tied a piece of white linen to the end of a pole. This I drove into the ground, in a place where it would be visible from the vessel. I arranged with my wife, that in case of any accident that should require my prompt assistance, they should take down the pole and fire a gun three times as a signal of distress, at which I would immediately turn back. But, with so many things to accomplish on board the vessel, it was probable that we should not, otherwise, return at night. In which case I also promised to make signals.

We embarked in silence, casting anxious looks on those we were quitting. Fritz rowed steadily, and I helped by rowing from time to time with the oar which served me for a rudder. When we had gone some distance, I remarked a current which was visible a long way. To take advantage of this current and to save our strength by means of it, was my first care. Little as I knew of the management of sea affairs, I succeeded in keeping our boat in the direction in which it ran. We were drawn gently on, till at length the lessening of its force obliged us again to take our oars. But our arms being now rested, we were ready for new exertions. A little afterward, we arrived at the cleft of the vessel, and fastened our boat securely to one of its timbers.

At once we went to the main deck, where we found all the animals we had left on board assembled. We added a fast supply of food and water for the animals, that no anxiety on their account might interrupt our enterprise. We renewed our own strength by a sufficient repast.

While we were eating, Fritz suggested that we contrive a sail for our boat. "In the name of Heaven," cried I, "what makes you think of this when we have so many things of indispensable necessity to arrange?"

"True, Father," said Fritz; "but I found it very difficult to row for so long a time, though I did my best. I observed that, though the wind blew strong against us, the current still carried us on. Now, as the current will be of no use on our way back, we might make the wind supply its place. Our boat will be very heavy when we have loaded it with all the things we mean to take away, and I am afraid I shall not be strong enough to row to land; so do you not think that a sail would be a good thing just now?"

"I perceive much good sense in your argument. The best thing is not to overload the boat, and thus avoid the danger of sinking, or of being obliged to throw some of our stores overboard. We will, however, set to work upon your sail. Come, let us begin."

I assisted Fritz to carry a pole strong enough for a mast, and another not so thick for a sail yard. I directed him to make a hole in a plank with a chisel, large enough for the mast to stand upright in it. I then went to the sail room, and cut a large sail down to a triangular shape. I made holes along the edges, and passed cords through them. We then got a pulley, and with this and some cords produced a sail.

"But now, Father," said Fritz, "I am thinking to make you a better rudder; one that would enable you to steer the boat both with greater ease and greater safety."

"Your thought would be a very good one," said I, "but I shall fix our oars in such a manner as to enable me to steer the raft from either end." Accordingly I fixed bits of wood to the stem and stern of the machine, in the nature of grooves, which were calculated to spare us a great deal of trouble.

We employed the rest of the day in emptying the tubs of the useless ballast of stones, and putting in their place what would be of service, such as nails, pieces of cloth, and different kinds of utensils, etc., etc. The prospect before us of an entire solitude made us devote our attention to securing as much powder and shot as we could, as a means of catching animals for food, and of defending ourselves against wild beasts.

The quantity of useful things in the store

chambers made it difficult for me to select among them, and I regretted that circumstances compelled me to leave some of them behind. Fritz, however, already meditated a second visit; but we took good care to secure knives, forks, and spoons, and a complete assortment of kitchen utensils. In the captain's cabin we found some services of silver, dishes and plates of high-wrought metal, and a little chest filled with bottles of many sorts of excellent wine. Each of these we put into our boat. We stripped the kitchen of gridirons, kettles, pots of all kinds, a small roasting jack, etc. Our last prize was a chest of choice eatables, containing Westphalia hams, Bologna sausages, and other savory food. I took some little sacks of maize, of wheat, and other grain, and some potatoes. We next added such implements as shovels, hoes, spades, rakes, harrows, etc. Fritz reminded me to increase our cargo by some hammocks and blankets; and such guns as he could find of a particular costliness or structure, together with some sabers and clasp knives. We took also a barrel of sulphur, a quantity of ropes, some small string, and a large roll of sailcloth. The vessel appeared to us to be in so wretched a condition that it was quite uncertain whether we should be able to approach her any more.

Our cargo was so large that the tubs were filled to the very brim. The first and last of the tubs were reserved for Fritz and me to seat ourselves in and row the boat, which sank very low in the water. However, we used the precaution of putting on our swimming jackets, for fear of any misfortune.

The day had been exhausting. Night suddenly surprised us, and we lost all hope of returning to our family the same evening. A large blazing fire on the shore soon greeted our sight—the signal agreed upon for assuring us that all was well. We returned the compliment, by tying four lighted lanterns to our masthead. This was answered by the firing of two guns; so that both parties had reason to be satisfied and easy.

Early the next morning Fritz prepared a substantial breakfast of biscuit and ham. But first recollecting that in the captain's cabin we had seen a telescope of superior size and power, we speedily conveyed it to the deck.

While fixing my eye to the glass, I discovered my wife coming out of the tent, looking attentively toward the vessel, and at the same moment caught sight of the flag upon the shore. My load of anxiety lifted; all were in good health, and had escaped the dangers of the night.

"Now that I have had a sight of your mother," said I to Fritz, "my next concern is to save the lives of some of the animals on board and to take them with us."

"Would it be possible to make a raft, to get them all upon it, and in this way get them to shore?" asked Fritz.

"How could we induce a cow, an ass, and a sow, either to get upon a raft, or, when there, to remain motionless and quiet?"

"Then here is another idea, Father. Let us tie a swimming jacket round the body of each animal, and throw one and all into the water; they will swim like fish, and we can draw them after us in the same manner."

"Right, very right, my boy. Let us not lose a moment in making the experiment."

We hastened to fix a jacket on one of the lambs, and threw it into the sea. Anxious yet curious, I followed the poor beast with my eyes. He sank at first, but he soon reappeared, shaking the water from his head, and in a few seconds was swimming.

"Victory!" I exclaimed, hugging my boy with delight. "These useful animals are all our own; let us adopt the same means with those that remain, but take care not to lose our little lamb." Fritz now tied on a swimming jacket. He took with him a rope, first making a slip knot in it. Overtaking the lamb, he threw the loop round his neck, drew him back to our boat, and then took him out of the water.

We next got four small water butts, emptied them, and carefully closed them again. I united them with a large piece of sailcloth, nailing a cask to each end, and strengthened it with a second piece of sailcloth. With this contrivance I destined to support the cow and the ass, the animal being placed in the middle, with a cask on either side. I added a thong of leather, stretching from the casks across the breast and haunches of the animal, to make the whole secure; and thus, in less than an hour, both my cow and my ass were equipped for swimming.

Of the smaller animals, the sow gave us the most trouble. We were first obliged to put a muzzle on her to prevent her biting; and then we tied a large piece of cork under her body. The sheep and goats were more accommodating, and we had soon prepared them for our adventure. And now we had assembled our whole company on the deck, in readiness for the voyage. We tied a cord to either the horns or the neck of each animal, and to the other end of the cord a piece of wood similar to the mode used for making nets, that it might be easy for us to draw the animal to us by the ropes if necessary.

We began with the ass, conducting him to the brink of the vessel, and then suddenly shoving him off. He fell into the water, and for a moment disappeared, then rose, swimming gracefully between his two barrels.

Next came the cow's turn: and as she was infinitely more valuable than the ass, my fears increased in proportion. The ass had swum so courageously, that he was already at a considerable distance from the vessel, so that there was sufficient room for our experiment on the cow. We had more difficulty in pushing her overboard; but she reached the water in as much safety as the ass, and was as perfectly sustained by the empty barrels. She made her way with gravity, and a sort of dignified composure.

We now proceeded with our whole troop, throwing them one by one into the water, where by and by they appeared in a group floating at their ease, and seemingly well content. The sow was the only exception. She became quite furious, set up a loud squalling, and struggled so that she was carried to a considerable distance toward the landing place we had in view.

With not a moment to lose, we put on our cork jackets, and descended without accident through the cleft, took our station in the boat, and were soon in the midst of our troop of quadrupeds. We carefully gathered all the floating bits of wood, fastened them to the stern of the machine, and thus drew them after us. When everything was adjusted, and our company in order, we hoisted our sail, which filling with a favorable wind, bore us toward the land.

Proud of our success, we were in high spirits, and made an excellent dinner. A sudden exclamation from Fritz filled me with alarm. "Oh, Heavens!" cried he. "We are lost! A fish of an enormous size is coming up to the boat."

"And why lost?" said I, half angry, and yet half partaking of his fright.

"Be ready with your gun, and the moment he is close upon us we will fire upon him." He had nearly reached the boat, and with the rapidity of lightning had seized the foremost sheep. At this instant, Fritz aimed his fire so skillfully that the balls of the gun were lodged in the head of the monster, which was an enormous shark. The fish half turned himself round in the water and hurried off to sea, staining the water red, which convinced us he had been severely wounded.

The animal being now out of sight, I resumed the rudder. And as the wind drove us straight toward the bay, I took down the sail, and continued rowing till we reached a convenient spot for our cattle to land. I had then only to untie the ends of the cords from the boat, and they stepped contentedly on shore. We happily followed their example.

Ernest and Jack now ran to the boat, shouting their admiration of the mast, the sail, and the flag. We began to unpack our cargo, while Jack stole aside and amused himself with the animals, took off the jackets from the sheep and goats, bursting into shouts of laughter at the ridiculous figure of the ass adorned with his two casks and his swimming apparatus, and braying loud enough to make us deaf.

Jack had round his waist a belt of metal covered with yellow skin, in which were fixed two pistols. "In the name of Heaven," I exclaimed, "where did you procure this curious costume, which gives you the look of a smuggler?"

"From my own manufactory," replied he, "and if you cast your eyes upon the dogs, you will see more of my specimens."

Accordingly I looked at them. Each had on a collar similar to Jack's belt, but the collars were armed with nails, the points of which were outwards, and exhibited a formidable appearance. "And is it you, Mr. Jack," cried I, "who have invented and executed these collars and your belt?"

"Yes, Father, they are indeed my invention, with a little of my mother's assistance with the needle."

"But where did you get the leather and the thread and the needle?"

"Fritz's jackal furnished the first," answered my wife, "and for the last, have I not an enchanted bag, from which I draw out such articles as I need?" I tenderly embraced her to express my thanks.

Perceiving that no preparations were making for supper, I told Fritz to bring us the Westphalia ham. Fritz returned, displaying with exultation the large ham, which we had begun to cut in the morning. "A ham!" cried one and all. "A ham! and ready dressed! What a nice supper we shall have!"

"I have something in my hand with which I shall make a pretty side dish," said my wife. "In the twinkling of an eye you shall see it make its entrance." She now showed us about a dozen turtles' eggs, and then hurried away to make an omelet of some of them.

"Look, Father," said Ernest, "if they are not the very same which Robinson Crusoe found in his island! See, they are like white balls, covered with a skin like wetted parchment! We found them upon the sands along the shore."

"Your account is perfect, my dear boy," said I. "By what means did you make so useful a discovery?"

"Oh, that is part of our history," interrupted my wife; "for I also have a history to relate, when you are ready to listen to it."

"Hasten then, my love, and get your pretty side dish ready, and we will have the history for the dessert. In the meantime I will relieve the cow and the ass from their jackets. Come along, boys, and help." They followed me gaily to the shore, and were not long in attending to the cow and the ass, but with the sow, our success was not so easy. No sooner was she untied than she escaped and ran so fast that none could catch her. Ernest sent the two dogs after her, who caught at her ears, and brought her back, making hideous noises. At last she suffered us to take off her cork jacket. We now laid everything across the ass's back, and returned to the tent; our slothful Ernest highly delighted that our loads were carried by a servant.

In the meanwhile, the kind mother had prepared the omelet, and spread a tablecloth on the end of the cask of butter, upon which she had placed some of the plates and silver spoons we had brought from the ship. The ham was in the middle, the omelet and the cheese opposite each other. Altogether a feast not to be despised by inhabitants of a desert island.

When we had finished our repast, I bade Fritz present our company with a bottle of the captain's Canary wine, and asked my wife for the promised history.

5. WE BUILD A BRIDGE

"YOU pretend," said my wife, with a little malicious smile, "to be curious about my history, yet you have not let me speak a single word in all this time. In the first day of your absence, nothing new took place. But this morning, when I was made happy by the sight of your signal, and had set up mine in return, I looked about in hopes of finding a shady place where we might now and then retire from the heat of the sun; but I found not a single tree. It will be impossible, said I to myself, to remain in this place with no shelter but a miserable tent, under which the heat is even more excessive.

"Why not undertake to do something that shall add some one comfort to our existence? I will pass over with my youngest sons to the other side of the river, and try to find some well-shaded agreeable spot, in which we may all be settled.

"I informed the boys of my plans for an excursion, and they lost not a moment in preparing themselves. They examined their arms, their gamebags, chose the best clasp knives, and cheerfully undertook to carry the provision bags, while I was loaded with a large flask of water and a hatchet, for which we might find a use. I also took the light gun which belongs to Ernest, and gave him in return a carbine which might be loaded with several balls at once. We took some refreshment, and sallied forth, with the two dogs for escort. We arrived at the place at which you had crossed the river, and succeeded in passing over. After having filled my flask with river water, we proceeded to the top of the hill which you described to us as so enchanting.

"In casting my eyes over the vast extent before me, I observed a small inviting wood. I had so long sighed for a little shade that I resolved to bend our course toward it; for this, however, it was necessary to walk along the river and turn at last upon the wood. We found traces of your footsteps, and took care to follow them till we had come to a place which seemed to lead directly to it.

"We soon reached the little wood. A prodigious number of unknown birds were skipping and warbling on the branches of the trees, and here the trees were of enormous height! No, my dear husband, you cannot possibly form an idea of the trees we now beheld! You must somehow have missed this, or so extraordinary a sight could not have escaped you. What appeared to us at a distance to be a wood was only a group of about fourteen trees, the trunks of which seemed to be supported in their upright position by arches being formed by the roots of the tree.

"Jack climbed upon one of these arch-formed roots, and with a packthread in his hand measured the actual circumference of the tree itself. More than twenty-eight feet. I made thirty-two steps in going round one of those giant productions at the roots, and its height from the ground to the place where the branches begin to shoot may be more than sixty feet. The twigs of the tree are strong and thick, its leaves bear some resemblance to the hazel tree of Europe, but I was unable to discover that it bears any fruit. The large breadth of shade invited us to make this spot the place to rest. I resolved to go no farther, but to enjoy its delicious coolness till it should be time to return. I sat down with my three sons around me and we took out our provision bags. A charming stream flowed at our feet, increased the coolness and beauty of the scene, and supplied us with a fresh and cooling beverage. If we could but contrive a kind of tent that could be fixed in one of the trees, we might well settle here. I had found nothing in any other direction that suited us so in every respect, and I resolved to look no further.

"When we had shared our dinner and were well rested we set out on our return, again keeping close to the river, half expecting to see along the shore some vestiges of the vessel which the waves might have washed up.

"As I expected, we found there pieces of timber, poles, large and small chests, and other articles, which I knew had come from the vessel. None of us, however, were strong enough to bring them away. We dragged all we could reach to the dry sands, beyond the reach of the waves at high water.

"We now perceived Flora turning over a round substance she had found in the sands, some pieces of which she swallowed from time to time. Ernest pronounced them to be turtles' eggs. We succeeded in collecting nearly two dozen of them. We then cast our eyes upon the sea, and to our astonishment perceived a sail. Ernest exclaimed that it was you and Fritz; and we soon had the happiness of seeing that it was indeed our well-beloved! We ran eagerly toward the river, arrived at the place of your landing, and had nothing further to do but to throw ourselves into your arms!"

The next morning we resumed the question of our change of abode "My own opinion is," said I, "that we had better remain here, where Providence seems to have conducted us. The place is favorable to our personal safety; we are on all sides protected by the rocks. It is an asylum inaccessible but by sea, or by the passage of the river. And it is near the vessel, from which we may continue to enrich ourselves. Let us have patience yet a little longer at least, till we have got all that can be removed, or that would be useful to us, from the ship."

My wife replied, that the intense heat of the sands was insupportable, and that by remaining, we lost all hope of procuring fruits of any kind, and must live on oysters, or on wild birds.

"As for the safety you boast of," pursued she, "the rocks did not prevent a visit from the jackals, and tigers or other animals might follow their example. Lastly, as to the treasures we might continue to draw from the vessel, I renounce them. We are already in possession of provisions and other useful things; and in truth, my heart is always filled with apprehension when you and Fritz are exposed to the danger of the sea."

"We will then think seriously of the matter; but let us have a good plan of operation before we leave this spot for your favorite wood. First, we must contrive a storehouse among the rocks for our provisions and other things, and to which, in case of invasion in the wood, we can retreat and defend ourselves. The next thing is to throw a bridge across the river, if we are to pass it with all our family and baggage."

"A bridge!" exclaimed my wife. "Can you

possibly think of such a thing? If we stay while you build a bridge, we may consider ourselves as fixed for life. Why should we not cross the river as we did before? The ass and the cow will carry all we possess upon their backs."

"But to keep what they carry dry, they must not perform their journey as they did from the vessel. For this reason, we must contrive a bridge. We shall want also some sacks and baskets to contain our different matters; you may therefore set about making these, and I will undertake the bridge, which, the more I consider, the more I find to be indispensable."

Thus, then, we decided the important question of removing to a new abode. We then fixed upon a plan of labor for the day, and awaked the boys. They were delighted with our project of building a bridge.

We now began to look about for breakfast. My wife milked the cow, and afterward gave some of the milk to each of the children. With a part of what remained she made a sort of sop with biscuits, and the rest she put into one of the flasks, to accompany us on our expedition. During this time, I was preparing the boat for another journey to the vessel to bring away a sufficient quantity of planks and timbers for the bridge. After breakfast we set out; and now I took with me Ernest as well as Fritz to accomplish our object in a shorter time.

We rowed stoutly till we reached the current, which soon drew us on beyond the bay. But scarcely had we passed a little islet than we perceived a prodigious quantity of sea gulls and other birds. Curious to discover what could be the reason, I steered for the spot, but the boat made but little way, and I hoisted my sail.

I approached near enough to step upon the land. After bringing the boat to anchor with a heavy stone, we stole softly up to the birds, feeding eagerly upon an enormous fish, which had been thrown there by the sea. So occupied were they with the feast that not one of them attempted to fly off. Fritz expressed his wonder at the monstrous size of the animal, and asked me by what means it could have got there?

"I believe," answered I, "that it is the very shark you wounded yesterday. See, here are the two balls which you discharged at its head."

"Yes, yes, it is the very same," said my

young hero joyously. "I well remember I had two balls in my gun, and here they are, lodged in its head."

Ernest drew out the iron ramrod from his gun, and by striking it to right and left among the birds, so on dispersed them. Fritz and I then cut several long strips of the skin from the head of the shark, with which we were proceeding to our boat, when I observed, lying on the ground, some planks and timbers which had recently been cast by the sea on this little island. On measuring the longest, we perceived they would answer our purpose; and with the assistance of the crow and a lever which we had brought with us, found means to get them into the boat, and thus spare ourselves a visit to the vessel. We bound the timbers together with the planks upon them, in the manner of a raft, and tied them to the end of the boat. Through this adventure, we were ready to return in four hours from the time of departure, after having done a good day's work.

Once more we landed safely on our shore and called to our family as loudly as we could. We were answered in turn, and in a few minutes my wife appeared between her two little boys returning from the river, each carrying a handkerchief in hand, filled with some new prize. Jack reached us before the rest; and his first act was to open the handkerchief he held, and pour out a large number of lobsters at our feet. A prodigious heap, and all alive, so that we were sure of excellent dinners for some days at least.

My wife set about dressing some of the lobsters, while Fritz and I untied the raft of timbers and planks, and moved them from the boat. I imitated the example of the Laplanders, in harnessing their reindeer for drawing their sledges. Instead of tracers, halters, etc., I put a piece of rope, with a running knot at the end, round the neck of the ass, and passed the other end between its legs, to which I tied the piece of wood which I wished to move. The cow was harnessed in the same manner, and our materials were drawn piece by piece to the spot chosen at the river for our bridge. It was a place where the shore on each side was steep, and of equal height. There was even on our side an old trunk of a tree lying on the ground, which I intended to use.

"Now then, boys," said I, "the first thing is to see if our timbers are long enough to reach to the other side. By my eye, I should think they are; but if I had a surveyor's plane, we might be quite sure, instead of working at a venture."

"But my mother has some balls of packthread, with which she measured the height of the giant tree," interrupted Ernest. "We could tie a stone to the end of one of them, and throw it to the other side of the river; then we could draw it to the very brink, and thus obtain the exact length for our timbers."

"Excellent!" cried I. "Run quickly and fetch the packthread." The stone was tied to the packthread and thrown across as we had planned; we drew it gently back to the river edge, marking the place where the bridge was to rest. We measured the string, and found that the distance from one side to the other was eighteen feet. It appeared to me, that I must allow three feet of extra length at each end for fixing them, making therefore in all twenty-four; and many of those we had brought were of this length. There now remained the difficulty of carrying one end across the stream; but we determined to discuss this while we ate our dinner.

We hurried through our meal, each being deeply interested in building the bridge.

Having decided on the means of laying our timbers across the river, first I attached one of them to the trunk of the tree by a strong cord, long enough to turn freely round the trunk; I then fastened a second cord to the other end of the timber, and tying a stone to its extremity, flung it to the opposite bank. I next crossed the river on the broken stones with a pulley, which I secured to a tree. I passed my second cord through the pulley, and recrossing the river with this cord in my hand, I harnessed the ass and cow to the end of the cord. I next drove the animals back from the bank of the river, and thus they drew the cord tied to the other end. Gradually, the other end of the plank advanced over the river. Presently, it touched the other side, and at length became fixed and firm by its own weight. In a moment Fritz and Jack leaped upon the timber, and crossed the stream with a joyful step upon this narrow but effective bridge.

The first timber being thus laid, a second and a third were fixed in succession. Fritz and I, standing on opposite sides of the river, placed them at such distances from each other as was necessary to form a broad and handsome bridge. We now laid some planks across and marked them quite close to each other. This was executed so expeditiously that our construction was completed in a very short time.

Our labor, however, had fatigued us. We returned to our home, partook heavily of an excellent supper, and went to bed.

6. WE CROSS OUR BRIDGE AND CONSTRUCT A LADDER

AS SOON as we were up and had breakfasted the next morning, I directed my sons to assemble our whole flock of animals, and to leave the ass and the cow to me, that I might load them with the sacks which my wife had made. I had filled these, and fastened them firmly on the back of one of the animals. We next began to put together all the things we should stand most in need of for the two or three first days in our new abode, working implements, kitchen utensils, the captain's service of plate, and a small provision of butter, etc., etc. I put these articles into the two ends of each sack, taking care that the sides should be equally heavy, and then fastened them on. I afterward added our hammocks to complete the load.

We were about to march, when my wife stopped me. "We must," said she, "contrive a place for our fowls among the luggage; also for our little Francis, who cannot walk so far. There is also my enchanted bag," said she, smiling, "for who can tell what may yet pop out of it for your good pleasure?"

I now placed the child on the ass's back, fixing the enchanted bag so as to support him, and I tied them so that the animal might even have galloped without danger of his falling off.

We packed and placed in the tent everything we were to leave, and for greater security, fastened down the ends of the sailcloth, by driving stakes through them into the ground. We ranged a number of vessels around the tent both full and empty to serve as a rampart. And thus we confided to the protection of Heaven our remaining treasures and took a solemn farewell of our first place of reception from the awful disaster of the shipwreck.

At length, we set out. Each of us carried a gun upon his shoulder, and a gamebag at his back. My wife led the way with her eldest son, the cow and the ass immediately behind them; the goats, conducted by Jack, came next, one carrying the little monkey on her back. After the goats came Ernest conducting the sheep, while I, as general superintendent, brought up the rear. The dogs for the most part pranced backward and forward, like adjutants to a troop of soldiers. Our march was slow, and somehow patriarchal, resembling our forefathers journeying in the deserts, accompanied by their families and their possessions.

Proudly we crossed our bridge. On the other side of the river the thick grass tempted our animals, who strayed from us to feed upon it. With the help of the dogs, we were able to bring them back to the line of our procession and continue our journey. For fear, however, of a similar occurrence, I directed our march to the left, along the seaside, where no grass would attract them.

But scarcely had we advanced a few steps on the sands, when our two dogs, which had strayed behind among the grass, set up a sort of howl. Fearing the dogs might be attacked by some dangerous wild beast, I advanced to their assistance. But youth is always full of ardor, and in spite of my warning, the boys eagerly jumped to the place from which the noise proceeded. In an instant Jack had turned to meet me, calling out, "Come quickly, Father, come quickly, here is a monstrous porcupine!"

Reaching the spot, I perceived that the dogs, with bleeding noses, were running around the animal. Jack took one of the pistols which he carried in his belt, and aimed it so exactly at the head of the porcupine that he fell dead on the instant.

The boys were at a loss for a means to carry away the carcass. They thought of dragging it along the ground. But after vainly attempting to take hold, "we must leave him behind," said they, "but it is a great pity."

While the boys were talking, my wife and I had hastened to relieve the dogs, examining the wounds inflicted by the quills and drawing out those that remained. Fritz had run on before with his gun, hoping to meet with some animal of prey. We followed him at our leisure, till at last we arrived at the place of the giant trees.

"Good heavens! What trees! I never heard of any so prodigious!" exclaimed one and all.

"I must confess," answered I, "I had no idea of the reality. To you be all the honor, my dear wife, of the discovery of this agreeable abode. The great task is the fixing of a tent large enough to receive us all in one of these trees so that we shall be perfectly secure from the invasion of wild beasts."

We began now to unburden our animals and ourselves. We took the precaution of tieing their forelegs together so that they might not go far away or lose themselves. We set the fowls at liberty, and then seating ourselves upon the grass, held a family council. I was somewhat uneasy on the question of our safety during the coming night and the chance of our being attacked by wild beasts. I accordingly observed to my wife that I would make an endeavor for us all to sleep in the tree that very night.

Meanwhile Fritz had stolen away to a short distance, and we heard the report of a gun. We recognized his voice crying out, "I touched him! I touched him!" and in a moment he came running toward us, holding a dead animal of uncommon beauty by the paws.

"Father, Father, look, here is a superb tiger cat," said he, proudly raising it in the air, to show it to the best advantage.

"Bravo!" cried I. "If you had not killed this animal, he would no doubt have demolished in one night our whole stock of poultry. Skin the animal carefully, so as not to injure it, particularly the parts which cover the fore-legs and the tail. You may then make yourself a belt with it. The odd pieces will serve to make some cases to contain our table utensils, the knives, forks, and spoons. Go then, boy, and put away its head, and we will see how to set about preparing the skin."

The boys left me no repose till I had shown them how to take off the skins of the animals without tearing them. In the meanwhile Ernest looked about for a flat stone as a sort of foundation for a fireplace, and little Francis collected some pieces of dry wood for his mother to light a fire.

Presently little Francis came running, with his mouth crammed full of something, and calling out, "Mamma, Mamma! I have found a nice fruit to eat, and I have brought you home some of it!"

"Little glutton!" replied his mother, quite alarmed. "What have you got there? For Heaven's sake, do not swallow the first thing that falls in your way. It may be poisonous." She made him open his mouth, and took out with her finger what he was eating with so keen a relish. With some difficulty she drew out the remains of a fig.

"I got it among the grass, Papa," said Francis, "and there are a great many more. I thought it must be good to eat, for the fowls and the pigeons, and even the pig, came to the place, and ate them in large quantities."

"You see then, my dear," said I to my wife, "that our beautiful trees are fig trees, at least the kind which are thus named at the Antilles." I cautioned the boys never to taste anything till they had seen it eaten by birds and monkeys. At the word monkeys, they all ran to visit the little orphan, whom they found seated on the root of a tree. Francis offered him a fig, which he first turned round and round, then smelled at it, and then ate it voraciously. "Bravo! Mr. Monkey," exclaimed the boys. "So these figs are good to eat!"

In the meanwhile my wife had been busy making a fire and preparing for our dinner.

While our dinner was being prepared, I employed my time in making some packing needles with some of the quills of the porcupine, which the boys had contrived to draw from his skin, and bring home.

I put the point of a large nail into the fire till it was red-hot. Then taking hold of it with some wet linen in my hand, by way of guard, I used it to perforate the thick end of the quills. I had soon the pleasure of presenting my wife with a large packet of long, stout needles, which were the more valuable as she intended to contrive some better harness for our animals, and had been perplexed for want of some larger needles.

I had singled out the highest fig tree and bade the boys try how high they could throw a stick or stone into it. I also tried myself; none of us could touch even the lowest branches. I perceived, therefore, that we should want some new inventions for fastening the ends of my ladder to them. Meanwhile I assisted Jack and Fritz in carrying the skin of the tiger cat to a near rivulet, where we confined it under water with some large stones. After this we returned and dined heartily on slices of ham and bread and cheese, under the shade of our beautiful trees.

Our repast ended. My wife began preparing the harness for the animals, that they might fetch wood from the seashore, or other articles of use to us. In the meantime, I set about suspending our hammocks to some of the arched roots of the trees, and spread a piece of sailcloth large enough to cover them, to preserve us from the dew, and from insects.

With the two eldest boys I hastened to the seashore, to choose out pieces of wood proper for the steps of my ladder. Ernest discovered some bamboo canes in a sort of bog. Completely cleared of dirt, and stripped of their leaves, I found that they were precisely what I wanted. I cut them with my hatchet on the spot, in pieces of four or five feet long. The boys bound them together in faggots, and we prepared to return with them to our tree.

I next required some straight and slender stalks, for the arrows I would need. At some distance, in a sort of thicket, I hoped to find some young pliant twigs which I might use.

We had hardly reached the spot when Flora threw herself furiously into the middle of the bushes. A troop of large and beautiful flamingos rose into the air with a loud rustling. Fritz fired instantly and two of the birds fell among the bushes. One of them was killed, the other was only slightly wounded in the wing. Unable to fly, he ran rapidly toward the swamp, and we feared he would escape. Fritz plunged up to his knees in the water, to pick up the dead flamingo he had killed, while I proceeded more cautiously in my pursuit of the wounded bird. Flora came to my assistance, and running on before, held the flamingo fast till I reached the spot, and took him into my protection. The bird made stout resistance, but at last I succeeded in tieing his feet and wings with my handkerchief, though he still fluttered about distressingly, trying to escape.

Fritz was not long in extricating himself from the swamp. He now appeared holding the dead flamingo by the feet. But I wished to preserve my bird alive. Holding the flamingo under my left arm, and my gun in my right hand, I jumped as best I could, to the swamp's edge at the risk of sinking every moment in the mud.

From some of the oldest of the stalks of bamboo, I now cut their hard pointed ends, to serve for the tips of my arrows, and cut two of the longest canes I could find to measure the height of our giant tree. On our returning, Ernest took charge of the canes, Fritz carried the dead flamingo, and I resumed the care of the living one.

We at length arrived once more at our giant trees and all were delighted at the sight of our new captures. My wife asked where we should get food enough for all the animals we brought home. "Some of them," I said, "will feed us, instead of being fed, and one will, I hope, prove able to find food for himself."

I examined his wound and found that only one wing was injured by the ball, but that the other had been slightly wounded by the dog in holding him. I applied some ointment to both, which seemed immediately to ease the pain. I then tied him with a long string to a stake I had driven into the ground, near the river, that he might go in when he pleased.

In the meantime, my little railers had tied the two longest canes together, and were endeavoring to measure the tree with them, vastly amused to find that they reached no farther than the top of the arch formed by the roots. I sobered them a little by recalling to Fritz's memory some lessons in land surveying he had received in Europe, and that the measure of the highest mountains, and their distance from each other, may be ascertained by the application of triangles and supposed lines.

Fixing my canes in the ground, and using string, which Fritz guided according to my directions, I found that the height of the lower branches of our tree was forty feet; a figure I was obliged to ascertain before I could determine the length of my ladder. I now set Fritz and Ernest to work, to measure our stock of thick ropes, of which I wanted no less than eighty feet for the two sides of the ladder; the two youngest collected all the small string we had used for measuring, and carried it to their mother.

I sat down on the grass, and began to make some arrows with a piece of the bamboo, and the short sharp points of the canes I had taken such pains to secure. As the arrows were hollow, I filled them with moist sand, to give a little weight, and lastly, I topped them with a bit of feather from the flamingo, to make them fly straight.

Just at this moment Fritz joined us, after measuring the ropes. Our stock of rope in all, was about five hundred fathoms, which I knew to be more than sufficient for my ladder.

I now tied the end of a ball of strong thread to an arrow, and fixing it to the bow, shot it into the tree so as to make the arrow pass over one of the largest branches and fall again to the ground. Thus I lodged my thread securely, while I had command of the end and the ball below. It was now easy to tie a piece of rope to the end of the thread, and draw it upward, till the knot should reach the same branch. Having thus made quite sure of being able to raise my ladder, we all set to work.

I cut a length of about one hundred feet from my parcel of ropes, an inch thick. This I divided into two equal parts, which I stretched along on the ground in two parallel lines, at the distance of a foot from each other. I then directed Fritz to cut portions of bamboo, each two feet in length. Ernest handed them to me, one after another. As I received them, I inserted them into my cords at the distance of twelve inches respectively, fixing them with knots in the cord, while Jack drove into each a long nail at the two extremities, to hinder it from slipping out again. Thus, in a very short time, I had formed a ladder of forty rounds in length, firm and compact.

I now tied it with strong knots to the end of the rope which hung from the tree and pulled it by the other, till our ladder reached the branch, and seemed to rest well upon it. All the boys wished to be the first to ascend upon it; but I decided on Jack, the nimblest and the lightest figure among them. Accordingly, his brothers and I held the ends of the rope and the ladder with all our strength, while Jack tripped up the rounds with ease, and presently took his post upon the branch. But he had not strength enough to tie the rope firmly to the tree. Fritz assured me that he could ascend as safely as his brother; but as he was much heavier, I was not altogether sure. I fastened the end of the ladder with forked stakes to the ground, and then advised him to divide his weight, by occupying four rounds of the ladder at the same time with his feet and hands. It was not long before we saw him side by side with Jack, forty feet above our heads, and both saluting us with exultant cries.

By passing the rope round and round the branch, Fritz fastened the ladder with so much skill and intelligence that I later ascended myself, to conclude the business he had begun. But first I tied a large pulley to the end of the rope, and carried it with me. When I was at the top, I fastened the pulley to a branch within reach, that I might be able the next day to draw up the planks and timbers for building my aerial castle. I executed all this by the light of the moon, and felt the satisfaction of having done a good day's work. I now descended my rope ladder, and joined my wife and children.

My wife presented me with her day's work—some traces, and a breast leather each for the cow and the ass. I promised her that we should all be completely settled in the tree the following day, and we then assembled to supper.

7. THE TREE HOUSE — A FAMILY WALK TO TENT HOUSE

THE NEXT morning after breakfast, we fell to work. My wife set off to the seashore with Ernest, Jack, and Francis, attended by the ass, to replenish our exhausted store of wood. I ascended the tree with Fritz, to make necessary preparations for my undertaking. Most of the branches grew close to each other, in horizontal direction. Those that did not, I cut off either with the saw or hatchet. I left those which spread themselves evenly upon the trunk, and had the largest circuit, as a support for my floor. Above these, at the height of forty-six feet, I found others upon which to suspend our hammocks; and higher still, there was a further series of branches, destined to receive the roof of my tent, which for the present was to be formed of nothing more than a large surface of sailcloth.

Our progress was very slow. It was necessary to raise certain beams to this height of forty feet, and here my pulley served to excellent purpose, and Fritz and I drew them up to the elevation of the tent, one by one. When I had already placed two beams upon the branches, I hastened to fix my planks upon them. I made my floor double, that it might have sufficient solidity if the beams should be warped from their places. I then formed a wall of staves of wood like a park paling, all round for safety. This operation, and a third journey to the seashore to collect the timber necessary, filled our morning so completely, that none of us had thought about dinner. We contented ourselves with a bit of ham and some milk, and returned to finish our aerial palace, which now made an imposing appearance. We unhooked our hammocks from the projecting roots, and by means of my pulley hoisted them up the tree, where they were soon hung on the branches, ready for our reception that very evening. The sailcloth roof was supported by the thick branches above. As it was of great size and hung down on every side, I nailed it to the paling on two sides, thus getting not only a roof, but two walls also. The immense trunk of the tree formed a third side, while in the fourth was the entrance to our apartment, and in this I left a large aperture, both as a means of seeing what passed without, and admitting a current of air to cool us.

Well satisfied with the execution of my plan, I descended with Fritz, who had assisted me throughout the whole; and as the day was not far advanced, and we had still some planks remaining, we set about contriving a large table, to be placed between the roots of the tree, and surrounded with benches. And this place we called our dining parlor.

Exhausted by the fatigues of the day, I threw myself on a bank, and my wife having seated herself near me, I thanked her for the tender care she was ever imposing on herself. And then I observed that the many blessings we enjoyed led the thoughts naturally to the beneficent Giver of them all, and tomorrow being a Sabbath day, we would rest from work, in obedience to His command, and otherwise keep it holy.

We now assembled round our table to supper, my wife holding in her hand an earthen pot, which we had before observed upon the fire, and the contents of which made us all curious. She took off the cover, and with a fork drew out of it the flamingo which Fritz had killed. She informed us that she preferred cooking it this way to roasting, because of Ernest, who had advised her to improve it by stewing. We rallied our glutton boy on this and his brothers named him the cook. However, the bird was excellent, and was eaten up to the very bones.

The boys now lighted one of the heaps of wood. I tied long ropes loosely round the necks of our dogs, purposing to mount to our tent with the ends in my hand, that I might let them loose upon the enemy at the first barking I should hear. Every one was eager to retire to rest, and I gave the signal for ascending the ladder.

The eldest boys were up in an instant, then came their mother's turn. She proceeded slowly and cautiously, and arrived in perfect safety. My own ascension was last, and the most difficult. For I carried little Francis on my back, and the end of the ladder had been loosened at the bottom, that I might be able to draw it up in the tent during the night. At last, however, I got to the top, and drew the ladder after me.

It appeared to us that we were in one of the strong castles of the ancient cavaliers, in which, when the drawbridge is raised, the inhabitants are secured from every attack of the enemy.

Notwithstanding this apparent safety, I kept our guns in readiness.

The next morning we descended the ladder, and breakfasted on warm milk. We served the animals with their meal and then all sat down on the tender grass, the boys full of impatient curiosity, their mother absorbed in silent reflection; while I was filled with the desire to impress upon the young minds of my children a subject I considered of the highest importance for their well-being.

All now standing up, I repeated aloud the church service, which I knew by heart, and we sang verses from the hundred-and-nineteenth Psalm. I then began the Great Parable of Creation with the words:

"My dear children, there was once a Great King . . ." and with the ending of the parable, a short prayer of benediction, I concluded the solemnity of our Sunday service.

The next morning the boys assembled round me with a petition that I would show them how to use arrows. We accordingly sat down on the grass; I took out my knife, and, with the remains of a bamboo cane, began to make a bow. I was well satisfied to observe them one and all take a fancy to shooting with an arrow. This exercise might possibly become our only means of protection and subsistence, for our provision of powder must at last be exhausted, or we might be deprived of it by accident. It was of the utmost importance to us to acquire other means of killing animals for food or attacking our enemies.

While I was finishing a bow, and silently reflecting on the subject, Ernest slipped suddenly away. At the same moment Fritz appeared, with the wetted skin of the tiger cat in his hand, and I began my instructions in the tanner's trade.

I told him the method of getting rid of the fat of the skin, by rubbing it over with sand, and placing it in running water till it had no longer any appearance of flesh, or any smell. Next, after rubbing it with soft butter, to make it supple, to stretch the skin in different directions. And also to make use of some eggs in the operation, if his mother could spare them. "You will not at first produce such excellent workmanship as I have seen in England; but with patience, you will have some decent-looking cases, and the pleasure of using the work of your own hands."

At this moment we heard the firing of a gun from our tent in the tree, and two birds at the same time fell dead at our feet. Surprised and alarmed, all eyes turned upward to the place. There we saw Ernest standing outside the tent, a gun in his hand, and heard him triumphantly exclaiming, "Catch them! Catch them there! I have hit them."

One of the dead birds was a sort of thrush, and the other was a very small kind of pigeon, very fat, and of a delicious taste. We now observed that as the wild figs ripened, they attracted these birds. I foresaw that our table would be furnished with a dish fit for a nobleman. I knew that, half-roasted, and put into barrels with melted butter thrown over them, they would keep a long time, and prove an excellent resource. My wife set about stripping the feathers of the birds, to dress them for our dinner. I seated myself by her side, and proceeded in my arrow-making.

Thus finished another day. Supper ended, and prayers said, we ascended the ladder in procession, and each got into his hammock to a tranquil sleep.

Jack had finished the trial of his arrows. They flew to admiration; and he practiced his new art incessantly. Little Francis waited with impatience. When I finished his bow, and prepared some little arrows for him, then I must make him a quiver. I took some bark from the branch of a tree, which came off in a round form; and folding the edges over each other, I stuck them together with glue produced from our soup cakes, stuck on a round piece for the bottom; and then tied to it a loop of string which I hung round his neck. He put his arrows into it, and, quite happy, took his bow and ran to try his skill. Fritz had also cleaned and prepared his materials for the cases, when his mother summoned us to dinner. We cheerfully placed ourselves under the shade of our tree, round the table I had manufactured. During the repast, I made the following proposition to the boys.

"What think you, my good friends," said I, "of giving a name to the place of our abode, and to the different parts of the country which are known to us?"

They all exclaimed at the excellent idea.

Father: "We shall begin with the bay by which we entered this country. What say you, Fritz? You speak first, for you are eldest."

Fritz: "Let us call it *Oyster Bay*. You remember what a quantity of oysters we found in it."

Jack: "Oh, no; let it rather be called *Lobster Bay,* for you cannot have forgotten what a large one it was that caught hold of my leg, and which I carried home to you."

My Wife: "Out of gratitude to God, who conducted us hither in safety, call it the *Bay of Safety*."

Father: "These words are appropriate, and please me extremely. But what name shall we give to the spot where we first set up our tent?"

Fritz: "Let us simply call it *Tent House*."

Father: "Very well. And the little islet at the entrance of Providence Bay, in which we found so many planks and beams that enabled us to make our bridge, how shall it be named?"

Ernest: "It may be called *Sea Gull Island*, or *Shark Island;* for it was here we saw those animals."

Father: "I am for Shark Island; for it was the shark that was the cause of the sea gulls being there."

Jack: "We could call the marsh, in which you cut the canes for our arrows, *Flamingo Marsh*."

Father: "Quite right, I think. But now comes the great question: What name shall we give to our present abode?"

Ernest: "It ought to be called simply *Tree Castle*."

Fritz: "No, no, that will not do at all; that is the same as if, when we wanted to name a town, we called it *The Town.* Let us invent a more noble name."

Father: "Will you let me decide the question for you? I think our abode should be called *The Falcon's Nest*; for you are not arrived at the dignity of eagles, but are, like the falcon, obedient, docile, active, and courageous. Ernest can have no objection to this; for, as he knows, falcons make their nests in large trees."

All exclaimed, clapping their hands, "Yes, yes; we will have it *The Falcon's Nest*! The sound is quite chivalrous; so health to Falcon's Nest!" they cried, all looking up to the tree, and making low bows. I poured out a small quantity of sweet wine, and presented it to each, to solemnize our baptism.

"Now then," said I, "for the promontory, where Fritz and I in vain wearied our eyes in search of our companions of the vessel; I think it may properly be called *Cape Disappointment.*"

All: "Yes, this is excellent. And the river with the bridge—"

Father: "If you wish to commemorate one of the greatest events of our history, it ought to be called *The Jackal's River;* for these animals crossed it when they came and attacked us, and it was there that one of them was killed. The bridge I should name *Family Bridge,* because we were all employed in its construction, and all crossed it together on our way to this place. Let me ask you all, will it not be a great pleasure to converse about the country we inhabit, now that we have instituted names as if everything belonged to us?"

Ernest: "It will be just as if we had farms and country houses all dependent upon our castle."

In this pleasing kind of chat, the time of dinner passed agreeably. As the evening advanced, and the intense heat of the day diminished, I invited my family to take a walk. "Leave your work for this time, my boys," said I, "and let us make a short excursion. Which way shall we direct our steps?"

Fritz: "Let us go to Tent House, Father. We are in want of powder and shot."

My Wife: "I too vote for Tent House. My butter is nearly gone, for Fritz took an unreasonable share for his new trade of tanning."

Father: "To Tent House, then. But not on our accustomed road along the seashore, but rather explore some other way. We will follow our own little stream as far as the wall of rocks, cross it by jumping from stone to stone, and so get to Tent House. We will return with our provisions by the road of Family Bridge, and along the seashore. This new route may possibly furnish some additional discoveries."

Our route along the stream was at first extremely agreeable, being sheltered by the shade of large trees, while the ground under our feet was a short and soft kind of grass. We proceeded slowly, looking about us to the right and left; the eldest boys often dashed on before, so that we sometimes lost sight of them. In this manner we reached the end of the wood. But the country now appearing to be less open, we thought it would be prudent to bring our whole company together.

On looking forward, we saw the boys approaching us at full gallop, and this time, for a wonder, the grave Ernest was first. They reached us panting for breath, and full of joy and eagerness.

Conversing on different subjects, we reached the long chain of rocks, over which our pretty Falcon's Stream made its escape in a cascade. We thus reached Jackal's River, and from there proceeded to Tent House, having with difficulty pushed our way through the high grass. We distinguished different families of grasses; the Indian fig in abundance, with its large broad leaf; aloes of different forms and colors; while that which pleased us best, was the crowned pineapple, of which we all partook with avidity.

Soon after, I discovered in the clefts of the rocks, the karata, many of which were now in blossom. The pith is used for tinder by the Negroes, who also make a strong kind of thread from the fibers of its leaves. Pleased with this discovery, and wishing to exhibit one of its uses to my children, I desired Ernest to take out my flint and steel.

I took a dried stalk of the tree, stripped off the bark, and there appeared a kind of dry spongy substance, which I laid upon the flint. Striking it with a steel, it instantly caught fire. The boys looked on with astonishment.

"Now, then," said I, "we have an article of greater usefulness. What materials will your mother use for sewing your clothes, when her thread from the enchanted bag is exhausted?"

My Wife: "I have long been uneasy, and would willingly exchange our greatest luxury for some hemp or flax."

Father: "You will find some excellent thread under the leaves of this extraordinary plant though the lengths of thread will be found not longer than the leaf."

I drew out of one of the leaves a strong piece of red thread, which I gave to my wife.

"How fortunate it is for us," said she, "that you have had the habit of reading and of study! But will it not be difficult to draw out the lengths of thread through the prickles that surround them?"

Father: "Not in the least. We shall put the leaves to dry. The useless part of the leaf will then separate by being beaten, and the mass of thread will remain."

I perceived Ernest holding a leaf upon the end of his knife and turning it about in all directions. "I wish I could know," he said at length, "what little scarlet animals these are on the leaf, which feed so eagerly upon it."

Father: "Ha, ha! Let me look at your leaf. I will wager that it is the insect called the cochineal."

Jack: "The cochineal! What a droll name! What is the cochineal, Father?"

Father: "It is an insect of the kind called suckers, or kermes. It lives by sucking the juice of the leaves of the Indian fig, which, no doubt, is the cause of its beautiful color, so much esteemed in dying; for nothing else produces so fine a scarlet."

We crossed Jackal's River stepping from stone to stone, and shortly arrived at Tent House, where we found everything as we had left it, and each went in pursuit of what he intended to take away. Fritz loaded himself with powder and shot; my wife and I and Francis employed ourselves in filling our pot with butter; Ernest and Jack looked about for the geese and ducks; but as they were become somewhat savage, the boys did not succeed in catching one of them. Thoughtful Ernest took small bits of cheese, tied them to pieces of string, and held them floating on the water. The voracious birds seized them, and Ernest drew them toward him, one by one, with the cheese in its bill, till he had caught the whole. Each bird was then tied in a pocket handkerchief, leaving the head at liberty, and fastened one to each gamebag, so that all had a share in carrying them.

We now set out loaded on our return. Our mutual jokes, and the general good humor which prevailed, served to shorten the walk, and none complained of fatigue till seated under our tree at Falcon's Stream.

8. GOURDS AND A KANGAROO — MORE STORES FROM THE WRECK

I HAD observed along the shore many pieces of wood, of which I thought I could make a kind of conveyance for our cask of butter and other provisions from Tent House to Falcon's Stream, and had determined to go early the next morning, before my family awoke. I had fixed upon Ernest for my assistant, and he promised to be ready at a very early hour.

At the first dawning I quietly awoke Ernest, and we descended the ladder. We roused the ass, and I made him draw some large branches of a tree, which I wanted for my undertaking.

We found the pieces of wood, cut them the proper length, and then laid them crossways on the branches, which we thus converted into a kind of vehicle. We added to the load a little chest, which we found half buried in the sands, quite close to the waves, and then returned to Falcon's Stream. When we reached our home, the chest we had brought was soon opened by a strong hatchet; for all were eager to see what was within. It contained only some sailor's clothes and some linen, and both were wet with the sea.

We then sat down tranquilly to breakfast, and to inspect the booty of the young sportsmen, who had shot about fifty ortolans and thrushes. But they had used so large a quantity of powder and shot that I stopped them. Instead I taught them how to make snares, to be suspended from the branches of the fig tree, and advised them to use for them the thread of the karata, which is as strong as horsehair.

Jack, who had suspended some of the snares to the branches of the tree came down again to bring us the acceptable intelligence that our pigeons had made a sort of nest there of some dry grass, and that it already contained several eggs. I therefore forbade the boys from firing into the tree. I also directed that the snares should be frequently examined, to see that the pigeons were not caught in them, as they might be strangled in their efforts to get loose.

Meanwhile the boys and I had been busily employed, and our work was completed. Two bent pieces of wood, the segments of a circle, which I fixed in their places by a straight piece of wood placed across, and firmly fixed to the bent pieces in the middle and at the rear, formed the outline of my machine. I then fastened two ropes in front, and here was a sledge as perfect as could be desired.

I had not raised my eyes from my work. Now, looking up, I perceived that my wife and two youngest boys had been stripping off the feathers from a quantity of birds.

She was in hopes, she said, that as I had now a sledge, I should not fail to go to Tent House after dinner to fetch the cask of butter, and in the meanwhile she was endeavoring to be ready with the birds, to do as I had advised, to half-roast them and preserve them in butter. I determined on going to Tent House the same day, requesting my wife to hasten the dinner for that purpose. She replied that this was already her intention, as she also had a little project in her head, of which I should be informed on my return. I had one too, which was to refresh myself, after the heat and fatigue of my labors, by a plunge into the sea. I wished that Ernest, who was to accompany me, should bathe also, while Fritz was to remain at home for the protection of the family.

We had harnessed the ass and the cow to our sledge, and, resting our guns upon our shoulders, began our journey. We took the road by the seashore, where the sands afforded better traveling for our vehicle than the thick wild grass. We reached Family Bridge, on Jackal's River, arrived at Tent House and unharnessed the animals to let them graze, while we set to work to load the sledge with the cask of butter, the cask of cheese, a small barrel of gunpowder, different instruments, small balls, and some shot.

It was late when we first observed that our animals, attracted by the excellent quality of the grass on the other side of the river, had repassed the bridge, and wandered out of sight. I directed Ernest to go with Flora and bring them back, intending in the meantime to look for a convenient place for bathing on the other side of Tent House.

I desired Ernest to fill a bag with some of the salt he had formerly observed here for the ass to carry. "During this time I will take the refreshment of bathing. And then it will be your turn to bathe, and mine to take care of the animals."

I returned to the rocks, and was not disappointed in my enjoyment. When I had dressed myself, and was returning to Ernest, I heard his voice, calling out, "Father, Father, a fish! A fish of monstrous size! Run quickly, Father,

I can hardly hold him! He is eating the string of my line!" I ran to the place from which the voice proceeded, and found Ernest lying along the ground, upon the extremity of a point of land, and pulling in his line, to which a large fish was hanging, struggling to get loose. I snatched the rod from his hand, for I feared the weight and activity of the fish might pull him into the water. I gave the line length, to calm the fish, and then contrived to draw him gently along into a shallow, from which he could no longer escape, and thus was secured. He appeared to weigh about fifteen pounds, and would afford the greatest pleasure to the good mother at Falcon's Stream.

While Ernest bathed, I had time to fill some more bags with salt. We then harnessed and loaded our animals, and resumed the road to Falcon's Stream.

We had proceeded about halfway, when Flora suddenly sprang off, and by her barking gave notice that she scented some game. We soon after saw her pursuing an animal which in endeavoring to escape made the most extraordinary jumps imaginable. The dog continued to follow; the creature, in trying to avoid him, passed within gunshot of the place where I stood. I fired, but its flight was so rapid that I did not hit. Ernest, at a small distance behind, hearing the report of my gun, prepared his own, and fired it off at the instant the singular animal was passing near him, seeking to hide among the tall herbage just by. He had fired so skillfully that the animal fell dead on the instant. I ran with extreme curiosity to ascertain what kind of quadruped it might be.

We examined the creature in silence. I could not be sure that I had ever seen an engraving or description of it in any natural history, or book of travels. It was as large as a sheep, with a tail like a tiger and a head like a mouse.

"What do you think is its name, Father?" cried Ernest. "I would give all the world to know."

Father: "And so would I, my boy. Let us again examine this interesting quadruped."

Ernest: "I think it can hardly be named a quadruped. The little forelegs look much more like hands, as is the case with monkeys."

Father: "They are, notwithstanding, legs. Let us look for its name among the animals who give suck. On this point we cannot be mistaken. Now let us examine its teeth."

Ernest: "Here are the four incisory teeth, like the squirrel."

Father: "Thus we see that it belongs to the

order of Nibblers. Now let us look for some names of animals of this kind."

Ernest: "Besides squirrels, I recollect only mice, marmots, hares, beavers, porcupines, and jumpers."

Father: "Jumpers! . . wait a moment—an idea strikes me. I will wager that our animal is one of the large jumpers, called kangaroos. This animal was first observed by the celebrated navigator, Captain Cook. You may have then killed an animal at once rare and remarkable. But now let us see how we shall manage to drag him to the sledge."

Ernest requested that I assist him to carry it, as he was afraid of spoiling its beautiful mouse-colored skin by dragging it on the ground. I therefore tied the forelegs of the kangaroo together; and by means of two canes, we contrived to carry it to the sledge, upon which it was securely fastened.

We arrived happily at Falcon's Stream, to the salutations of our family. I gave a treat of salt to each of our animals, and made an excellent supper on our little fish, and some vegetables. The labors of the day had disposed us all to seek repose. We therefore said our prayers at an early hour, mounted our ladder, and were soon asleep.

I rose with the first crowing of the cock, descended the ladder, and set about skinning the kangaroo, taking care not to deface its beautiful smooth coat. My family were assembled about me and calling out "Famine," before I had finished my work. Breakfast over, I ordered Fritz to get ready for Tent House to prepare the boat, and again proceed to the vessel.

We took Ernest and Jack a little way with us, and then sent them back with a message to their mother—that we might be forced to pass the night on board the vessel. It was most essential to get from it, if yet afloat, all that could be saved.

We got into the boat, and, gaining the current, quickly cleared Safety Bay, and reached the wreck, whose open side offered us an ample space to get on board. When we had fastened our boat, our first care was to select fit materials to construct a raft to carry a considerable burden. We found a sufficient number of water casks, emptied them, replaced the bungs carefully, and threw the casks overboard, after securing them with ropes to keep them together at the vessel's side. We then placed a sufficient number of planks upon them to form a firm and commodious platform, or deck, to which we added a gunwale of a foot in depth all round, to secure the lading. Thus we contrived a handsome raft, in which we could stow three times as much as in our boat. This laborious task had taken up the whole day, short of a minute or two to eat some cold meat we had provided. In the evening, Fritz and I were so weary, that, having taken all due precaution in case of a storm, we lay down in the captain's cabin, on a good elastic mattress. We both slept heavily, side by side, till broad daylight opened our eyes. We rose, and set to work to load our raft.

We began with stripping the cabin of its doors and windows; next we secured the carpenter's and gunner's chests, containing all their tools and implements. Those we could remove with levers and rollers were put entire upon the raft, and we took out of the others what rendered them too heavy. One of the captain's chests was filled with costly articles, which, no doubt, he had meant to dispose of to the opulent planters of Port Jackson, or among the savages. In the collection were several gold and silver watches, snuffboxes of all descriptions, buckles, shirt buttons, necklaces, rings; in short, an abundance of all the trifles of European luxury. But the discovery that delighted me most was a chest containing some dozens of young plants of every species of European fruits, which had been carefully packed in moss for transportation—pear, plum, almond, peach, apple, apricot, chestnut trees, and vine shoots. We discovered a number of bars of iron, and large pigs of lead, grinding stones, cart wheels ready for mounting, a complete set of farrier's instruments, tongs, shovels, plowshares, rolls of iron and copper wire, sacks full of maize, peas, oats, vetches, and even a little hand mill. We found a sawmill in a separated state, but each piece numbered, and so accurately fitted that nothing was easier than to put it together for use.

With difficulty and hard labor, we finished our loading, having added a large fishing net, quite new, and the vessel's great compass. With the net, Fritz found two harpoons and a rope windlass, such as they use in whale fishery. He asked me to let him place the harpoons, tied to the end of the rope, over the bow of our tub boat, and thus be in readiness in case of seeing any large fish; and I indulged him in his fancy.

Having executed our undertaking, we stepped into the tub boat, and pushed out for the current, drawing our raft triumphantly after us with a stout rope, which we had carefully and securely fastened at its head.

9. THE TORTOISE HARNESSED — ANOTHER TRIP TO THE WRECK

THE WIND was favorable, and briskly swelled our sail. The sea was calm, and we advanced at a considerable rate. Fritz had for some time fixed his eyes on something floating on the water. I soon perceived that it was a tortoise, which had fallen asleep in the sun on the surface of the water. Fritz entreated me to steer softly within view of so extraordinary a creature, and I readily consented. But as his back was toward me, and the sail between us, I did not observe his motions, till a violent jerk of the boat, a sudden turning of the windlass, accompanied by a rapid motion of the boat, gave me the necessary explanation. "For Heaven's sake, what are you about, Fritz?" I exclaimed.

"I have caught him!" cried Fritz, not hearing one word I had been saying. "The tortoise is ours; it cannot escape, Father! Is not this, then, a valuable prize, for it will furnish dinners for us all for many weeks?"

I soon perceived that the harpoon had caught the animal, which, feeling itself wounded, thus agitated the vessel in its endeavors to get away. I quickly pulled down the sail, and seizing a hatchet, sprang to the boat's head to cut the rope, and let the harpoon and the tortoise go. But Fritz caught hold of my arm, begging me to wait. He proposed watching himself, with the hatchet in his hand, to cut the rope suddenly should any sign of danger appear. I yielded to his entreaties.

Drawn along by the tortoise, we proceeded with hazardous rapidity, but the creature was making for the sea. I therefore again hoisted the sail, and as the wind was to the land, and very brisk, the tortoise found resistance of no avail. He accordingly fell into the track of the current, and drew us straight toward our usual place of landing, and, by good fortune, without striking upon any of the rocks. The tide threw us upon a sandbank, but the boat, though driven with violence, remained upright in the sand.

I stepped into the water, which did not reach far above my knees, when suddenly the tortoise gave a plunge, and then disappeared. Following the rope, I presently saw him stretched at length at the bottom of the water, where it was so shallow that I cut off his head with the hatchet.

Being now near Tent House, Fritz gave a halloo, and fired a gun, to summon our relatives. The mother and her three young ones soon appeared, running toward us. Upon which Fritz jumped out of the boat, placed the head of our sea prize on the muzzle of his gun, and walked to shore, which I reached at the same moment.

I requested my wife to go with two of the younger boys to Falcon's Stream, and fetch the sledge and the beasts of burden, to put at least part of our booty from the ship safely under shelter the same evening. A tempest, or even the tide, might sweep away the whole during the night. We took every precaution in our power by fixing the boat and the raft, now, at the time of the receding tide, as securely as we could without an anchor.

The sledge arrived, and we placed the tortoise upon it, and also some articles of light weight, such as mattresses, pieces of linen, etc. On reaching our abode, we immediately turned the tortoise on his back, that we might strip off the shell, and make use of some of the flesh while it was fresh. Taking my hatchet, I separated the upper and under shell all round, which were joined by cartilages. The upper shell of the tortoise is extremely convex; the under, on the contrary, is nearly flat. I cut away sufficient flesh of the animal for a meal, and laid the rest carefully on the under shell, which served as a dish, recommending to my wife to cook what I had cut off, with no other seasoning than a little salt, I promised that she would produce a luxurious dish.

Fritz: "I thought, Father, of cleaning the shell thoroughly, and fixing it by the side of our river, and keeping it always full of pure water for my mother's use, when she has to wash the linen, or cook our victuals."

Father: "Excellent, excellent, my boy! And we will execute the idea as soon as we can prepare some clay, as a solid foundation for it."

Ernest: "When the water tub is complete, I will put some roots I have found to soak a little in it, for they are now extremely dry. I do not exactly know what they are. They look something like the radish, or horse-radish; but the plant from which I took them was almost the size of a bush."

Father: "If my suspicion is right, you have made a beneficial discovery. I think your roots are manioc, of which the natives of the West

Indies make a sort of bread or cake which they call cassava.

"But it possesses harmful properties without a certain kind of preparation. Try to find the same place, and bring a sufficient quantity for our first experiment."

We had finished unloading the sledge, and I bade the three eldest boys accompany me to fetch another load before it grew dark. Having reached the raft, we took from it as much as the sledge could hold. One object of my attention was to secure two chests which contained the clothes of my family. I reckoned also on finding in one of the chests some books on interesting subjects, and principally a large handsomely printed Bible. I added to these, four cart wheels and a hand mill for grinding, which, now that we had discovered the manioc, I considered of signal importance.

On our return to Falcon's Nest, we found my wife ready with an ample and agreeable repast. Before she had well examined our new stores, she drew me, with one of her sweetest smiles, by the arm.

"Step this way," said she, "this is the work I performed in your absence," pointing to a large cask half sunk in the ground, and the rest covered over with branches of trees. She then applied a small corkscrew to the side, and filling the shell of a coconut with the contents, presented it to me. I found the liquor equal to the best canary I had ever tasted. "How then," said I, "have you performed this new miracle? I cannot believe the enchanted bag produced it."

"Not exactly," replied she, "an obliging white wave threw it on shore. The boys had little difficulty in getting the cask to Falcon's Stream, where we dug this place in the earth to keep it cool."

My wife now proposed that all should be regaled with some of the delicious beverage. I completed my day's work by drawing up the mattresses we had brought from the ship by means of a pulley, to our chamber in the tree. When I had laid them along to advantage, they looked so inviting that I could scarcely resist my desire to rest.

But now the savory smell of the tortoise called me. I hastened down, and we all partook heartily of the luxurious treat. We returned thanks to God, and speedily retired to sound repose upon the mattresses.

After breakfast the next morning we completed the unloading of the raft, that it might be ready for sea on the flowing of the tide. We were not long in taking two cargoes to Falcon's Stream. At our last trip the water was nearly up to our craft, and shortly after, the tide was high enough for us to row off. Instead of steering for Safety Bay to moor our vessels there securely, I was tempted by a fresh sea breeze to go out again to the wreck. But it was too late to undertake much, and I was unwilling to cause my dear partner uneasiness by passing another night on board. I therefore determined to bring away only what could be obtained with ease and speed, and we searched hastily through the ship for any trifling articles that might be readily removed. Jack was up and down everywhere, and when I saw him again, he drew a wheelbarrow after him, shouting that he had found a vehicle for carrying our wild roots.

But Fritz next disclosed still better news, which was, that he had discovered, behind the bulkhead amidship, a pinnace (a small craft, the fore part of which is square), taken to pieces, with all its appurtenances, and even two small guns for its defense. This intelligence so delighted me that I quitted everything else to run to the bulkhead. But I instantly perceived that to put it together, and launch it, would be an Herculean task. I collected various utensils, a copper boiler, some plates of iron, tobacco graters, two grinding stones, a small barrel of gunpowder, and another full of flints, which I much valued. Jack's barrow was not forgotten; two more were afterward found and added, with straps belonging to them. All these articles were hurried into the boat, and we re-embarked with speed, to avoid the land wind that rises in the evening.

Arrived at Falcon's Stream, my wife exhibited a good store of tuberous roots, which she had got in during our absence, and a quantity of the manioc roots.

"But now," said I, "for some supper and repose, and tomorrow, I shall reward the boys with the novelty of a new trade to be learned."

I waked them very early, reminding them of my promise.

"What is it? What is it?" they exclaimed all at once, springing out of bed, and hurrying into their clothes.

Father: "It is the art of the baker, my boys. Hand me those iron plates that we brought yesterday from the vessel, and the tobacco graters also. Ernest, bring hither the roots you found. But first, my dear, I must request you to make me a small bag of a piece of strong wrapper cloth."

My wife set instantly to work to oblige me.

But having no great confidence in my talents for making either bread or cakes, she first filled a copper boiler with roots, and put it on the fire, that we might not be without something to eat at dinnertime. In the meanwhile I spread a piece of coarse linen on the ground. I gave each of the boys a grater, to rest on the linen, and then to grate the roots of manioc. In a short time each had produced a considerable heap of a substance somewhat resembling pollard.

My wife had completed the bag. I had it well filled with what we called our pollard, and she closed it securely by sewing up the end. I was now to contrive a kind of press. I cut a long, straight, stout branch. I then placed a plank across the table we had fixed between the arched roots of our tree, and on this I laid the bag. I put other planks again upon the bag, and then covered all with the large branch bark-free. The thickest extremity of this I inserted under an arch, while to the other, I suspended all sorts of heavy substances, such as lead, our largest hammers, and bars of iron, which, acting with great force as a press on the bag of manioc, caused the sap it contained to issue in streams.

We then opened the bag, and took out a small quantity of the pollard, which already was dry enough. We stirred the rest about with a stick, and then replaced it under the press. The next thing was to fix one of our iron plates, which was of a round form, and a little hollow, so as to rest upon two blocks of stone at a distance from each other; under this we lighted a large fire, and when the iron plate was completely heated, placed a portion of the dough upon it with a wooden spade. As soon as the cake began to be brown underneath, it was turned, that the other side might be baked also.

When the cake was cold, we broke some of it into crumbs, and gave it to two of the fowls, and a larger piece to the monkey, who nibbled it with perfect relish.

The first thing after dinner was to visit our fowls. Those which had eaten the manioc were in excellent condition as was the monkey. "Now then to the bakehouse, young ones," said I, "as fast as you can scamper." The grated manioc was soon emptied out of the bag, a large fire was quickly lighted, and I placed the boys where a flat surface had been prepared for them. I gave to each a plate of iron and the quantity of a coconut full to make a cake apiece, and they were to try who could succeed the best. They were ranged in a half circle round me, that they might observe how

I proceeded. The result was not discouraging for a first experiment, though now and then a cake was burned. But these served to feed the pigeons and the fowls, which hungrily hovered round us.

The rest of the day was employed by the boys in making several turns with their wheelbarrows, the ass, and our sledge in drawing to Tent House the remaining articles we had brought from the ship.

10. THE PINNACE AND THE CRACKER

FROM the time of discovering the pinnace, my desire to return to the vessel grew irresistible. It was absolutely necessary to collect all my hands to get her out of the wrecked vessel.

After breakfast, then, we set out. We took with us an ample provision of potatoes and cassava, and arms and weapons of every kind. We reached Safety Bay, scattered some food for the geese and ducks, put on our cork jackets, and soon after stepped gaily into our tub raft. Fastening the new boat by a rope to her stern to be drawn along, we put out for the current, fearing that the wreck had disappeared; but it still stood firm between the rocks.

On board, we all repaired to the bulkhead. The cabinet which contained the pinnace was in the interior of the ship, and timbers of prodigious bulk and weight separated it from the breach. What was to be done?

The cabinet was lighted by several small fissures in the timbers, which, after a few minutes to accustom the eye, enabled one to see sufficiently to distinguish objects. I discovered, with pleasure, that all the pieces of which she was composed were so accurately arranged and numbered that I hoped to be able to collect and put them together, if allowed the necessary time, and a convenient place. I therefore decided on the undertaking, and we immediately set about it.

We passed an entire week in this arduous undertaking. I embarked every morning with my three sons, and returned every evening, and never without some small addition to our stores. We were now so accustomed to this that my wife bade us good-by without concern, and we left Tent House without anxiety.

At length the pinnace was completed, and

in condition to be launched. The question was, how to manage this. She was an elegant little vessel, perfect in every part. She had a small neat deck, and her masts and sails were no less exact and perfect than those of a little brig. It was probable she would sail well, from the lightness of her construction, and in consequence drawing but little water. We had pitched and towed all the seams and had even taken the pains to mount her with two small cannon of about a pound weight and, in imitation of larger vessels, had fastened them to the deck with chains.

But in spite of the delight we felt, the commodious, charming little vessel still stood fast, enclosed within four walls. Nor could I conceive a mode of getting her out. We thought to cut away all intervening timbers, but we had neither strength nor time for such a proceeding. From one moment to another, a storm might arise and engulf the ship, timbers, pinnace, ourselves, and all. Despairing, then, of being able to find means, I thought of a project, which could only be tried with tremendous hazard and danger.

I had found on board a strong iron mortar, such as is used in kitchens. I took a thick oak plank, and nailed to different parts of it some large iron hooks. With a knife I cut a groove along the middle of the plank. I sent the boys to fetch some matchwood from the hold, and cut a piece sufficiently long to continue burning at least two hours. Placing this train in the groove of my plank I filled the mortar with gunpowder, pitched it all around and then laid the plank upon it. And lastly, I made the whole fast to the spot with strong chains, crossed by means of the hooks in every direction. Thus I accomplished a sort of cracker[1] from which I expected a happy result. I hung this machine of mischief to the side of the bulkhead next to the sea, having taken care to choose a spot in which its action could not affect the pinnace. When the whole was arranged, I sent the boys to the raft for safety. Though they had assisted in forming the cracker, they had no suspicion of its intended use.

I set fire to the match, the end of which projected far enough beyond the plank to allow me sufficient time to escape, hurried aboard the raft, and set sail.

On our arrival at Tent House, I immediately put the raft in readiness to return speedily to the wreck when the noise of the cracker should inform me that my scheme had taken effect. We set busily to work emptying her, and very

[1] Bomb.

soon our ears were assailed with the noise of an explosion of such violence that my wife and the boys, who were ignorant of the cause, were dreadfully alarmed. "What can it be? What is the matter?—What can have happened?"—cried all at once. "It must be cannon. It is perhaps the captain and the ship's company who have found their way hither! Or some vessel in distress? Can we go to its relief?"

The boys lost not a moment in jumping into their tubs, and I soon followed them, after having whispered a few words to my wife, to tranquilize her mind during the trip we had now to engage in. We rowed rapidly out of the bay. With the vessel in sight, I observed with pleasure that the part of her which faced Tent House was undamaged, and that no sign of smoke appeared. We advanced in excellent spirits; but instead of rowing to the breach, we proceeded round to the side, on the inside of which we had placed the cracker.

The horrible scene of devastation we had caused now broke upon our sight. The greater part of the ship's side was shattered to pieces and splinters covered the surface of the water. In the midst of a scene of terrible destruction, our elegant pinnace seemed unharmed. Entering the new breach, we found that the pinnace had wholly escaped injury, and that the fire was entirely extinguished.

I then examined the breach and the pinnace, and perceived that it would be easy, with the help of the crow and the lever, to lower her into the water. In putting her together, I had used the precaution of placing her keel on rollers. Before letting her go, however, I fastened the end of a long thick rope to her head, and the other end to the most solid part of the wreck, for fear of her being carried out too far. We put our whole ingenuity and strength to this undertaking, and soon joyfully watched our pinnace descend gracefully into the sea.

Two whole days more were spent in completely equipping and loading the beautiful little barge we had now secured. When she was ready for sailing, I could not resist the earnest importunity of the boys to salute their mother, on their approach to Tent House, with two discharges of cannon. These accordingly were loaded, and the two youngest placed themselves, with a lighted match in hand, close to the touchholes, to be in readiness. Fritz stood at the mast, to manage the ropes and cables, while I took my station at the rudder. We put off, full of joy demonstrated by loud huzzas. The wind was favorable, and so brisk that we glided with the rapidity of a bird along the mirror of the water. While my young ones were transported with pleasure by the speed, I was filled with fear of disaster.

Our old friend the tub raft had been deeply loaded, and fastened to the pinnace, and it now followed as an accompanying boat. We took down our large sail as soon as we entered Safety Bay, to have the greater command in steering the pinnace. And soon the smaller ones were lowered one by one to avoid being thrown violently upon the rocks along the coast. Thus, proceeding at a slower rate, we had greater facilities for managing the important affair of the discharge of the cannon. When we arrived within a certain distance, "Fire!" cried Commander Fritz. The rocks behind Tent House returned the sound. "Fire!" said Fritz again. Ernest and Jack obeyed, and the echoes again majestically replied. Fritz at the same moment had discharged his two pistols, and all joined instantly in three loud huzzas.

"Welcome! Welcome! Dear ones," was the answer from the anxious mother, almost breathless with astonishment and joy. "Welcome!" cried also little Francis, with his feeble voice, as he stood clinging to her side. We now tried to push to shore with our oars and my wife and little Francis hastened to the spot to receive us.

Fritz now assisted his mother on board. When they had all stepped upon the deck, they saluted, by again discharging the cannon, and at the same moment conferring on the pinnace the name of their mother—*The Elizabeth.*

My wife was particularly gratified by these adventures, and applauded our skill and perseverance. "But," said she, "we have not remained idle while the rest were so actively employed. Dear ones, come with me and see what we have done."

We jumped briskly out of the pinnace and complied. Taking little Francis by the hand, she led the way, and we followed gaily. She conducted us up an ascent of our rocks, and at the spot where the cascade is formed from Jackal's River, she displayed to our astonished eyes a handsome kitchen garden, laid out properly in beds and walks.

"This," said she, "is the pretty exploit we have been engaged in. In this spot the earth is so light, being principally composed of decayed leaves, that Francis and I had no difficulty in working in it, and then dividing it into different compartments; one for potatoes, one for manioc, with smaller shares for lettuces of various kinds, and some plants of the sugar cane."

I stood transported in the midst of so perfect an exhibition of the zeal and industry of this most amiable of women! I could only exclaim that I should never have believed in the possibility of such a project in so short a time, and with so much privacy as to leave me wholly unsuspicious of its existence.

The pinnace was anchored on the shore, fastened with a rope, by her head, to a stake. When all our stores were disposed of, we journeyed to Falcon's Stream, taking with us everything that wanted for our comfort.

11. GYMNASTIC EXERCISES AND THE GOURD WOOD

MY SONS resumed the exercise of the shooting of arrows, increasing their bodily strength and agility. To this I added the exercises of running, jumping, getting up trees, both by means of climbing by the trunk, or by a suspended rope, as sailors are obliged to do to get to the masthead. We began at first by making knots in the rope, at a foot distance from each other; then we reduced the number of knots, and soon we contrived to succeed without any. I next taught them an exercise which required two balls of lead, fastened one to each end of a string about a fathom in length.

"I am endeavoring," said I, while all eyes were fixed upon me, "to imitate the arms used by the Patagonians, of the most southern point in America. But, instead of balls, they tie two heavy stones, one at each end of a cord, but considerably longer than the one I am working with. If they wish to take an animal alive, and without hurting it, they throw it so as to make it run several times round the neck of the prey, occasioning a perplexing tightness. They then throw the second stone, and they scarcely ever miss their object. The second operation is to twist itself about the animal to impede his progress, even though he were at full gallop. The stones continue turning, carrying with them the cord. The poor animal is at length so entangled that he can neither advance nor retire, and thus falls a prey to the enemy."

I tried the effect of my own instrument upon a small trunk of a tree which we saw at a certain distance. My throws entirely succeeded; and the string with the balls at the end so completely surrounded the tree that the skill of the Patagonian huntsmen required no further illustration. Each of the boys made a similar instrument; and in a short time Fritz became quite an expert in the art.

The next morning, with a high wind, and the sea violently agitated, I rejoiced to find myself in safety in my home, with no out-of-door occupation. We now fell to close examination of all our possessions at Falcon's Stream. My wife showed me many things she had herself added during my repeated absences from home. Among these was a pair of young pigeons, lately hatched, and already beginning to try their wings, while their mother was again sitting on her eggs. From these we passed to the fruit trees we had laid in earth to be planted. I arranged with the boys to assist me to plant all the young trees, and we set about it at once.

When we had finished, the evening was too far advanced for our walk to the wood of the gourds to provide ourselves with vessels for our provisions. By sunrise the next morning we set out, full of good humor and high spirits. Turning round Flamingo Marsh, we soon reached the pleasant spot. Fritz took a direction a little farther from the seashore, followed Turk into the tall grass, and both disappeared. Soon we heard Turk's loud barking. A large bird sprang up, and almost at the same moment a shot from Fritz brought it down. But though wounded it was not killed; it raised itself, and ran off with incredible swiftness. Turk followed, and seizing the bird, held it fast till Fritz came up. The captive was large in size, and strong. It struck the dogs, or whoever came near, with its legs, with so much force, that none dared approach. Fortunately I reached the spot in time to give assistance, and was pleased to see that it was a female bustard of the largest size.

To secure the bird without injuring it, I threw my pocket handkerchief over its head. As it could not now see me, I got near enough to pass a string with a running knot over its legs, which I drew tight, to prevent further mischief from such powerful weapons. I gently released its wing from Turk's mouth, tied both wings close to the bird's body, and the bustard was ours.

As we advanced I used the hatchet to free a passage in the tall grass for the ass. The heat also increased, and we were all complaining of thirst, when Ernest, of the useful discoveries, made one that was most agreeable.

He found a kind of hollow stalk, of some height, which grew at the foot of trees, and entangled our feet in walking. Cutting one, he was surprised to see a drop of pure fresh water issue at the cut. He showed it to us, put it to his lips, and found it pure. I then fell to examining the phenomenon myself, and soon perceived that the want of air prevented a more considerable issue of water. I made some incisions, and presently water flowed out as if from a small conduit. I tried dividing the plants longways, and they soon gave out water enough to supply even the ass, the monkey, and the bustard.

Arrived at the wood of gourds, we were not long in finding the spot that Fritz and I had once visited. My wife had requested some vessels to contain milk, a large flat spoon to cut out butter by pieces, and next, some pretty plates for serving it at table, made from the gourd rinds.

The boys gathered gourds of a sufficient number, and we began our work. Some had to cut; others to saw, scoop out, and model into agreeable forms. Each tried what he could best present. I made a pretty basket large enough to carry eggs, with one of the gourds, and a certain number of vessels, with covers, to hold our milk. Also some spoons to skim the cream. My next attempt was some bottles large enough to hold fresh water, and these occasioned me more trouble than all the rest. It was necessary to empty the gourd through the small opening of the size of one's finger, which I had cut in it. After loosening the contents with a stick, I was obliged to get them out by friction with shot and water well shaken on the inside. Lastly, to please my wife, I undertook to make the set of plates she required for her use. Fritz and Jack engaged to make hives for the bees, and nests for the pigeons and hens. For the nests, they took the largest gourds, and cut a hole in front, the size of the bird for whose use it was intended. The pigeons' nests were intended to be tied to the branches of our tree; those for the hens, the geese, and the ducks, were to be placed between its roots, or on the seashore to represent a hencoop.

Our work, added to the heat of the day, had made us all thirsty; but we found nothing on this spot like our fountain plants, as we had named them.

Eagerly Ernest proposed to look for water. It was not long before we heard him calling loudly to us, and saw him returning in great alarm. "Run quick, Father," said he, "here is an immense wild boar."

I then cried out to the boys to call the dogs quickly. "Halloo, here, Turk!" and Ernest conducted us to the place where he saw the boar. It was gone, but we soon heard the cry of the dogs. They had overtaken the runaway, and the most hideous growling now assailed our ears. We advanced with caution, holding our guns in readiness to fire. Presently the animal appeared, with the two brave creatures, each holding one of his ears between its teeth.

But it was not a boar, but our own sow which had run away and so long been lost! After the first surprise we laughed heartily, and hastened to disencumber our old friend of her two adversaries.

But here our attention was attracted to a kind of small potato which we observed lying thick on the grass around us, and which had fallen from some heavily laden trees. The fruit was of different colors like the poisonous apple called the *mancenilla;* but the sow ate them with so much eagerness, and the tree which bore them having neither the form nor foliage ascribed by naturalists to the mancenilla, I doubted this. My sons put some of the fruit in their pockets, to experiment with them on the monkey.

Now again, from extreme thirst, we sought

for water in every direction. Jack sprang off, and sought among the rocks, hoping to discover some little stream, but scarcely had he left the wood than he bawled to us that he had found a crocodile.

"A crocodile!" cried I, with a hearty laugh. "You have a fine imagination, my boy. Who ever saw a crocodile on such scorching rocks as these, and no water near?"

But instead of a crocodile, I saw before me a large sort of lizard, named by naturalists *Leguana*, or *Iguana*, a mild-natured animal, an excellent food, and rare prize for their mother. Fritz was taking aim with his gun, but I prevented him.

"Let us try," said I, "another sort of experiment; as he is asleep, we need not be in a hurry."

I cut a stout stick from a bush, to the extremity of which I tied a string with a running knot. I guarded my other hand simply with a little switch, and cautiously approached. When I was very near to him, I began to whistle a lively air, taking care to make the sounds low at first, and to increase in loudness till the lizard was awakened. The creature appeared entranced with pleasure as the sounds fell upon his ear, and raised his head to discover the source. I now advanced step by step, continuing with music, which fixed him like a statue to the place. At length when I was near enough, I tickled him gently with my switch, still continuing to whistle, one after the other, the different airs I could recollect. The lizard was bewildered by the charms of the music. I dexterously seized the moment when he raised his head, to throw my noose over him. Now the boys drew near also, and wanted instantly to draw it tight and strangle him at once. This I forbade.

Continuing to whistle my most affecting melodies, I plunged my switch into one of his nostrils. The blood flowed in abundance, and soon deprived him of life, without his exhibiting the least appearance of being in pain. On the contrary, to the last moment, he seemed to be still listening to the music.

After a moment's reflection, I perceived that I had better carry so large and valuable a prize across my shoulders. And an amusing figure I made with so singular an animal on my back and with his tail dragging on the ground.

On our return, we met my wife and little Francis. We had forgotten to give them notice of our approach by firing our gun, and they imagined some terrible disaster must have befallen us. We had so many things to tell, that, till reminded by my wife, we forgot to mention that we had failed to procure any water. My sons had taken out some of the unknown apples from their pockets, and they lay them on the ground beside us. The monkey, Knips, soon scented them, and fell to chewing some with great eagerness. I threw one or two to the bustard, who also ate them without hesitation. Being now convinced that the apples were not of a poisonous nature, the boys ate them and found them excellent. I suspected that they might be the fruit called guava, esteemed in hot countries. The apples relieved our thirst; but increased our hunger. Lacking time to prepare a portion of the lizard, we contented ourselves with the cold provisions we had brought with us.

The evening was now far advanced. It seemed prudent to leave the sledge, which was heavy laden, till the following day, when I could return and fetch it. I loaded the ass with the bags which contained our new sets of porcelain, the lizard, which I feared might not keep fresh so long, and little Francis, who began to complain of being tired. I left to my wife and Fritz the care of confining the bustard so that she could walk before us without danger of escaping.

Our little caravan then took the direction

of a straight line to Falcon's Stream. The course of our route now lay along a wood of majestic oaks, and the ground was covered with acorns. My young travelers tasted them, and finding them both sweet and mild, I reckoned them as a new kind of food.

We arrived at Falcon's Stream before it was completely dark, concluded the day with a plain repast, contrived a comfortable bed for the bustard by the side of the flamingo, and then stretched our weary limbs upon the homely couch in the giant tree.

12. WE EXPLORE BEYOND THE ROCKS — USEFUL OCCUPATIONS

MY FIRST thought, the next morning, was to fetch the sledge from the wood. I wished to penetrate a little farther into the land beyond the wall of rocks to see the general extent and form of our island. Fritz and Turk accompanied me. We set out very early in the morning, and drove the ass before us to draw home the sledge.

As we were picking up some acorns, different birds of exquisite plumage flitted about us. Fritz fired and brought down three, to learn their species. One was the great blue Virginia jay, and the other two were parrots, a superb red and a green and yellow.

At the guava trees, where we had left the sledge, we found our treasures safe, and entered upon our intended project of penetrating beyond the wall of rocks.

We pursued our way at the foot of these rocks to a pretty little grove, the trees of which were loaded with large quantities of an extraordinary berry, entirely covered with a minute meal or farina. I knew of a sort of bush this plant resembled, the berries of which, when boiled, yield a material resembling wax. It grows in America, and is called the candleberry tree.

Soon our attention was claimed by a brown bird scarcely larger than a chaffinch. These birds appeared to exist as a republic, there being among them one common nest. We saw one of these partly hidden nests, formed of plaited straws and bulrushes intermixed. It enclosed great numbers of inhabitants, and was built round the trunk of a tree. A kind of roof formed of roots and bulrushes was carefully knit together, and the sides were small apertures, seemingly intended as doors and windows to each particular cell of the general nest. From a few of these apertures issued small branches, which served the birds as points of rest for entering and returning. The appearance of the whole was like an immensely large open sponge.

While we were attentively examining this interesting little colony, numbers of a very small kind of parrot were hovering about the nest. Their gilded green wings, and the variety of their colors were beautiful; they seemed to be perpetually disputing with the colonists, and trying to prevent their entrance into the building. They attacked them fiercely, and even pecked at us, if we advanced a hand to the structure. Fritz climbed to the nest, and thrust his hand into one of the apertures, to seize whatever living creature it should touch in that particular cell. What he most desired was to find a female brooding, and to carry both her and the eggs away. Several of the cells were empty, but finally he found one, received a violent peck from an invisible bird, and hastily withdrew his hand. However, he ventured a second time to pass his hand into the nest, and succeeded in seizing the resisting bird. He drew it through the aperture, buttoned it securely in his pocket, and slid down the tree to safety. The signals of distress sent forth by the prisoner collected a multitude of birds from their cells, who surrounded him, uttering loud cries, and attacking him with their beaks, till he had made good his retreat. He now released the prisoner, and we discovered him to be a beautiful green parrot. Fritz hoped to present him to his brothers, who would make a cage and tame him and teach him to speak.

On the road home, we agreed that from the circumstance of this young bird's nesting within the structure it appeared probable that the bright species belonged in the nest, and that the brown-colored birds were intruders endeavoring to displace them.

We reached a wood in which the trees resembled the wild fig tree. But a kind of gum issued in a liquid state from the trunk of the tree, and became immediately hardened by the air. This discovery awakened Fritz's attention. In Europe he had often made use of the gum produced by cherry trees, either as a cement or varnish, in his youthful occupations. He thought he could do the same with this gum.

As he walked, he tried unsuccessfully to soften it with his breath, but he discovered it to be elastic. He was struck with surprise, and sprang toward me exclaiming, "Look, Father! Is this not the very thing we formerly used to rub out bad strokes in our drawings?"

"Ah! What do you tell me?" cried I with joy. "Such a discovery would be valuable indeed, if it is the true caoutchouc tree which yields the Indian rubber. Quick, let me examine it." Having satisfied myself of our good fortune, I had now to explain that caoutchouc is a kind of milky sap, which runs from its tree from incisions made in the bark.

"This liquid is collected in vessels and afterward made to take the form of dark-colored bottles, of different sizes, such as we have seen them, in this manner. Before the liquid has time to coagulate, some small earthen bottles are dipped into it a sufficient number of times to form the thickness required. These vessels are then hung over smoke, which completely dries them, and gives them a dark color. The mold is then broken and the pieces shaken out through the neck. There remains the complete form of a bottle. In the same way we may be able to make shoes and boots without seams. We must consider some means of restoring masses of the caoutchouc to its liquid form, for spreading upon the molds, or we may endeavor to draw it in sufficient quantities, in its liquid state, from the trees themselves."

We now found that it was impossible to pass through the thick bushes of bamboo, and as we had found no passage beyond the wall of rocks, we turned left toward Cape Disappointment, and the luxurious plantations of sugar canes. We each cut a large bundle of the canes, which we threw across the ass's back with the gamebag of wax berries. We soon arrived on the well-known shore of the sea, to an open and a shorter path, and reached the wood of gourds. There we found our sledge loaded as we had left it. We took the sugar canes and berries from the ass and fastened them to the sledge, harnessed the ass, and the patient animal began to draw toward home.

On the following day I began to manufacture my candles. I set myself to recollect all I had read on the subject, and soon perceived that I lacked a little fat to mix with the wax to be procured from the berries, for making the light burn clearer, but I was compelled to do without it. I put as many berries into a vessel as it would contain, and set it on a moderate fire, while my wife made some wicks with the threads of sailcloth. An oily matter, of a pleasing smell and light green color, rose to the top of the liquid; and we skimmed it off into a separate vessel, keeping it warm. We continued this process till the berries were exhausted, and had produced a considerable quantity of wax. We next dipped the wicks one by one into it, while it remained liquid, and then hung them on the bushes to harden. In a short time we dipped them again, repeating the operation till the candles were increased to the proper size. They were then put away till sufficiently hardened for use. We burned one of the candles that evening, and were well satisfied.

Our success in this last enterprise encouraged us to think of another—the way to make fresh butter of the cream we every day skimmed from the milk. We stood in need of a churn to turn the cream in, but I recollected what I had read of the method used by the Hottentots for making butter. Instead of their sheepskin sewed together at its extremities, I emptied a large gourd, washed it clean, filled it with cream, and stopped it close with the piece I had cut from the top. I placed my vase of cream on a piece of sailcloth with four corners, and tied to each corner a stake. I placed one boy midway between each stake, and directed them to shake the cloth briskly and steadily for a certain time. This pleased them mightily. They were singing and laughing all the time. In an hour, taking off the cover, we had some excellent butter.

I had now to propose to my sons a more difficult piece of work than we had hitherto accomplished. It was the construction of a cart, to carry our effects from place to place instead of the sledge, which was so tiring to load and draw. We wasted both time and timber, but produced what from courtesy we called a cart, and it answered the purpose.

By this time we had nearly exhausted our stock of clothes and we were compelled once more to descend on the vessel for some chests fit for our use. We wished also to take another look at her, and, if practicable, to bring away a few pieces of cannon.

The first fine day my three eldest sons and I reached the wreck without any striking adventure, and found her still fixed between the rocks but somewhat more shattered. We secured the chests of clothes, and whatever remained of ammunition stores—powder, shot, and even such pieces of cannon as we could remove, while those that were too heavy we stripped of their wheels, which might be extremely useful.

But it was necessary to spend several days in visits to the vessel, returning constantly in the evening, enriched with everything of a portable nature which the wreck contained. Doors, windows, locks, bolts—nothing escaped our grasp. The ship was now entirely emptied, with the exception of the large cannon, and three or four immense copper caldrons. By degrees we contrived to tie the heaviest articles to two or three empty casks well pitched, which would thus be sustained above water. I supposed that the wind and tide would convey the beams and timbers ashore, and thus without effort we should be possessed of a sufficient quantity of materials for erecting a building at some future time. When these measures were taken, I planned to blow up the wreck. We accordingly prepared a cask of gunpowder, which we left on board for the purpose. We rolled it to a favorable place, made a small opening in its side, and on quitting the vessel, inserted a piece of matchwood, which we lighted at the last moment. We then sailed with all possible expedition for Safety Bay, where we arrived in a short time.

About nightfall, a majestic rolling sound like thunder, accompanied by a column of fire and smoke, announced that the ship so concerned with our peculiar destiny, which had brought us to the desert, and furnished us there with such vast supplies for general comfort, was that instant annihilated, and gone forever.

At this moment, love for the country that gave us birth, sank with a new force into our hearts. The ship had disappeared forever. Could we then hope ever to behold that country more? We had made a sort of jubilee of witnessing the spectacle. The boys had skipped about in joyful expectation. But the noise was heard, the smoke and sparks were seen, and a sudden change took place in our minds and hearts. In mournful silence all rose, as at a common impulse, and took the road to Tent House.

Early in the morning I went with the boys to see the effects of the explosion. In the water and along the shore lay abundant vestiges of the departed wreck. And the empty casks, caldrons, and cannon, all tied together were floating in a large mass upon the water. We jumped instantly into the pinnace, with the tub boat fastened to it, and made a way through the wreckage to the mass, which from its great weight moved slowly upon the waves. Fritz flung some rope round two four-pounders, and fastened them to our barge. He secured also an enormous quantity of poles, laths, and other useful articles; and with this rich booty we returned to land.

We performed three more trips bringing away more cannon, caldrons, fragments of masts, etc., all of which we deposited for present convenience in Safety Bay. And now began our most fatiguing operations—moving the numerous and heavy stores from the boats to the Tent House. We separated the cannon and the caldrons from the tub raft, and from each other, and left them in a place accessible to the sledge and the beasts of burden. With the help of the crow we succeeded in getting the caldrons upon the sledge, and by replacing the four wheels we had taken from the cannon, we found it easy to make the cow and the ass draw them.

The largest of the boilers or copper caldrons we found most useful. We placed all our barrels of gunpowder on their ends in three separate groups, at a short distance from our tent. Round the whole we dug a little ditch to draw off the moisture from the ground, and then put one of the caldrons turned upside down upon each. This completely answered the purpose of a powder outhouse. The cannon were covered with sailcloth, upon them we laid heavy branches of trees. The larger casks of gunpowder we prudently removed under a projecting piece of rock, and covered them with planks till we should have leisure to plan an ammunition storehouse—an earnest hope.

My wife made the agreeable discovery that two of our ducks and one of the geese had been brooding under a large bush, and at the time were conducting their little families to the water. The sight of the little creatures carried our thoughts to Falcon's Stream and of our return. Fixing the next day for our departure, we set about making preparations.

The fruit trees forming the avenue to Falcon's Stream were not vigorous in appearance; they curved a little in the stalk, and needed support. I proposed, therefore, to walk to Cape Disappointment to cut some bamboo.

Accordingly, the following morning we set out. I desired to explore more thoroughly this part of our island, and therefore made some preparations for sleeping, should we find the day too short for all we wished to accomplish. I fixed some planks across the cart for Francis and his mother to sit upon should they be tired, and was careful to provide the different implements we might want; some rope machinery I had contrived for climbing trees, some provisions, water in a gourd flask, and one bottle of wine from the captain's store.

I thought we could not do better than to halt at the caoutchouc or gum elastic trees and endeavor to collect a quantity of the sap for the different utensils and the impenetrable boots and shoes. For this I had taken care to bring with me several of the largest gourd rinds. I made deep incisions in the trunks, and fixed some large leaves of trees, partly doubled together lengthways to the place, to serve as a sort of channel to conduct the sap to the gourds ready to receive it. Soon we perceived the sap begin to run out as white as milk, and in large drops. We hoped on our return to find the vessels full with a sufficient quantity of the ingredient for a first experiment.

Leaving the sap running, we pursued our way to the wood of cocoa trees. From there we passed to the left, intending to stop halfway between the bamboos and the sugar canes, intending to gather a provision of each. On clearing the wood, we found ourselves in an open plain with the sugar-cane plantation on our left, and on our right those of bamboo, interspersed with various kinds of palm trees, and, in front, the magnificent bay formed by

Cape Disappointment, which stretched far out into the sea.

The view was of such exquisite beauty that we determined to choose it for our resting place, and the central point of every future excursion.

It was now evening. As we had determined to pass the night in this enchanting spot, we began to think of forming some large branches of trees into a sort of hut, as is practiced by the hunters in America, to shelter us from the dew and the coolness of the air. Suddenly the ass, who we had been grazing quietly, picked up his heels and pranced about, and set off at a full gallop. Unfortunately, Turk and Flora, whom we sent after him, entered the plantation of the sugar canes, while the ass had preferred the direction of the bamboos on the right.

The following morning we breakfasted on some milk from the cow, some potatoes, and a small portion of Dutch cheese. It was decided that one of the boys and myself, attended by the two dogs, should seek the ass through the bamboo plantation. I took with me the agile Jack, and we forced ourselves through the intricate entanglements of the bamboo plantation. Greatly fatigued, we at last discovered the print of the ass's hoofs on the soil. After another hour of vain search, we reached the edge of the plantation, in an open space, which bounded the great bay. Here a considerable river flowed into the bay. The ridge of rocks, which we constantly see, extended here to the shore, terminating in a perpendicular precipice, and leaving only a narrow passage between the rocks and the river. During every flux of the tide, this must be under water, but at that moment it was dry and passable.

The probability that the ass would prefer passing by this narrow way, to the hazard of the water, determined us to follow in the same path. Also we were curious about what might be found on the other side of the rocks, whether they formed a boundary to our island, divided it into two portions, or whether land or water lay beyond. At length we reached a stream which issued foaming from a large mass of rock, and fell in a cascade into the river, and after a long time we found a part where we could cross. On the other side, the soil was again sandy, and mixed with a fertile kind of earth. In this place we no longer saw naked rock, but the print of the ass's hoofs were again visible on the ground.

We saw with astonishment prints of other animals, much larger and different from those of the ass. We followed the traces to a plain at a great distance, to our wondering eyes a terrestrial paradise. We ascended a hill, and with the assistance of a glass, beheld an extensive range of country, of every kind of rural beauty, in profound tranquillity.

We perceived at a great distance some specks upon the land, that seemed to be in motion. As we drew nearer, we saw they were wild buffaloes. In alarm I remained fixed to the spot. By good luck the dogs were far behind us, and the buffaloes gave no sign of fear or of displeasure at our approach. They stood perfectly still, with their large round eyes fixed upon us in vacant surprise. Those which were lying down got up slowly, but not one seemed hostile. The dogs' absence was most likely the means of our safety, as we had time to draw back quietly, and prepare our firearms. It was not, however, my intention to make use of them in any way but for defense. Recollecting to have read that the sound of a gun drives buffalo to a state of desperation, I thought only of retreating, and did so with my poor Jack, for whom I was more alarmed than for myself.

Unfortunately Turk and Flora ran up to us. The buffaloes instantly and all together set up such a roar as to make our nerves tremble. They struck their horns and their hoofs upon the ground, tearing it up and scattering it in the air. Turk and Flora ran, in spite of all our efforts, into the midst of them, and, laid hold of the ears of a young buffalo, which was nearer to us than the rest. Though the creature set up a tremendous roar and flung up his heels, they held him fast, and were dragging him toward us. Our only hope seemed now to lie in terrifying the buffaloes by the noise of our musketry, which might excite them to flight. With palpitating heart and trembling hands, we fired both at the same moment. The buffaloes, terrified by the sound and by the smoke, remained for an instant motionless, and then one and all betook themselves to flight with incredible rapidity, and were soon out of sight. We were left with only one of their terrible species near us. This one, a female, was no doubt the mother of the young buffalo which the dogs had seized. She had drawn near on hearing its cries, and had been wounded by our guns, but not killed. The creature was in a furious state. She took aim at the dogs, and with her head on the ground, as if to guide her by the scent, was advancing in her rage, and would have torn them in pieces, if I had not fired upon her with my double-barreled gun, and thus put an end to her existence.

The young buffalo still remained a prisoner, with his ears in the mouths of the dogs, and the pain occasioned him to be so furious that I was fearful he might do them some injury. I determined to advance and give them what assistance I could; but I scarcely knew in what way to rescue them.

I had the power of killing him with a pistol at a stroke. But I had a great desire to preserve him alive, and to tame him as a substitute for the ass. I stood perplexed, when Jack suddenly drew from his pocket his string with balls, and, taking a few steps backward, threw it so skillfully as to entangle the buffalo completely, and throw him down. I then tied his legs two and two together with a very strong cord, the dogs released his ears, and from this moment we considered the buffalo our own.

But how were we to get the buffalo home? The best way would be to tie his forelegs together so that he could not run, yet loose enough for him to walk. "And," I pursued, "we will next adopt the method practiced in Italy; you will think it somewhat cruel, but the success will be certain. And afterward we will make amends by the kindest care and treatment. Hold strongly the cord which confines his legs that he may not be able to move."

I then called Turk and Flora, and made each again take hold of the ears of the animal. Taking hold of the snout, I made a hole in the nostril with my sharp-pointed knife, into which I quickly inserted a string. This I immediately tied so closely to a tree that the animal was prevented from the least motion of the head, which might have inflamed the wound and increased his pain. I drew off the dogs the moment the operation was performed. The creature, furious, would have run away, but the stricture of the legs and the pain in the nostril prevented it.

Unwilling to leave so fine a prey as the dead buffalo, I carefully took off the skin from the four feet. I remembered that the Americans use these skins, which are soft and flexible, as boots and shoes, and I considered them precious. I lastly cut the tongue and some of the flesh of the animal with the skin on, and salted it, and abandoned the rest to the dogs. After washing myself in the river, we sat down under the shade of a large tree, and ate the rest of our provisions.

With the saw Jack cut down a quantity of enormous reeds, but he took pains also to choose the smallest. "What shall we do," said I, "with these small-sized reeds?"

"I am thinking of some candlesticks for my mother, who will set a high value on them," answered Jack.

"This is a good thought," said I. "For your kindness and your inventiveness, I will assist you to empty the reeds without breaking them."

We had so many and such heavy articles to remove that I dismissed for that day all thoughts of looking further for the ass. I began now to think of untying the young buffalo, and saw with pleasure that he was asleep, which proved that his wound was not extremely painful. As I began to pull him gently with the string, he gave a start; but he afterward followed me without resistance.

We repassed the river in safety, and regained the narrow pass at the turn of the rocks. We proceeded with caution; once safely on the other side, we quickened our pace and soon arrived at the hut.

The day concluded with supper, and sound repose.

13. HOLLOW IN THE GREAT TREE

THE NEXT morning my wife told me that the boys had ascended Cape Disappointment with her, and had brought down an immense palm tree. It lay on the ground, covering a space of at least seventy feet in length.

Fritz was in high spirits too on another account. He carried on his wrist a young bird of prey of beauteous plumage, taken from a nest in one of the rocks near Cape Disappointment. Young as the bird was, it had already all its feathers, which had not yet received their full coloring. It answered to the description I had read of the beautiful eagle of Malabar, and I viewed it with admiration. Meeting with one of these birds is thought a lucky omen, and I was desirous to have it trained like a falcon, to pursue smaller birds. Fritz had already covered its eyes, and tied a string to its foot, and I advised him to hold it often, on his hand, and to tame it with hunger, as falconers do.

When all the narratives were concluded, I

ordered a fire to be lighted, and a quantity of green wood to be piled on it, to raise a thick smoke, over which to hang the buffalo meat I had salted, to dry and preserve it for future use. The young buffalo was beginning to browse, and we gave him also a little of the cow's milk, and in a few days sliced roots, which he greedily devoured. The pains from the wound in his nose seemed to have subsided, and we hoped he would soon become tame.

We left our meat suspended over the smoke of the fires during our sleep. We tied the young buffalo by the side of the cow, and were pleased to see them agree and live in peace together. At night the dogs were set upon the watch, and we did not get up till after sunrise.

After a moderate breakfast, I found that my young ones had some projects in their heads, and neither they nor their mother were ready to follow my plans.

"Ernest assures me," said my wife, "the tree we felled is a sago tree. If so, the pith would be an excellent ingredient for our soups. Do, my dear, examine it, and let us see if we can turn it to account."

I found she was right, and it was necessary to employ a day in the business. Moreover, besides the use of the farinaceous pith, by emptying the tree I could obtain two large troughs for the conveyance of water from Jackal's River to my wife's kitchen garden at Tent House, and thence to my new plantations of trees.

I now desired them to bring me the graters they had used for the manioc, and their help; the palm tree must be raised from the ground by fixing at each end two small crosspieces or props to support it. To split it open as it lies would be too difficult. I shall want wooden wedges to keep the cleft open while I am sawing it, and afterward a sufficient quantity of water.

"There is the difficulty," said my wife. "Our Falcon's Stream is too far off, and we have not yet discovered any spring in the neighborhood of this place."

"That is of no consequence, Mother," said Ernest. "I have seen so many plants which contain water, that will fully supply us if I could only get vessels enough to hold it."

We now produced the enormous reeds we had brought home. Being hollow they would answer the purpose of vessels, and Ernest and Francis at once set to work. They cut a number of the plants, which they placed slantingly over the brim of a vessel, and while one was filling, they were preparing another. With our united strength the rest of us soon succeeded in raising the heavy trunk, and the top of it was then sawn off. We next split it through the whole length, and soon reached the pith or marrow that fills up the middle of the trunk from end to end. When divided, we laid one half on the ground, and pressed the pith together with our hands, so as to make temporary room for the pith of the other half of the trunk, which rested still on the props. We wished to empty it entirely, that we might employ it as a kneading trough, leaving merely enough of the pitch at both ends to prevent a running-out; and then we proceeded to form our paste.

My young manufacturers brought water, and poured it gradually into the trough, while we mixed it with the flour. In a short time the paste appeared sufficiently fermented, and I then made an aperture at the bottom of the grater on its outside, and pressed the paste strongly with my hand. The farinaceous parts passed with ease through the small holes of the grater, and were received in reed vessels which my boys conveyed directly to their mother, who spread out the small grains upon sailcloth to dry in the sun. Thus we procured a good supply of a wholesome and pleasant food.

We next loaded the cart with our tools and the two halves of the tree. Night coming on, we retired to our hut, and early next morning were ready to return to Falcon's Stream. Our buffalo now commenced his service, yoked with the cow in place of the ass, and was very tractable. It is true, I led him by the cord in his nose, and thus restrained him whenever he was disposed to deviate from his duty.

Returning the same way as we came, in order to load the cart with berries, wax, and elastic gum, I sent Fritz and Jack ahead with one of the dogs, to cut an ample road through the bushes for our cart. The two water conductors, which were very long, somewhat impeded our progress but we reached the wax and gum trees with tolerable speed, and halted to place our sacks of berries in the cart. The elastic gum had not yielded as much as I expected, from the too rapid thickening caused by the hot sun. However, we obtained about a quart, which sufficed for the experiment of the impenetrable boots I had so long desired.

We set out again through the little wood of guavas cleared by our pioneers. Suddenly we heard a dreadful barking from our vanguard, and Fritz and Jack hastened toward us. I began to fear a tiger or panther near at hand. I prepared myself for a conflict. I advanced at the head of my troop to a thicket into which I was going to fire promiscuously, when Jack, who had thrown himself on the ground to have a better view, got up in a fit of laughter. "It is only," exclaimed he, "our old sow, playing tricks on us." Half vexed, half laughing, we broke into the thicket. There our old companion stretched supinely on the earth, round her seven little creatures, littered a few days, sprawled about, contending with each other for a hearty meal. This discovery gave us considerable satisfaction.

And now a general consultation about this new family took place. It was decided that for the present the sow and her young should stay in their retreat.

We then took to our road, and arrived at Falcon's Stream in safety. It was necessary to tie up the buffalo again, to inure it by degrees to confinement, and the handsome Malabar eagle shared the same fate. Fritz chose to place it near the parrot, on the root of a tree. He fastened it with a piece of packthread, of sufficient length to allow it free motion, and uncovered its eyes. Till then the bird had been tolerably quiet, but the instant it was restored to light it fell into a rage that surprised us. It proudly raised its head, its feathers became ruffled, its eyeballs seemed to whirl in their orbits, and dart out vivid lightnings. All the poultry were terrified and fled. But the poor luckless parrot was too near the sanguinary creature to escape. It was seized and mangled by the formidable hooked beak of the eagle.

Fritz's passionate anger would have killed the murderer on the spot, had not Ernest entreated him to spare its life: "Parrots," said he, "we shall find in plenty, but never so magnificent a bird as this eagle which we may train for hawking. Why did you uncover his eyes? Falconers keep them covered six weeks, till they are completely tamed."

On Ernest's advice, Fritz took some tobacco and a pipe, of which we had plenty in the sailors' chests, and began to smoke, at the same time gradually approaching the unruly bird. As soon as it was somewhat composed, he replaced the fillet over the eyes, and smoked close to its beak and nostrils so effectually that it became motionless on the spot, and had the exact air of a stuffed bird. Fritz thought it dead, and was angry with his brother. But I told him it would not hold on the perch if it were lifeless, and that its head alone was affected—and so it proved. The favorite came to itself by degrees, and made no noise when its eyes were unbound. It looked at us with an air of surprise, but no fury, and grew tamer and calmer every day.

We next began a business which I and my wife had long been thinking of. She found it difficult to use our rope ladder, and apprehensive lest one of the children make a false step, and be lame forever.

I reflected on what was possible. I had thought of constructing winding stairs within the immense trunk of the tree, if it should be hollow. I had heard the boys talking of a hollow in our tree, and of a swarm of bees issuing from it, and I now went to examine the extent of the cavity. The boys sprang up, and climbed to the tops of the roots like squirrels, to strike at the trunk with axes, and to judge its hollowness from the sound.

But the whole swarm of bees, alarmed at the noise, issued forth, buzzing with fury, attacked the disturbers, stung them, stuck to their hair and clothes, and put them to flight, uttering lamentable cries. My wife and I had some trouble to cover their wounds with fresh earth to allay the smart. Jack, of the rash temper, had struck fiercely upon the bees' nest, and so serious was his injury, it was necessary to cover the whole of his face with linen. Ernest got up the last and was the first to run off when he saw the consequences, and thus avoided any but a sting or two. But some hours elapsed before the other boys could be relieved from the acute pain.

When they grew a little better, they teased me to hasten the measures for obtaining possession of the honey. In the meantime the bees were still buzzing furiously round the tree. I prepared tobacco, a pipe, some clay, chisels, hammers, etc. I took the large gourd long intended for a hive, and fitted a place for it, by nailing a piece of board on a branch of the tree; I made a straw roof for the top, to screen it from the sun and rain; and as all this took up more time than I was aware of, we deferred the attack of the fortress to the following day, and got ready for a sound sleep, which completed the cure of my wounded patients.

Next morning, almost before dawn, all were up and in motion. The bees had returned to their cells, and I stopped the passages with clay, leaving only a sufficient opening for the tube of my pipe. I then smoked enough to stupefy, without killing, the little warlike creatures.

At first a humming was heard in the hollow of the trees, and a noise like the gathering tempest, which died away by degrees. All became calm, and I withdrew my tube without the appearance of a single bee. Fritz had got up by me; we then began with a chisel and a small ax, to cut out of the tree, under the bees' hole of entrance, a piece three feet square. Before it was entirely separated, I repeated the fumigation lest the noise we had just been making revived the bees. As soon as I supposed them lulled again, I separated from the trunk the piece I had cut out like a window, through which the inside of the tree was open to view.

We were filled with astonishment on beholding the immense and wonderful work of this colony of insects. The whole interior of the tree was lined with fine honeycombs, which I cut off with care, and put in the gourds the boys constantly supplied. I put the upper combs, in which the bees had assembled in clusters and swarms, into the gourd which was to serve as a hive, and placed it on the plank I had purposely raised. I came down, bringing with me the rest of the honeycombs, with which I filled a small and well-washed cask. Some I kept out for a treat at dinner, carefully covering the barrel, so that the bees, attracted by the smell, could not get to it.

At the table we regaled ourselves plentifully with the delicious treat, and my wife then put by the remainder. I placed a board at the aperture, and burned a few handfuls of tobacco on it, which drove them back whenever they attempted to return. Gradually they became reconciled to their new residence, where their queen no doubt had settled herself. I now advised that all should watch during the night over the whole provision of honey. And to this end we threw ourselves on our beds, in our clothes, to take an early doze.

On awakening about nightfall, we found the bees quiet in the gourd, or settled in clusters upon near branches, and we set out to work. The cask of honey was emptied into a kettle, except a few prime combs, which we kept for daily consumption. The remainder, mixed with a little water, was set over a gentle fire, reduced to a liquid, strained and squeezed through a bag, and afterward poured back into the cask, and left to cool. In the morning the wax was entirely separated, and had risen to the surface in a compact and solid cake, that was easily removed. Beneath was the purest, most beautiful and delicate honey that could be seen. The cask was then sealed carefully, and put into cool ground near our wine vessels.

This task accomplished, I revisited the hive, and found everything in order; the bees going forth in swarms, and returning loaded with wax, from which I judged they were forming fresh edifices in their new dwelling place.

I had been surprised that the numbers occupying the trunk of the tree should find room in the gourd, till I perceived the clusters upon the branches, and concluded a young queen was among them. In consequence, I procured another gourd, into which I shook them, and placed it by the other. Thus I had two fine hives of bees in activity.

We examined the inside of the tree. I sounded it with a pole from the opening I had made; it penetrated with no resistance to the branches above and a stone fastened to a string sounded the bottom, descending unhampered to the roots. Thus we ascertained the height and depth of the cavity. The trunk had wholly lost its pith, and most of its wood internally. It seems that this species of tree, like the willow in our climates, receives nourishment through the bark, for it did not look decayed, and its far-extended branches were luxuriant and beautiful. I determined to begin the construction of our stairway in its capacious hollow that very day.

We began to cut into the side of the tree, toward the sea, a doorway equal in dimensions to the door of the captain's cabin, which we had removed with all its framework and windows. We next cleared away from the cavity all the rotten wood, and rendered the interior even and smooth, leaving sufficient thickness for cutting out resting places for the winding stairs, without injuring the bark. I then fixed in the center the trunk of a tree about twenty feet in length, and a foot thick, in order to carry my winding staircase round it. On the outside of this trunk, and the inside of the cavity of our tree, we formed grooves, at which the boards were to be placed to form the stairs. These were continued till I had got to the height of the trunk round which they turned. I made two more apertures at suitable distances, thus completely lighting the whole ascent. A second trunk was fixed upon the first, firmly held with screws and transverse beams. It was surrounded, like the other, with stairs cut slopingly, made to the level of our bed-chamber into which I made a door.

To render the staircase more solid and agreeable, I closed the spaces between the stairs with plank. I then fastened two strong ropes to assist in case of slipping. I fixed the sash windows taken from the captain's cabin in the apertures we had made to give light to the stairs, and happily completed my design.

A few days after the commencement of our

undertaking, our brave Flora whelped us six young puppies. I kept but a male and female to keep up the breed. A few days later, the two she-goats gave us two kids, and our ewes five lambs. So that now we saw ourselves in possession of a pretty flock.

Next to the winding stairs, my chief occupation was the management of the young buffalo, whose wound in the nose was quite healed, so that I could lead it at will with a cord or stick passed through the orifice, as the Caffrarians do. I preferred the stick, which answered the purpose of a bit, and I resolved to break this spirited beast for riding as well as drawing. It was already used to the shafts, and very tractable in them. But I had more trouble in inuring him to a rider, and to wearing a girth, made of the old buffalo's hide. I tacked a sort of saddle of sailcloth to the girth, and upon it a burden, gradually increased, until he carried large bags of roots, salt, and other articles.

The monkey was his first rider, and stuck close to the saddle, in spite of the plunging and kicking of the buffalo. Francis was then tried, but throughout his excursion I led the beast, for safety. Jack was next. I passed the stick through the buffalo's nose, tied strong packthread at each end of it, and put this newfangled bridle into the hands of the young rider, directing him how to use it. Ernest, Fritz, and lastly myself, got on successively. His trotting shook us to the very center, the rapidity of his gallop turned us giddy, and our lessons in horsemanship were reiterated many days before the animal could be ridden with either safety or pleasure. At last, my three oldest boys mounted it together, and the strength and swiftness of our saddled buffalo were prodigious.

We now began to manufacture our impenetrable boots without seams, of the elastic gum. I began with a pair for myself; and I encouraged my children to form some flasks and cups that could not break.

They made some clay molds, which they covered with layers of gum according to the instructions I had given them. I filled a pair of stockings with sand, and covered them with a layer of clay, which I dried in the shade, and then in the sun. I then fixed a sole of buffalo leather, well-beaten, and studded round with tacks, under the foot of the stocking. After this I poured the liquid gum into all the openings; on drying, this produced a close adhesion between the leather and stocking sole. I next smeared the whole with a thick coat of gum. As this layer dried, I put on another, till I had applied enough. After this I emptied the sand, drew out the stocking, removed the hardened clay, shook off the dust, and thus obtained a pair of seamless boots, as finished as if made by the best English workman, being pliant, warm, soft, smooth, and completely waterproof.

We had also constructed a fountain, a perpetual source of pleasure to all of us. In the upper part of the stream we built with stakes and stones a kind of dam, that raised the water sufficiently to convey it into the palm tree troughs. Afterward, by means of a gentle slope, it glided on to our dwelling place, where it fell into the tortoise-shell basin, which we had elevated on stones to a convenient height. And it was so contrived that the redundant water passed off through a cane pipe fitted to it. I placed two sticks athwart each other for the gourds, that served as pales, to rest on. And we thus produced, close to our abode, an agreeable fountain, delighting with its rill, and supplying us with a pure crystal fluid, unencumbered with leaves and earth or muddied by our waterfowls.

14. TRAINING THE WILD ASS — FLAX AND THE RAINY SEASON

ONE morning, we were putting the last touch to our winding staircase, when we heard at a distance the howlings of wild beasts, or of some creature at its last gasp.

We loaded our guns and pistols and placed them together within our tree. The howlings having ceased an instant, I descended well-armed, and put on our two faithful guardians their spiked collars and side guards. I assembled our cattle about the tree to have them in sight, and I then reascended to look around for the enemy's approach.

At this instant the howlings were renewed, closer to us. Fritz listened attentively, then threw down his gun, and burst into a loud laughter, exclaiming, "Father, it is our ass, come back to us! Listen! Do you not hear his melodious braying?" A fresh roar raised loud peals of laughter amongst us. Shortly after, our old friend Grizzle moved toward us leisurely, stopping now and then to browse. To our great joy, he was accompanied by one of his own species, of very superior beauty, which I knew to be a fine onager, or wild ass. Without delay I descended the ladder with Fritz, and we consulted on means of taking the stranger captive.

I got ready a long cord with a running knot, one end of which I tied fast to the root of a tree. The noose was kept open with a little stick slightly fixed in the opening, so as to fall of itself on the cord being thrown round the neck of the animal, whose efforts to escape would draw the knot closer. I also prepared a piece of bamboo about two feet long, which I split at the bottom, and tied fast at the top, to serve as nippers. I told Fritz my project of catching the onager in the noose, which I gave him to manage, being nimbler and more expert than myself. The two asses drew nearer and nearer to us. Fritz, holding in his hand the open noose, moved softly from the tree where we were concealed, and advanced to the length of the rope.

The onager first sprang backward, then stopped; Fritz now remained quite still, the animal continued to browse. Soon Fritz held out a handful of oats mixed with salt, and our ass instantly ran up and greedily devoured its favorite food. The other drew near, raised its head, breathing strongly, and came up so close that Fritz succeeded in throwing the rope round its neck.

The motion and stroke so affrighted the beast that it sprang off, but was soon checked by the cord, which almost stopped its breath. It could go no farther, and sank panting for breath upon the ground. I hastened to loosen the cord to prevent its being strangled, and threw our ass's halter over its head. I fixed the nose in my split cane pincers, which I secured at the bottom with packthread.

Thus I succeeded in subduing the first alarm of this wild animal. Then I wholly removed the noose, fastened the halter with two long ropes to two trees near us, on the right and left, and let the animal recover itself.

In a few moments the onager got up again, striking out furiously with its heels to free itself, but the pain of its nose, squeezed in the bamboo, forced it to lie down again, exhausted. Now Fritz and I undid the cords, fastened the now quieted onager between two roots closely connected, so as to make its escape impossible. We also confined Grizzle's forelegs with a rope, and then fastened him beside the onager, with plenty of good food before him for solace. My boys exulted in the idea of riding the onager, and in the fortunate result of Grizzle's flight. We named the onager *Lightfoot.*

A triple brood of our hens had given us more than forty chicks to my wife's great satisfaction. Some she kept under her zealous care, while others were sent to feed and breed in the desert, where we could find them as desired for our use.

This increase of our poultry reminded us of the need to build covered sheds for all our bipeds and quadrupeds between the roots of our great tree.

The rainy season, which is the winter of these countries, was drawing near, and to avoid loss of our stock, it was requisite to shelter it.

We began by forming of bamboo canes a kind of roof above the arched roots of our tree, the longest and strongest supported the roofing in the place of columns, the smaller laid more closely. I filled up the interstices with moss and clay, and a thick coat of tar over the whole formed a compact and solid covering. I then made a railing round it to form a balcony, under which, between the roots, were various stalls, sheltered from rain and sun; these could easily be shut and separated from each other by means of planks nailed upon the roots.

Part served as a stable and yard, part as an eating house, a storeroom, etc., and as a hayloft, to keep our hay and provisions dry. Afterward we filled these places with everything useful that might give us employment when confined by the weather.

One evening I went round by the wood of oaks with Ernest and Fritz, to fill our empty sacks with many sweet acorns. Ernest was accompanied by Knips the monkey, and Fritz, horsemanlike, was on the onager, Lightfoot.

When we reached the oaks and were busily employed, the monkey skipped unperceived into an adjoining bush. It had been there some time, when we heard loud cries of birds and flapping of wings. I dispatched Ernest to reconnoiter. In an instant we heard him exclaim, "Come quickly, Father! A fine heath-fowl's nest, full of eggs."

Fritz ran up directly, and in a few moments brought out alive the male and female heath-fowl, both very beautiful. I rejoiced at this discovery, and helped my son to tie their wings and feet, and held them while he returned to the bush for the eggs. Now Ernest came forward, driving the monkey before him, and carrying his hat with the utmost care. He had stuck his girdle full of narrow sharp-pointed leaves. On coming up to me he uncovered his hat, crying out, "Here, Father, are some heath-fowl's eggs. I found them concealed under these long leaves. I am going to take the eggs home. They will please my mother, and these leaves will amuse Francis, for they are like swords, and he will like them for a plaything."

It was now time to think of moving homeward. Fritz with the acorns, on Lightfoot, Ernest carried the eggs, I took charge of the hen, and we proceeded to Falcon's Stream. At home, our first care was the eggs. The female bird was too frightened to sit upon them, but fortunately we had a hen that was hatching. Her eggs were immediately removed, and the new ones put in their place. The female heath-fowl was put into the parrot's cage, and hung up in the room, to accustom it to our society. In less than three days all the chickens were hatched. As they grew up I plucked out the large feathers of their wings, lest they take flight, but they and their real parent gradually became domesticated, daily accompanied our feathered stock in search of food, and regularly came back at night to the roost I had prepared for them.

Francis for a short time was highly amused with his sword leaves, and then grew weary of them, and they were thrown aside. Fritz picked up some that were quite soft and withered, pliable as a riband in his hand. "Francis," said he, "you can make whips of your sword grass, to use in driving your goats and sheep." Fritz accordingly helped him to divide the leaves, and plait them into whip-cords.

Examining them closely, I found they were composed of long fibers. The discovery led me to surmise that this supposed sword grass might be the flax plant of New Zealand. My wife expressed the liveliest joy at this discovery. "This," said she, "is the most useful thing you have found. Bring me all you can of these leaves. I will make you stockings, shirts, clothes, thread, ropes—in short, give me flax, looms, and frames, and I shall find use for all of it." I could not help smiling at the scope she gave to her imagination on the bare mention of flax. Fritz whispered to Jack, and both went to the stable. One mounted Lightfoot, the other the buffalo, and they galloped off toward the wood.

In a quarter of an hour they were back; they had foraged the woods, and heavily loaded their cattle with the precious plant, which they joyfully threw at their mother's feet. All would assist her in preparations for the work she was to engage in, and the first would be in steeping the flax.

Next morning the ass was put to the small light cart, loaded with bundles of leaves, and the family gaily followed with shovels and pickaxes. We stopped at Flamingo Marsh, placed our bundles in the water, pressing them down with stones. We left them till it was time to set them in the sun to dry, and thus render the stems soft and easy to peel.

In a fortnight we took the flax out of the water, and spread it on the grass in the sun. It dried so rapidly that we were able to load it on our cart the same evening, and carry it to Falcon's Stream, where it was put by till we had time to make the beetles, wheels, reels, carding combs, etc., required for the manufacture. This task was left for the rainy season, to employ present time in collecting animals. Occasional slight showers had already come on; the temperature became gloomy and variable, the skies dark, and stormy winds warned us to get ready all that might be wanted.

Our first care was to dig up a full supply of yams and other roots for bread, with plenty of coconuts and some bags of sweet acorns. It occurred to us, while digging, that the ground being thus opened and manured with the leaves of plants, we might sow in it to advantage the remainder of our European corn. The season, moreover, was proper for sowing, and planting the embryo grain. We planted the palm trees we had discovered and formed a large handsome plantation of sugar canes, so as to have hereafter everything useful and agreeable around us.

Unfortunately, the weather changed sooner than we expected. The rain fell in heavy torrents that seemed to change the whole face of the country into a lake.

The first thing to be done was to fix our residence at the bottom of the tree, between the roots and under the tarred roof I had erected. We were forced to take down our hammocks, mattresses, and every article that could be injured by the rain; and most fortunate were we in having made the winding stairs, which sheltered us during the removal. The stairs served afterward for a kind of lumber room; we kept in it most of our culinary vessels, which my wife fetched as she wanted them. Our little sheds between the roots, constructed for the poultry and the cattle, could scarcely contain us all. We were half-stifled with smoke whenever we kindled a fire, and drenched with rain when we opened the doors. For the first time since our disaster, we sighed for the comfortable houses of our dear country.

We dismissed from our livestock those animals that, native to the country, would provide for themselves. Not to lose them, we tied bells round their necks, and Fritz and I sought and drove them in every morning when they did not spontaneously return.

Our only remedy for the smoke was to open the door when we made a fire; and we did without fire as much as we could, living on milk and cheese, and only making one to bake our cakes, and to boil enough of our favorite roots and salt meat to last us a number of days. Our dry wood was also nearly expended. Not having provided sufficient hay and leaves for our European cattle, which we kept housed, the cow, the ass, the sheep, and the goats (the two last greatly increased in number), we were forced to give them our tuberous roots and sweet acorns. However, this imparted a delicate flavor to their milk. After milking, cleaning and feeding the animals, we made flour of the manioc root, with which we filled the large gourds.

Fortunately, we had laid in a huge store of candles. When darkness fell, we got round the table, where a large taper fixed on a gourd gave us an excellent light. My wife pursued her occupation with the needle. I was forming a journal recording the narrative of our shipwreck and residence in this island while my family reminded me of various incidents belonging to the story. Ernest wrote off my pages in a clear legible hand. Fritz and Jack drew from memory the plants and animals which they had observed; while one and all taught little Francis to read and write. The day's devotional reading in the Holy Bible was performed by each in turn, and we then retired to rest.

It was unanimously resolved on, however, that we would not pass another rainy season exposed to the same evils.

The choice of a fresh abode now engrossed our attention, and Fritz came forward triumphantly with a book he had found in the bottom of our clothes chest. "Here," said he, "is our best counselor and model, *Robinson Crusoe*; as far as I remembered, he cut himself a habitation out of solid rock. Let us see how he proceeded; we will do the same with greater ease, for he was alone, and we are six in number."

The final result of our deliberations was to survey the rocks round Tent House, and to examine whether any of them could be excavated for our purpose.

Our last job for the winter was a beetle for my wife's flax, and some carding combs. I filed large nails till they were even, round, and pointed; I fixed them at equal distances in a sheet of tin, and raised the side of it like a box. I then poured melted lead between the nails and the sides to give firmness to their points, which came out four inches. I nailed this tin on a board, and the machine was fit to work. My wife was impatient to use it, and it became in time a source of inexhaustible delight.

15. SPRING — SPINNING — HOUSE IN THE SALT ROCK MINE

AFTER many gloomy weeks of rain, the sun darted its benign rays on the earth, and the air became mild and serene. The beauteous verdure began to shoot forth on every side.

Our summer occupations commenced by arranging and thoroughly cleaning Falcon's Nest. The stairs were cleared, the rooms between the roots reoccupied, and we were left with leisure to proceed to other employments. Our sons led the cattle to the fresh pastures, while I carried the bundles of flax into the open air, where, by heaping stones together, I contrived an oven sufficiently commodious to dry it well. The same evening, we all set to work to peel, and afterward to beat it and strip off the bark, and lastly to comb it with my carding machine. I took this laborious task and drew out such distaffs full of long soft flax ready for spinning that my enraptured wife ran to embrace me, requesting me to make her a wheel without delay, that she might enter upon her favorite work.

Early in life I had practiced turnery for my amusement. Now as I had not forgotten the arrangement and component parts of a spinning wheel and reel, I accomplished those two machines to her satisfaction. She fell eagerly to spinning, allowing herself no leisure, and scarcely time to prepare our dinners.

At Tent House, we found the ravages of winter more considerable even than at Falcon's Stream. The tempest and rain had beaten down the tent and made havoc among our provisions. Luckily our handsome pinnace had been for the most part spared. It was still at anchor, ready to serve us in case of need; but our tub boat was too shattered to be of any further service.

We were grieved to find two barrels of gunpowder wholly useless, but the remaining one was in tolerable condition. This, our only wealth, should not be exposed to such loss in winter quarters.

Fritz and Jack were determined to make me undertake the excavation of the rock, but I had no hopes of success. Robinson Crusoe found a spacious cavern that merely required arrangement. No such cavity was apparent in our rock. Still, I resolved to attempt to cut off a recess to protect the gunpowder. I accordingly set off one day, accompanied by my two boys. We took with us pickaxes, chisels, hammers, and iron levers, to try what impression we could make on the rock. I chose a part nearly perpendicular; the view from it was enchanting, for it embraced the whole range of Safety Bay, the banks of Jackal's River, and Family Bridge. I marked out with charcoal the opening we wished to make, and we began the heavy toil of piercing the quarry.

We made so little progress the first day, that we were tempted to relinquish the undertaking. Persevering, however, hope revived, as the stone was of softer texture as we penetrated deeper. The rays of the sun upon the rock had hardened the external layer, but when I had cut about a foot in depth, we could loosen it with a spade like dried mud. My boys assisted me with a spirit and zeal beyond their years.

After a few days of labor, we had already advanced seven feet into the rock. Fritz removed the fragments in a barrow, and discharged them in a line before the place, to form a sort of terrace; I enlarged the aperture; Jack, the smallest of the three, was able to get in and cut away below. He had with him a long iron bar sharpened at the end, which he drove in with a hammer to loosen a piece at a time. Suddenly he bawled out, "It is pierced through, Father! Fritz, I have pierced it through!"

"Let us hear, what have you pierced? The mountain? Not peradventure your hand or foot, Jack?" said I.

"No, no, it is the mountain," cried Jack. "I have pierced the mountain."

Fritz now ran to him. "Come, let us see then. It is no doubt the globe at least you have pierced," said he. "You should have pushed on your tool boldly, till you reached

Europe. I should have been glad to peep into that hole."

"Well, then, peep you may, but look how far the iron is gone in, and tell me if it is all my boasting."

"Come hither, Father," said Fritz, "this is really extraordinary. His iron bar seems to have got to a hollow place. See, it can be moved in every direction."

I approached, and working the bar about, made a sufficient aperture for one of my sons to pass through. The rubbish fell within the cavity, which I judged, from the falling of the stones, was not much deeper than the part we stood on. I began to feel a giddiness from the foul air, and was compelled to withdraw quickly.

Under my direction the boys now hastened to gather some dry moss, which they made into bundles. They then set fire to them, and threw the blazing moss into the opening. The fire was extinguished at the very entrance, thus proving bad air within.

I recollected that we had brought from the vessel a chest that was full of grenades, rockets, and other fireworks, for the purpose of making signals, as well as for amusement. I took some of these, together with an iron mortar for throwing. Out of the opening I laid a train of gunpowder and set fire to the end, which reached to where we stood. A general explosion took place, and an awful report reverberated through the dark recess. The lighted grenades flew about on all sides like brilliant meteors, rebounding and bursting with a terrific sound. We then sent in the rockets, which hissed in the cavity like flying dragons, disclosing to our astonished view its vast extent. We beheld too, numerous dazzling bodies that sparkled suddenly, as if by magic, and disappeared like lightning, leaving the place in total darkness.

After the fireworks, I tried lighted straw. To our great satisfaction, the bundles thrown in were entirely consumed; we could then reasonably hope nothing was to be feared from the air. But there still remained the danger of plunging into some abyss, or into a body of water. I deferred our entrance into the recess till we had lights to guide us.

I dispatched Jack on the buffalo to Falcon's Stream to tell his mother and brothers of our discovery, directing him to return with them, bringing all the tapers.

In three or four hours they came up. I immediately lighted some of the tapers, each taking one in his right hand, an implement in his left, another taper in his pocket, and some flint and steel. Thus we entered the rock.

The most magnificent spectacle presented itself. The sides of the cavern sparkled like diamonds, the light from our tapers was reflected from all parts, and had the effect of a grand illumination. Innumerable crystals of every length and shape hung from the top of the vault, which, uniting with those of the sides, formed pillars, altars, and a variety of other splendid masses. We might have fancied ourselves in the palace of a fairy, or an illuminated temple.

The floor was level, covered with a white and very fine sand, completely dry. All this led me to hope the spot would be healthy, convenient, and eligible for our proposed residence. I now conjectured about the crystallizations shooting out on all sides, and from the arch roof. Impatient to try an experiment, I discovered with great joy, by breaking a portion of one of them, that I was in a grotto of *sal-gem,* that is, rock salt, found in the earth in solid crystallized masses, generally above a bed of gypsum, and surrounded by layers of fossils or rock. The discovery of this fact pleased us all exceedingly. The shape of the crystals, their little solidity, and finally their saline taste, were decisive evidences.

Many schemes were formed for converting this magnificent grotto into a convenient and agreeable mansion for our abode. Some voted for our immediate establishment there, but it was resolved that Falcon's Stream should still be our headquarters till the end of the year.

The lucky discovery of a previously existing cavern in the rock had considerably lessened our labor. I had more room than was wanted for the construction of our dwelling, but to render it habitable was our object. The upper bed of the rock in front of the cavern was soft, and could be worked with moderate effort. Being now exposed to the air and heat of the sun, it would no doubt become by degrees hard and compact, with openings for doors and windows in the front. I had previously marked out the openings to be cut for the frames, to be grooved for greater convenience and solidity. I took care not to break the stone taken from the apertures, and to preserve it in large pieces, and these I cut with saw and chisel into oblongs an inch and a half in thickness, to serve as tiles. I laid them in the sun, and they hardened quickly. I then removed them, and my sons placed them in order against the side of the rock, till wanted for our internal arrangements.

When I could enter the cavern freely with a good doorway, and it was sufficiently lighted by windows, I erected a partition. With ample room for my design, I laid out the interior in the following manner. A very considerable space was first partitioned off in two divisions. The one on the right was appropriated to our residence, that on the left was to contain kitchen, stables, and workroom. At the end of the second division, where windows could not be placed, the cellar and storeroom were to be formed; the whole separated by partition boards, with doors of communication, to give us a pleasant and comfortable abode.

The residence side was divided into three apartments; the first, next the door, was the bedroom for my wife and me, the second a dining parlor, and the last a bedroom for the boys. As we had only three windows, we put one in each sleeping room; the third was fixed in the kitchen, where my wife would often be. I contrived a good fireplace in the kitchen near the window. I pierced the rock a little above, and four planks nailed together served for a chimney.

We made the workroom near the kitchen of sufficient dimensions for undertakings of some magnitude; it served also to keep our cart and sledge in. Lastly, the stables, which were formed into four compartments, to separate the different species of animals, occupied all the bottom of the cavern on this side. On the other were the cellar and magazine for the gunpowder.

During these employments we found several advantages. Immense turtles were often seen on the shore, where they deposited their eggs —a real treat—in the sand. We got possession of the turtles themselves for livestock, to feast on whenever we pleased. As soon as a turtle was seen, one of my boys cut off its retreat. Meanwhile, without doing it any injury, we turned the turtle on its back, passed a long cord through the shell, and tied the end of it to a stake fixed close to the edge of the water. This done, we set the prisoner on its legs again. It hastened into the sea, but could not go beyond the end of the cord, but apparently it found food with more facility along shore than out at sea.

A number of sea dogs came into Safety Bay in search of prey. The fish is not good food, but its skin, tanned and dressed, makes excellent leather. I was in great need of it for straps and harnesses to make saddles for Fritz and Jack to ride the onager and buffalo, and to cut up into soles, belts, and pantaloons; and the fat yielded good lamp oil to be substituted for tapers in the long evenings of winter, and for tanning and rendering the leather pliant.

This time I improved our sledge for carrying stores from Falcon's Stream to Tent House. I raised it on two beams, on axle trees, at the extremities of which I put the four gun-carriage wheels I had taken off the cannon from the vessel. Thus I obtained a light and convenient vehicle, of moderate height, on which boxes and casks could be placed.

We set out all together to pass our Sunday at Falcon's Stream, and once more offered our pious thanks to the Almighty.

16. WE BUILD TWO FARMHOUSES

THE WORK of our dwelling went on, with the hope of our being settled within it by the time of the rainy season.

From the moment I discovered gypsum to be the basis of the crystal salt in our grotto, I foresaw great advantages from it. I tried to find a place in the continuation of the rock, which I might blow up. I soon had the good fortune to meet with a narrow slip between the projections of the rock, which I could easily convert into a passage to our workroom. I found also on the ground fragments of gypsum, and removed them to the kitchen. We baked a few of the pieces at a time when we made a fire for cooking. By rubbing it into a powder when cold we obtained a considerable quantity, which I put carefully into casks for use in finishing the interior of our dwelling. My notion was to form the walls for separating the apartments of the squares of stone I had already provided, united with a cement of this new ingredient.

One day Jack and I perceived immense quantities of large fish moving slowly toward the banks of Jackal's River. I distinguished the largest to be sturgeon, while the smallest were salmon. "What say you now, Father?" said Jack. "This is nothing like your little paltry fry! A single fish of this troop would fill a tub!"

"No doubt," answered I; and with great gravity, "Prithee, Jack, step into the river, and fling them to me one by one, to take home to salt and dry."

He looked at me for a moment to see if I could possibly be in earnest, then, "Wait a moment, Father," cried he, "and I will do so." He sprang off like lightning toward the cavern, from where he soon returned loaded with a bow and arrows, the bladders of the sea dogs, and a ball of string, to catch, as he assured me, every one of the fishes. I looked on with interest and curiosity. He tied the bladders round at certain distances with a long piece of string, to the end of which he fastened an arrow and a small iron hook; he placed the large ball of string in a hole in the ground at a sufficient distance from the water's edge, and then he shot off an arrow, which the next instant stuck in one of the largest fishes. At his shout of joy, Fritz joined us. "Well done, brother Jack," cried he; "let me, too, have my turn." He ran back and fetched the harpoon and the windlass, and returned with Ernest. We were pleased with their arrival, for the salmon Jack had pierced struggled fiercely; but, aided by Fritz and Ernest, we succeeded in drawing it to a bank, where I put an end to it.

This fortunate beginning inspired us all. Fritz seized his harpoon and windlass, I wielded a trident, Ernest prepared the large fishing rod, and Jack his apparatus and his arrow, and the bladders, which were so effectual in preventing the fish from sinking when struck. Such numbers of fish that were that we had only to choose among them. Jack's arrow struck a large sturgeon, secured with great difficulty, while I was obliged to go up to the middle in the water to manage two that I caught. Ernest, with his rod and line and a hook, had taken two smaller ones. Fritz, with his harpoon, struck a sturgeon at least eight feet in length, and all our skill and strength was necessary to conduct him safe to shore, where we harnessed the buffalo to him with strong cords to draw him to Tent House.

Now we began to plan for constructing a small boat as a substitute for the tub raft, to come close in to shore. I desired to make it, as the savages do, of the rind of a tree. We therefore searched for a tree of capacious dimensions, not one likely to yield us fruit, to refresh us with its shade, or to adorn the landscape round our dwelling.

We all arrived at Falcon's Stream, intending to pass the night. The grain my wife had so plentifully sowed had sprung up luxuriantly. We reaped barley, wheat, rye, oats, peas, millet, and lentils—sufficient to enable us to sow again plentifully at the proper season. The plant that yielded most was maize, a proof that it best loved the soil. Its splendid golden ears attracted the voracity of the feathered birds, and the moment we drew near, a dozen at least of large bustards sprang up with a loud rustling noise, which awakened the attention of the dogs. They plunged into the thickest parts, and routed numerous flocks of birds of all kinds and sizes, who took hastily to flight. Among the fugitives were some quail, who escaped by running, and lastly several kangaroos, whose prodigious leaps enabled them to elude the dogs.

Before we recovered from our surprise, the prey was beyond our reach. Without further loss of time, Fritz took the bandage from his eagle's eyes (for the bird always accompanied him perched upon his gamebag), and showed him with his hand the bustards still flying. The eagle took rapid flight. Fritz jumped like lightning on the back of his onager, galloped in the direction the bird had taken, and we soon lost sight of him.

The eagle soon had his prey in view. He mounted above one of the bustards in a direct line, then darted suddenly down. The bustards flew about in utter confusion, but the eagle remained steady in pursuit of the bird he had fixed upon his prey. He alighted on the unlucky bustard, fixed his claws and his beak in its back, till Fritz, arriving full gallop, got down from the onager, replaced the bandage on the eagle's eyes, seated him once more upon the gamebag, and having relieved the poor bustard from his persecutor, shouted to us to come. We ran speedily to the place.

We now hastened forward to Falcon's Stream, and dressed the wounds of the bustard. It was a male, and we foresaw giving him for a companion to our solitary female bustard, now completely tame. I threw a few more bundles of maize into the cart, and soon we arrived at our tree.

The rest of the day was employed in picking the grains of the different sorts of corn from the stalks. We put what we wished to keep for sowing into some gourd shells, and the Turkey wheat was laid carefully aside in sheaves till we should have time to beat and separate it. Fritz observed that we should also want to grind it; and I reminded him of the hand mill we had secured from the wrecked vessel.

"But, Father," exclaimed Fritz, "the hand mill is so small, why should we not contrive a water mill, as they do in Europe? We have surely rapid streams of water in abundance."

"Such a mechanism is more difficult than you imagine, my boy. Still, if it is worth further attention, we have abundance of time, when our harvests produce plentiful crops of corn. Meantime, think of tomorrow's excursion, for we should set out by sunrise."

We began our preparations. My wife chose some hens and two fine cocks, with the intention of leaving them at least to produce a colony at a considerable distance from our dwelling places. I visited our beasts, and selected four young pigs, four sheep, two kids, and one male of each species. We could well afford to spare these individuals for the experiment. We thus evaded the burden of their support, and could find them at will.

We took this time a new direction. We were often obliged to turn aside or halt, while I cut a passage with my hatchet, but these accidents led to discoveries; among others, some roots of trees curved by nature to serve both for saddles and yokes for our beasts of burden. I put several in the cart.

In about an hour we found ourselves in the extremity of the wood and in view of a singular phenomenon. A small plain, or rather a grove of low bushes, to appearance almost covered with flakes of snow, lay extended before us. Fritz, who had darted forward on his onager, now returned with one hand filled with tufts of a most excellent species of cotton, so that the whole surface of low bushes was in reality a plantation. The pods had burst from ripeness, the winds had scattered and the ground was strewed with their flaky contents; they had gathered in tufts on the bushes, and they floated gently in the air.

The joy of this discovery was beyond words. We collected as much cotton as our bags would hold, and my wife filled her pockets with the seed, to raise it in our garden at Tent House.

We now proceeded towards a high point of land which skirted the wood of gourds, and commanded a view of the adjacent country. I conceived a wish to erect a farmhouse in the vicinity of the cotton plantation and the gourd wood, which furnished so many of the utensils for daily use throughout the family. I found the high ground in all respects favorable to my design.

My plan for a building was approved by all; we pitched our tent, and cooked our victuals. When we had eaten, I looked about for a group of trees, at such fit distances from each other as would assist me in my plan. I found exactly what I wanted, quite near to the spot we had felt to be so enviable. I returned to my companions, whom I found busily employed in preparing excellent beds of the cotton, upon which we all retired to rest.

The trees that I had chosen for the construction of my farmhouse were for the most part one foot in diameter in the trunk. They grew in a tolerably regular parallelogram, with its longest side to the sea, the length twenty-four feet, and the breadth sixteen. I cut little hollow places or mortises in the trunks, at the distance of ten feet, one above the other, to form two stories. The upper one I made a few inches shorter before than behind, that the roof might be in some degree sloping; I then inserted beams five inches in diameter respectively in the mortises, and thus formed the skeleton of my building. We next nailed some laths from tree to tree, at equal distances from each other, to form the roof, and placed on them a covering composed of pieces of the bark of trees, cut into the shape of tiles, and in a sloping position, for the rain to run off in the wet season. As we had no great provision of iron nails, we used for the purpose the strong pointed thorn of the acacia, which we had discovered and cut down the day before. A quantity of them, laid in the sun to dry, became as hard as iron, and did essential service.

After our next meal we resumed our undertaking of the farmhouse. We formed the walls with matted reeds interwoven with pliant laths to the height of six feet. The remaining space to the roof was enclosed with only a simple grating, to admit air and light, and a door was placed in the middle of the front. We next arranged the interior with as much convenience as time would allow. We divided it halfway up by a partition wall into two unequal parts; the largest for the sheep and goats, and the smallest for ourselves, should we wish to pass a few days here. At the farther end of the stable we fixed a house for the fowls, and above it a sort of hayloft for the forage.

Before the entrance door we placed two benches, contrived of odd pieces of wood, to rest ourselves under the shade of the trees. Our own apartment was provided with a couple of the best bedsteads we could make of twigs of trees, raised upon four legs, two feet from the ground, and destined to receive our cotton mattresses. We contented ourselves for the present with these slight hints of a dwelling; additions could be made hereafter.

I had imagined we should accomplish what we wished at the farm in three or four days; but we found that a week was necessary, and our victuals fell short before our work was done. Fritz and Jack were dispatched to Falcon's Stream and to Tent House, to fetch new supplies of cheese, ham, potatoes, dried fish, manioc bread, for us, and also for the animals we had left there.

During the absence of our purveyors, Ernest and I followed the winding of a river toward the middle of the wall of rocks. Our course was interrupted by a marsh which bordered an enchantingly picturesque lake. The swampy surface was covered with wild rice, ripe on the stalk, which attracted large flocks of birds. As we approached, a loud rustling was heard; we distinguished on the wing, bustards, Canada heath-fowl, and great numbers of smaller birds, and succeeded in bringing down five or six of them.

Presently Master Knips jumped from Flora's back, and plucked something from thick-growing plants along the ground, then ate it voraciously. We found he had discovered there the largest and finest kind of strawberry, called in Europe the *Chili,* or *pine strawberry.*

When we reached the lake we found a quantity of swans gliding over its surface. Their color, instead of white, like those of our country, was a jetty black, while six large feathers of the wings were white. Their glossy plumage, reflected on the water, produced the most astonishing effect.

We returned to the farm at the same time with Fritz and Jack, and produced our welcome offering of strawberries and our specimen of rice. We filled the stable with forage, laid a large provision of grain for the fowls within their house, and began arrangements for our departure.

The following day, we directed our course toward the eminence in the vicinity of Cape Disappointment. From this point we viewed the country which surrounded Falcon's stream —a rich landscape, comprehending sea, land, and rocks. We agreed that on this beautiful spot we would build a second cottage. A spring of the clearest water issued from the soil near the summit, and flowed over its sloping side. "Let us build here," I exclaimed, "and call the spot—*Arcadia,*" to which my wife and all agreed.

We again set to work, building with incredible rapidity. This cottage contained a dining room, two bedchambers, two stables, and a storeroom for preserving all kinds of provisions for man and beast. We formed the roof square, with four sloped sides, and the whole had really the appearance of a European cottage, and was finished in the short space of six days.

What now remained to be done was to fix on a tree fit for my project of a boat. After much search, I at length found one of prodigious size, its lowest branches high on the trunk.

It was, however, no very encouraging prospect I had before me, the stripping off a piece of the bark that should be eighteen feet in length, and five in diameter. We fastened our rope ladder by one end to the nearest branch, to enable us to work with the saw at any height from the ground. We cut quite round the trunk in two places, at eighteen feet and at the foot, and then took out a perpendicular slip from the whole length between the circles. Thus we could introduce the proper implements for raising the rest by degrees, till the bark was entirely separated from the tree. We toiled with increasing anxiety, at every moment dreading that we should not be able to preserve the bark from breaking. When we had loosened about half, we supported it by means of cords and pulleys; and when all was at length detached, we let it down gently, and with joy beheld it lying safe on the grass.

Our business was next to mold it to our purpose, while the substance continued moist and flexible.

The boys observed that we had now nothing more to do than to nail a plank at each end, and our boat would be as those used by the savages; but for my own part, I could not be contented with a mere roll of bark for a boat. I made the boys assist me to saw the bark in the middle of the two ends, the length of several feet. These two parts I folded over till they ended in a point. I kept them in this form by the help of the strong glue made from fish bladders, with pieces of wood nailed fast over the whole. This operation tended to widen the boat in the middle, and thus render it of too flat a form. By straining a cord all round, we reduced it to its due proportion, and in this state we put it in the sun, to harden and fix.

At the end of the wall of rocks we then planted a sort of fortification of trees, which should discourage the invasion of savages, allow us to keep our pigs on the other side, and thus secure our different plantations from the chance of injury. In addition, we placed a slight drawbridge across the river beyond the narrow pass, which we could let down or take up at pleasure on our side.

We now returned to Arcadia, and after a night's repose loaded the sledge with the boat and other matters, and returned to Tent House.

We resumed the completion of the boat. In two days she had received the addition of a keel, a neat lining of wood, a small flat floor, benches, a small mast and triangular sail, a rudder, and a thick coat of pitch on the outside, so that the first time we saw her in the water, we were all charmed at her appearance.

Before the rainy season we completed the grotto. We made the internal divisions of planks, and that which separated us from the stables, of stone. We collected or manufactured all sorts of materials, beams and planks, reeds, and twigs for matting, pieces of gypsum for plaster, etc., etc., for use in winter occupations.

At length the time of the rainy season was near at hand, and we thought of it with pleasure.

We plastered over the walls of the principal apartments on each side with the greatest care. We then ventured to make some carpets with the hair of our goats. To this effect we smoothed the ground in the rooms we intended to distinguish with great care. We spread over it some sailcloth, which my wife joined in breadths, and fitted exactly. Next we strewed the goats' hair, mixed with wool obtained from the sheep, over the whole; on this surface we threw some hot water, in which a strong cement had been dissolved. The whole was then rolled up and was beaten for a considerable time with hard sticks. The sailcloth was now unrolled, and the inside again sprinkled, rolled, and beaten as before. This process was continued till the substance had become a sort of felt, which could be separated from the sailcloth, and was then put in the sun to harden. We thus produced a very tolerable substitute for a carpet. We completed two, one for our parlor, and the other for our drawing room, as we jocosely named them.

Thus we had made the first steps toward a condition of civilization. Separated from society, condemned, perhaps, to pass the remainder of life in this desert island, we now possessed the means of happiness, with an abundance of necessaries, and many of the comforts of civilized living.

17. ANNIVERSARY OF OUR DELIVERANCE

ONE MORNING, I occupied myself by counting up the time that had passed away since our shipwreck. Calculating the dates I found that the next day would be just two years since the hand of God had saved us from a watery grave. I resolved to celebrate the day with all the pomp our situation would permit.

At supper I announced the holiday for the morrow. The announcement of a holiday surprised and overjoyed my children, and their mother was astonished to find that we had been on the island two years.

On the morrow we rose and dressed as decently as our scanty means afforded, and proceeded to breakfast. After our daily prayer I announced to my family the amusements of the day.

"You have practiced for some time," said I, "in wrestling, running, slinging, and horsemanship. You shall this day contend, before your mother and me, and the crown shall be given to the victor."

I then organized the different combats which were to take place. First came firing at a mark.

For this we arranged on the ground a rudely shaped piece of wood, with two bits of leather at each side of the top, which we called a kangaroo. Jack did wonders, he shot away one of the ears of our pretended kangaroo! Fritz just grazed the head, and Ernest lodged his ball in the middle of the body.

Another proof of skill consisted in firing at a ball of cork which I threw up in the air. Ernest cut the ball to pieces. Fritz also shot well, but Jack could not hit it. We then tried the same thing with pistols, shortening the distance, and again I complimented my boys upon the progress they had made since last year.

In slinging, Fritz carried off the prize. After that came archery; and here all—even little Francis—distinguished themselves. Next came the races; and I gave them for a course the distance between Family Bridge and Falcon's Nest.

"The one that arrives first," said I to the runners, who gathered about me, "will bring me, as proof of his victory, my knife, which I left on the table, under the tree." I then gave the signal, by clapping my hands three times. My three sons set out, Jack and Fritz with all their natural impetuosity. On the contrary, Ernest, reflective, set off slowly at first, but gradually augmented his pace. I perceived that he had his elbows pressed firmly against his body—a mark of prudence.

Jack returned first, but he was mounted on his buffalo, and the onager and the ass followed him.

"How now," said I, "is this what you call racing? It was your legs, and not those of the buffalo, that I wished to exercise."

"Bah!" cried he, jumping from the back of his courser, "I knew I would never get there, so as the trial of horsemanship comes next, I thought that, being near Falcon's Nest, I would bring our coursers back with me."

Fritz came next, all out of breath and covered with sweat. But it was Ernest who brought the knife to me.

"How come you have the knife," said I, "when Fritz got here before you?"

"The thing is simple," answered Ernest. "In going, he could not long keep up the pace he started with, and soon stopped to breathe, while I ran on and got the knife; but in coming back, Fritz pressed his arms against his sides, and held his mouth shut, as I had done, and then the victory depended upon our relative strength. Fritz is sixteen while I am but thirteen, and of course he arrived first."

I praised the two boys for their skill, and declared Ernest conqueror.

But now Jack, mounted on his buffalo, demanded that the riding exercises commence.

"To the saddle, to the saddle, my lads," he bellowed.

Fritz mounted his onager, and Ernest took the ass, but although they tried all their skill, Jack distanced them both. A practiced groom could not have managed a thoroughbred horse with more ease and grace than he did his bull. Just as I was about to proclaim Jack victor, little Francis rode into the arena, mounted on his young bull "Broumm," who was not more than three or four months old. My wife had made him a saddle of kangarooskin, with stirrups adjusted to his little legs, and there he sat, a whip in his right hand, and the bridle of his animal in the left.

"Gentlemen," said the little cavalier, "will you now permit me to make a trial of horsemanship before you?"

The assembly loudly applauded and the boy, cool and calm, commenced to maneuver his courser. My wife looked on with maternal pride, and Francis was unanimously proclaimed an excellent horseman.

After the horsemanship, the swimming occupied some time.

They also climbed the trees, and I announced that the rewards would now be distributed.

Every one hastened to the grotto, which had been lighted up with all the torches we possessed. My wife, as queen of the day, was installed in an elevated seat, decorated with flowers, and I called up the laureates to receive the rewards, which their mother distributed to each one with a kiss.

Fritz—conqueror at shooting and swimming—received a superb English rifle, and a hunting knife, which he had long wished for. Ernest had for the reward of the race a splendid gold watch. Jack—the cavalier—obtained a magnificent pair of steel spurs and a whip of whalebone. Little Francis received a pair of stirrups and a box of colors as a reward for the industry he had displayed in educating his bull.

When this distribution was finished, I rose, and, turning to my wife, presented her with a beautiful English workbox which contained pins, needles, scissors, etc.

"Receive," said I, "my excellent companion, also a reward; for your services and endurance during the years with the tender love of myself and the children."

The day was finished as it had begun—with songs and expressions of joy. We were all happy, all contented. And we all thanked in our hearts the Lord who had been so merciful toward us.

18. THE DOVECOT

WE ALL remembered the bountiful provision of blackbirds and ortolans at Falcon's Nest the preceding year. The time had now arrived for their reappearance. To secure this delicious provision for the coming winter, we resolved to leave the grotto and move nearer to the spot.

Our provision of India rubber was exhausted, and before I set out I wished to give our waterproof boots a new coat. I sent Fritz and Jack to the wood of India-rubber trees, where I thought they would find, ready drawn, a sufficient quantity of the gum. We had made large incisions in the trees, and placed calabashes shaded with green branches under them to receive it, as the sun hardens the gum immediately. Suddenly my wife exclaimed, "I have forgotten to give the boys a calabash for the gum, for they cannot bring it home in the flat dishes we put there. I mean to go directly, and see whether my gourds are ripe." I asked her what she meant by saying "my gourds."

She then informed me that she possessed a superb plantation of gourds, the seeds of which she had found among our European grains, and planted in her kitchen garden. She led the way. We found a quantity of bottle-shaped gourds, selected the ripest, in useful forms, and emptied them out. We made bottles, and plates, and saucers, using alternately the knife and the saw.

The sun had already begun to decline, when the young messengers returned, the one mounted on the onager, the other on the buffalo.

"Well," said I, "have you made out well?"

"Oh, yes, very well," said Fritz, in a singular tone, and showed us what they had brought —a root of anise that Jack had in his buffalo pouch; a root wrapped up in leaves, which they called "monkey root"; two calabashes of India rubber, and another half full of turpentine; a sack full of wax berries; and a crane, which Fritz's eagle had killed.

Jack told us how he had obtained the anise and the turpentine. I then asked them concerning the "monkey root" they had brought; Fritz answered:

"I can assure you that it far surpasses manioc, both in smell and savor. We discovered it close by the farmhouse, where a company of monkeys were regaling themselves on it."

The monkey root, or ginseng, made its appearance at supper, and was pronounced excellent; but as its aromatic nature made it more of a medicine than an article of food, I forbade its frequent use.

The next morning I took a certain quantity of the liquid India rubber, which I mixed with the turpentine, and placed the mixture over the fire. And while the glue was thickening, I sent the boys into the copse to gather a quantity of little twigs which I needed. The abundance of game suggested another idea, and I resolved to try an imitation of the Americans in Virginia, the experiment of a hunt with torches; it would be perhaps more successful than taking the birds by snares.

I then taught the boys to plunge a packet of five or six twigs, by the aid of a pair of pincers, into the glue for snares. When I had a sufficient quantity, Jack and Fritz climbed into the tree and placed the branches of fig trees, covered with the snares, among the limbs of the tree. It was not long before we saw the unfortunate ortolans falling to the ground in numbers, their legs and wings stuck fast in the glue. But, although the fowling was so abundant, the labor was very fatiguing, for the branches to which Fritz and Jack had to climb were as much as sixty or seventy feet from the ground. While I was arranging the material for making the torches, Jack brought me a beautiful bird, much larger than an ortolan, which had been taken in the snare.

Ernest had already recognized it. "I am very sure it is one of our European pigeons, one of the young ones of those who built their nests last year in the branches of the tree."

I took the bird from Jack's hands, rubbed the ends of his wings and his feet with ashes to clean them from the glue, and put him in a cage. We captured others, and at night we had in our possession two fine pairs of wood pigeons.

But, notwithstanding our hard labor during the day, we were not able to fill more than one barrel. The bark of two or three of the fig trees where the birds roosted decided the matter. After supper, and a few minutes of rest, I commenced my preparations. These consisted of two or three long bamboo canes, two bags, torches of resin, and some sugar canes. Fritz regarded me incredulously. With these strange instruments, how could I realize the prodigies I prophesied?

We set out, and night soon overshadowed the earth. Arrived at the foot of the trees that we had chosen, I lighted up my torches, and scarcely had the flame begun to burn, than a cloud of ortolans fell around us, and began to fly wildly around the flickering flames.

I then armed each boy with a bamboo cane, and set them an example by striking right and left among the mass of ortolans. They fell as thick and fast as rain, and we soon filled two large bags. Our torches, however, would only last long enough to light us back to Falcon's Nest. We placed the heavy sacks crosswise on the bamboo poles, and thus carried them very easily.

We arrived safely at Falcon's Nest, looked over our game, and terminated the sufferings of those poor birds that had not been killed by the blows. The next day, every one put his hand to work of cleaning and preparing our game—a disagreeable, although necessary, task. We filled two barrels with ortolans, half-roasted, and packed down in butter.

My wife took care of my pigeons, and approved of a dovecot. The wagon was loaded with provisions, and all that was necessary for an excursion of some days, and we set out for the grotto.

As soon as we arrived, I chose that part of the rock next our grotto as the situation of our dovecot. With the softer rock we soon made an excavation ten feet high, and large enough to contain twenty pairs of pigeons; two perches ran through the whole length, and projecting out in front, with a board nailed across, formed a platform, which we protected by a slight roof; a door with a hole to admit light closed the front; and a rope ladder suspended from one of the perches enabled us to mount and look after the inhabitants. It cost us several weeks of constant labor to finish the construction, fix the boards strongly in their places, cover the inside with a coat of plaster to prevent humidity, and arrange the perches, the nests, etc.

"There is the edifice," said I to Fritz. "We must find a way to force our wild stranger pigeons to dwell in the new habitation and bring their companions with them."

A pigeon merchant gave me the secret which I am about to put into practice. I have never tried it. It consists in perfuming a new dovecot with anise. The pigeons are so fond of the odor of this plant that they will return every night to its perfume. And thus they insensibly change their country life for that of the pigeon house.

"Nothing can be easier," replied Fritz. "The plant of anise that Jack brought will do the business. We can break the seeds on a stone, and release the aromatic oils."

"I think as you do," I answered. We then made the oil of anise and with it rubbed the door of the dovecot, the perches, wherever the pigeons could touch either feet or wings. I then placed in the middle of the dovecot a sort of dough with anise, salt, and clay, and we put in the pigeons. We shut them up, with provisions for two days, to enjoy at their leisure the odor of the anise.

When our boys returned from our kitchen garden they flew to the ladder, eager to get a sight of the new inhabitants. The two windows of isinglass which I had placed in the door were raised and I saw with pleasure that our prisoners appeared quite tame.

Two days passed. On the morning of the third day Fritz rubbed fresh anise on the door, which was made to rise up and down by means of a pulley. Without saying anything about our preparations, we awoke the still-sleeping family. I then announced that the day of liberty for our prisoners had arrived, and now they were to be free.

All now took their stations. I gave the cord of the door into Jack's hands, described a magic circle with a wand, and after having murmured a pretended conjuration, I ordered Jack to pull up the cord.

The pigeons poked their heads cautiously out of the hole, advanced on the platform, and suddenly soared up to such a height that they were lost to our sight. But in a few moments they again flew down, and settled, tranquilly, upon the platform they had just quitted.

This incident, which I did not expect, gave new proofs to my children of my dealings in magic, and I cried out, most seriously, "I knew very well, when they flew up in the clouds, that they were not lost."

"How could you possibly know that?" said Ernest.

"Because my charms have attached them to the dovecot," was my answer.

"Charms!" cried Jack. "Are you, then, a sorcerer, Papa?"

"Simpleton!" replied Ernest. "Who ever heard of sorcerers?"

At that moment the two Molucca pigeons suddenly quitted their European brothers, and flew off rapidly in the direction of Falcon's Nest.

"Adieu, gentlemen," cried Jack, as they darted away, "adieu, a pleasant trip to you."

My wife and Francis deplored the loss of our two handsome pigeons, while I, looking as serious as possible, stretched out my hands, and, turning to the direction in which the pigeons flew, murmured, half aloud, the following words: "Fly, little ones, fly far, far away; till tomorrow you may stay; but then, return with your companions."

I then turned toward my family, who stood stupefied with astonishment.

The other pigeons appeared completely tamed. They had found the dovecot of Europe with its shelter, and there they gladly remained.

We passed the rest of the day in the neighborhood of the dovecot, conversing on sorcery and the question of the pigeons. Evening came, and the European pigeons slept alone in their palace. We supped gaily, and retired to rest in anxious expectation of the morrow, which must establish either my defeat or my triumph.

The next day I felt a little doubtful about the return of the birds and anxiously awaited the evening. About noon, we saw Jack running furiously toward us, screaming out: "He has returned! He has returned!"

"Who? Who?" was eagerly asked.

"The blue pigeon!" he answered. "The blue pigeon! Quick! Quick! Come and see him!"

We ran to the dovecot. Besides the blue pigeon, we found with him on one of the exterior perches of the house, his mate, whom he was endeavoring to persuade to venture into the interior. He would put in his head, and then return to her, until at last we had the satisfaction of seeing her enter the pigeon house.

My sons would have immediately closed the door, but I prevented them, saying, "How are the other pigeons to enter if we close the door?"

"I begin to think," said my wife, at last, "that there is something extraordinary in this; I cannot comprehend it."

"It is chance—pure chance," interrupted Ernest.

"Chance" replied I, laughing; "that will do for one time; when the other pigeon returns this evening, with his mate, will you think that chance?"

"Impossible!" he answered. "The same phenomenon could not happen twice in a day."

Fritz suddenly interrupted us. His eagle

eyes had perceived the bird we were expecting.

"What do you say now, my little doctor?" I said to Ernest. "Both pigeons have now returned.

"I do not know what to say," he answered seriously. "It certainly appears extraordinary. But as for sorcery being employed, I will not believe it."

"If a third pair of Molucca pigeons should visit us today, would you call that chance also?"

Ernest did not answer, but he was far from being convinced.

We returned to our occupations, and had worked about two hours, when our little Francis came with a message from his mother to hasten to the dovecot.

We did so. My wife, after cautioning us to make no noise, pointed out to us two superb birds, whom those in the interior were endeavoring to persuade to enter.

"I give up," said Ernest, at last. "I beg of you, Papa, to explain all."

I explained to him, in detail, all that we had done. Jack laughed heartily on hearing that his anise plant had been the charm which had so puzzled them; I urged him to follow Ernest's example, and not believe everything so readily.

In the following days we saw, with joy, that the new inhabitants were permanently settled, and had already begun to construct their nests. Among the articles they gathered for that purpose was a sort of long, gray moss. I recognized it as a substitute from India for horsehair, in the manufacture of mattresses.

This discovery pleased my good wife, and afforded promise of some fine mattresses.

We found, from time to time, in the soil of the dovecot, nutmegs which, doubtless, the pigeons of Molucca had brought over. We washed and planted them without much hope of their ever germinating.

19. JACK'S ADVENTURE AND NARROW ESCAPE — THE RAINY SEASON

JACK one day set off on a lone expedition. We soon saw him returning, covered from head to foot with a thick, black mud, and dragging after him a bundle of Spanish rushes, likewise covered with mud.

"Where have you been," said I, "to dirty yourself so?"

"In Flamingo Marsh."

"What in the name of common sense were you doing there?"

"I wanted to get some Spanish osiers to make nests for the pigeons."

"A praiseworthy intention," said I.

"If it had not been for these bundles of rushes I should certainly have lost my life. I wanted some thin, flexible rushes, and I jumped from hummock to hummock in the marsh until I slipped in, and found myself up to my knees. I screamed at the top of my voice, but nobody heard me, except my jackal, who came running up to me howling with all his might.

"At last I took my knife from my pocket, and cut two large bundles of willow, placing one under each arm. They served me as a sort of hold. Then, exerting all my strength, by moving my body, my arms, and my legs, I managed to raise myself up a little. All this time my jackal stood on the edge of the marsh, howling. I whistled him to me, and, grasping hold of his tail at last, with great difficulty, I reached terra firma."

"God be praised, my poor child," said I, "that you have been preserved to us!"

His mother hastened to wash and clean the poor adventurer. His entire suit was put to soak in the Jackal's River, and we also washed the rushes.

I profited by the willows that Jack had brought, to commence the construction of a weaving machine that my wife had long expected of me.

Two rushes, split lengthwise, and wound round with packthread, so that they would dry without bending, formed four bars to make that part of the machine called the "combs." I made my sons cut me a quantity of little pieces of wood, to make the teeth for the combs; and when I had procured these first materials, I put them aside, saying nothing to anybody concerning their destined use, as I wished the machine to be a surprise to my wife.

Our onager gave birth to a beautiful little ass of its species. I gave it the name of "Rapid," as I designed him particularly for the saddle; and we saw with pleasure that his limbs were all beautifully proportioned.

The approach of the rainy season and the remembrance of the trouble we had in collecting our animals last year, induced us to accustom our animals to return to their homes at the sound of a conch shell, in which I had placed a bit of wood, like a flute.

Among the comforts with which we had surrounded our winter habitation, we still lacked a reservoir of pure water, which we were obliged to bring from Jackal's River. To remedy the inconvenience before the rains came on, we established a fountain, as we had done at Falcon's Nest. Bamboo canes, fitted into one another, served us for canals. We rested them on crutches of wood, and a barrel sunk in the ground became a basin. My wife was just as contented with the little fountain as if it had been built of marble.

We hastened to get in everything necessary before the season of rains. The grain, the fruits of all sorts which surrounded our habitation, potatoes, rice, guavas, sweet acorns, pineapples, anise, manioc, bananas. We sowed our seeds as we had done the year before, hoping that the European sorts would sprout quicker and more easily on account of the moisture of the atmosphere.

My wife made us sacks of canvas which we filled, and, by the aid of our patient beasts, emptied into large hogsheads. I resolved on a more regular cultivation next year. We had a pair of buffalos for all the labor that would have to be done, and all that was required was a double yoke, which I intended to make during our winter seclusion.

Now the rains had already commenced, and for the space of fifteen days we were witnesses of a scene of whose majesty and terrific grandeur man cannot form an idea. The trees bent to the terrible blasts, the lightning and the thunder were mingled with the wind. It seemed to us that the storm of last year had been nothing in comparison to it. Nevertheless, the winds began to calm, and the rain, instead of beating down upon us in torrents, began to fall with the uniformity which would last for twelve long weeks.

We devoted our attention first to a crowd of minor wants. Our apartments were all on one floor, but the ground had not been carefully leveled, and we set to work to fill up the cavities and cut away the projections. The fountain I had made did not answer the purpose, and the one great necessity of a good supply of water was as yet unprovided for. We made tables and chairs, and prepared for all exigencies to render our long confinement as supportable as possible. But there was yet an inconvenience we had not foreseen. We wanted light. There were but three openings in the grotto, besides the door, and all the rest of our habitation was plunged in the most complete darkness. Three or four more windows were necessary, but they could not be made before the return of fine weather, and I devised the following remedy for the defect.

Among the bamboos that I had procured as leaders for the water was one of great size, which I had preserved. This bamboo I found by chance was just the height of our grotto. I trimmed it, and planted it in the ground about a foot deep, surrounding it with props to make it steady. Jack then climbed the pole with a hammer, a pulley, and a rope, and, after having driven the pulley into the roof of the grotto, and thrown the cord over it, he descended safely to the ground. I then suspended to one end of the cord a large oil lantern which we found in the ship. Thanks to the thousand reflectors which lined the sides of the rock, our grotto was as light as if it had been broad day.

The light was an immense benefit to us, and enabled us to carry on our different occupations with zeal and comfort.

Ernest and Francis charged themselves with the task of arranging our library, and disposing the works we had saved from the wreck on its shelves. Jack aided his mother in the kitchen, and Fritz, being stronger than his brothers, assisted me in the workroom.

We arranged there a superb English turning lathe, with all its equipments. I now could put my knowledge of the art of wood-turning to some use. We also constructed a forge. Anvils were fixed in large blocks of wood, and all the tools of the wheelwright and the cooper were laid out in long array on the racks I had put up next the wall. I was proud of the businesslike appearance of our shop and often did I congratulate myself that I had sufficiently acquainted myself with mechanics.

The grotto every day grew more agreeable. We had our workroom, our dining room, and our library, where we could refresh our minds. The cases we had saved from the ship contained a quantity of books which had belonged to the captain and officers. Besides Bibles and books of devotion, we found works on history, botany, philosophy, voyages, and travels, some enriched with engravings, which were a real treasure to us. We also had maps, several mathematical and astronomical instruments, and a portable globe.

We all knew a little French, for this is as much in use as German throughout Switzerland. Fritz and Ernest had commenced to learn English at Zurich, and I had myself paid some attention to the language, in order to superintend their education. I now urged them to continue their studies, as English was the language of the sea, and there were very few ships that did not contain someone who understood it. Jack who knew nothing at all began to pay some attention to Spanish and Italian. As for myself, I labored hard to master the Malay tongue, for the inspection of charts and maps convinced me that we were in the neighborhood of these people.

Our grotto grew every day so comfortable that the children could not think of any name suitable to call it by. We came to the conclusion that it should be called simply "Felsenheim" —dwelling in the rock.

20. CLOSE OF THE RAINY SEASON — A WHALE — CORAL

THE END of August brought a renewal of the bad weather. The rain, the winds, the thunder redoubled with new fury. How happy we were in the habitation we had made. But at last the weather became more settled; the clouds dissipated; the rain ceased; and we were able to venture out from our grotto.

We promenaded upon the belt of rocks that extended all along the coast and took pleasure in scaling the highest peaks. Fritz, whose eye almost rivaled that of his eagle, perceived, upon the little island in Flamingo Bay, a black spot that he thought was a shipwrecked vessel. We walked down to the seashore, emptied the rain water from the canoe, and set off to inspect it. What was our surprise to see an enormous whale, lying on his side upon the strand.

Being ignorant whether he was dead or sleeping, I thought it prudent to steer for the other side of the island. There were two roads to choose to reach the whale—one by climbing over the rocks; the other longer, but less fatiguing. I took the first path, and commanded the boys to take the other, as I wished to examine fully this little island, which wanted but trees to render it charming. From this elevation I could see the whole coast, from Tent House to Falcon's Nest, a spectacle which made me almost forget the whale. When I reached the other side my children came running toward me, their hats full of shells and coral, which they had picked up on the beach.

"Note how the sea has thrown these frail,

light things upon our shores," said I, "and also a monster whose bulk is so immense."

When we returned home I told my wife of my resolution to return to the whale that afternoon; she cheerfully declared that she would accompany me. I was enchanted, and we hastened to prepare the necessary provisions and articles for a stay of two days; for perhaps we might be detained on the island.

After dinner, being reminded that we yet had four tubs in our boat to hold the blubber of the whale, I fastened them to the stern of the canoe; and after having armed my sons with knives, hatchets, and saws, and all the cutting instruments I could find, we weighed anchor, and directed our course toward the island and the whale.

Our whale looked like those of Greenland—the back greenish black, the stomach yellowish, the fins and tail black. It measured between sixty and seventy feet long, and about forty in diameter. My children were astonished that the head formed a third of the whole creature. Its mouth was immense, and its jaws, which were full twelve feet in length, were furnished with "dewlaps," which in Europe form an article of commerce as whalebone. Fritz was struck by the smallness of the monster's eye, no larger than that of an ox, while the opening by which his immense mouth communicated with his throat was scarcely the diameter of an arm.

Fritz and Jack entered the head of the whale, and with the hatchet and saw, cut out the "dewlaps," and more than two hundred pieces of different sizes. Meanwhile Ernest and I cut several feet deep into the fat which covered the sides of the animal. We literally swam in grease, for walls of solid fat rose on each side of us. A multitude of winged robbers flew round and round our heads, then approached and boldly snatched pieces of fat from our hands. The birds were very troublesome, but my wife, saying that their down would be useful, I knocked down some with a club, and threw them into the boat. I cut from the back of the whale a long and large band of skin, to make harnesses for the ass and the two buffaloes. We set out for the coast with the new cargo we had acquired. It was precious treasure, but far from agreeably obtained.

The next morning we again embarked in the canoe, but this time Francis and his mother were left behind, for I intended to procure some parts of the whale's immense intestines.

Now we took care to strip off every article

of clothing, excepting our pantaloons. Then, like true butchers, we opened the animal. I cut the intestines in pieces of from six to twelve feet long, and, after having turned them inside out, washed them and rubbed them well with sand. Placing them in the boat with the birds and a new cargo of whale blubber, we set sail for Felsenheim. I had taken so much trouble to obtain the whale's intestines as I wished to use them as vessels to contain the oil.

Next day at dawn we were all up and ready for work. The four tubs of fat were raised from the ground, and, applying strong pressure, we squeezed out as much of the oil as possible; and as this was the finest and purest, we filled one or two of the entrails with it. The rest, emptied into a large iron kettle, over a slow fire, was soon reduced to liquid, and emptied from the kettle into the entrails.

While we were occupied in our manufacture of oil, my wife proposed that we establish a new colony on the island of the whale. "We will put some fowls there," said she; "they will be safe from their two great plagues, the monkeys and the jackals."

The children were so enchanted that they wanted to start immediately.

"Not so fast," said I. "First, I have conceived an idea of fitting a propeller machine to the canoe, to save your arms some labor, and quicken our speed. Let us proceed with it."

The machine that I constructed was not a masterpiece of execution, but it answered the purpose very well. A handle attached to the wheel put the machine in motion, and two large flat pieces of whalebone, nailed together in the form of a cross, and fixed at each end of the axle, resembled the wheels of a steamboat. When the handle was turned, the wings of whalebone beat against the surface of the water, and drove the canoe forward.

My children were in transports of joy when the canoe glided over the surface of the water, and I was astonished myself at the rapidity of our course. The day was too far advanced to admit going to the island of the whale, but I promised on the morrow, a grand trial of our vessel by an excursion by sea, to the farmhouse at Prospect Hill, for the purpose of inspecting our colony there.

At day's first dawning everybody was ready. We gaily quitted the shore, and the strong current of Jackal's River soon brought us to the sea. The breeze was good, everything promising a favorable sail. We soon perceived

Shark Island, the sandbank where the whale was stranded, and in a short time found ourselves in sight of Prospect Hill.

When we had arrived opposite the "Wood of Monkeys," I ran the boat into a little creek, and landed to replenish our stock of coconuts. With keen pleasure we heard the crowing of the cocks through the woods, announcing the neighborhood of the farmhouse. We gathered our coconuts, and there we directed our course.

Everything was in order. But we were astonished at the wildness of the sheep and goats, who fled at our approach. My sons began to run after them, soon grew tired, drew from their pockets the strings with balls attached, and captured three or four of the fugitives. We distributed some potatoes and a handful of salt among them. In return they yielded us several bowls of most delicious milk.

We dined at Prospect Hill. Leaving my wife to prepare for our departure, I started out with Fritz to gather some sugar cane, and dig up some roots to plant on Whale Island.

We weighed anchor, hoisted the sail, and thanks to the breeze we were soon in sight of Whale Island.

My first care was to plant the roots I had brought from Prospect Hill, but my companions ran off to gather shells. My good wife supplied their places, and we two began our labors. We had scarcely commenced when Jack came running up to us, all out of breath. "Papa, Papa," cried he, "come here—quick, I have discovered the skeleton of a mammoth!"

I burst into a laugh, and informed my boy that his skeleton was nothing more than the carcass of our whale.

"No, no," he replied, "they are not fish bones, but those of some immense animal."

I consented at last to go; but another voice stopped my progress.

"Run, run—this way," screamed Fritz, from some distance. "Quick—a monstrous turtle that we are not strong enough to turn." I caught up two hand spikes and ran to the spot, where I found Ernest struggling with a huge turtle, which he held by one leg. Despite all his efforts, it had reached the border of the sea, and I arrived just in time. Throwing one of the spikes to Fritz, we were able to turn the animal on its back.

It really was enormous; about eight and a half feet in length, and could not possibly weigh less than five hundred pounds. How should we be able to carry it away?

Jack continued teasing me to go and see his mammoth. It really was our whale, but the birds of prey had not left a morsel of flesh on the bones, which had blanched in the sun.

Returning to our plantation, it was too late to finish our work that night. We buried the roots, yet unplanted, in the ground; the giant turtle was now our grand object. I brought the boat round to where he lay extended on his back, and, forming a circle round him, we debated means of transporting him.

"Zounds! Gentlemen," said I, "instead of carrying this monster, let him conduct us back to Felsenheim." I commenced empting out the barrel of water we had brought. Then, turning the turtle over on his feet, we fastened the barrel to his back, so that it was impossible for him to sink and draw us with him. A cord, passed through a hole which we broke in the upper shell, served me for reins, and without losing time we all embarked for home. I placed myself in the prow of the canoe, with a hatchet to cut the cord in case of need.

Our course was accomplished rapidly and safely. Arriving at Felsenheim, our first care was to secure our turtle by strong ropes. But as we could not keep him long in this way, we finished his life the next morning, and his enormous shell was destined to serve as a basin to our fountain in the grotto. It was very difficult to detach the flesh from the shell, but it was a superb piece of meat, full six feet by three, and afforded us many a delicious pot of soup. We inquired into all our works on natural history, and we came to the conclusion that our turtle was the giant green turtle, the largest of all.

21. A DANGEROUS VISITOR—THE ASS FALLS VICTIM

OUR garments had become so tattered and torn that I was forced to construct a weaving machine for my wife.

The machine was of incalculable benefit to us, though it was neither perfect nor handsome. As we had none of the wheat flour that the weavers use to make paste to harden the warp and prevent the threads from tangling, I substituted fish glue. From this fish glue I also made window panes, not calculated, it is true, for windows exposed to the rain. But they answered for ours, in their deep embrasures, protected from storm.

Encouraged by success, I resolved to try my hand at another thing. We had need of yokes, saddles, and bridles. I established myself as a saddler. Kangaroos and sea dogs furnished me with the necessary leather. For wadding I used the moss that the Molucca pigeons had discovered for us. But as this moss would have matted together, and grown hard under the rider, I employed my sons to twist it into cords. Left for some time, and then untwisted, we thus obtained frizzed hair, as elastic as horsehair. In a short time we had saddles and stirrups, bits and bridles, yokes and collars.

My restless young people begged me to take them hunting in the country. But I put the matter off for other work—the making of baskets, a number of which we needed to carry our rice, roots, grain, etc. Our first clumsy attempts we reserved for our potatoes. When we were skillful enough, I ventured to use those Spanish rushes that had cost Jack so dear, and we made a number of fine baskets.

"Papa," said Fritz, "an idea has struck me. Why cannot we make a litter of rushes for Mama, and then she will be able to accompany us in our distant excursions?"

"Really," I replied, "a litter would be more convenient than the back of the ass, and easier than the cart. We will try what can be done."

Immediately the buffalo and the bull were brought out. Two poles, which supported a large basket, were suspended by cords on each side, and Ernest jumped in to make the first trail. Jack mounted Storm, who was placed at the head, and Francis, Broumm, who supported the hinder part, and they set off. The basket, balanced between the poles, resembled a luxurious carriage on its springs of steel.

We returned to our basketmaking. Suddenly Fritz started up.

"There is some large animal on the other side of the river," said he, "to judge from the dust it has raised, it is plainly coming in this direction."

"I cannot imagine what it is," I answered.

"Probably two or three sheep, or, perhaps, our sow, frolicking in the sand," observed my wife.

"No, no," replied Fritz, quickly. "It is some singular animal. It rolls and unrolls itself alternately. See, it is raising itself up, and looks like a huge mast in the dust."

I ran for the spyglass and directed it toward the dust.

"I can see it plainly," said Fritz. "What do you think of it, Papa?"

"That we must fly as fast as possible, and entrench ourselves in the grotto. It is a serpent—a huge serpent, advancing directly for us."

"Shall I run for the guns?"

"No, the serpent is too powerful to permit of our attacking him."

We hastened to the grotto, and prepared to receive our enemy. It was a boa constrictor. It advanced so quickly that it was too late to take up the boards on Family Bridge.

Watching all his movements, we saw the reptile stretching out his enormous length along the bank of the river. From time to time he would raise the forepart of his body twenty feet from the ground, and turn his head gently from right to left, as if seeking his prey, while he darted a triple-barbed tongue from his half-open jaws. He crossed the bridge, and directed his course straight for the grotto. We had barricaded the door and the windows as well as we were able, and ascended by our interior entrance into the dovecot. We passed our muskets through the holes in the door, and waited silently for the enemy.

The boa stopped about thirty paces directly

in front of our position. Ernest, more through fear than through any warlike ardor, discharged his gun. Jack and Francis followed his example; and my wife, whom the danger had rendered bold, also discharged her gun.

The monster raised his head. But either because none of the shots had touched him, or because the scales of his skin were impenetrable, he appeared unharmed. Fritz and I then fired, without effect, and the serpent glided away with inconceivable rapidity toward the marsh which our ducks and geese inhabited, and disappeared in the rushes.

I could think of no way to rid ourselves of the boa and our united forces were as nothing against such an enemy.

The fear of our terrible neighbor kept us shut up three days in our retreat—three long days of anguish—during which time I suffered no one to open the door without my permission, and I allowed no one to go beyond the reservoir of the fountain.

The monster had given us no signs of his presence. We would have supposed him departed, but the birds assured us of his presence. Every evening the whole colony of ducks and geese directed their course to the bay, making a terrible noise, and sailed away for Whale Island, where they found a safe asylum.

I was afraid that a direct attack might cost us our lives of one or more of our little family. Our dogs could do nothing against such a foe; and to have exposed any one of our beasts of burden would have been certain destruction to it. We were in a most deplorable situation when our poor old jackass came to our aid.

The fodder in the grotto had diminished frightfully. It was necessary to nourish the cow, so necessary to our subsistence, and some must be taken from the other animals. In this dilemma I resolved to set them at liberty, and let them provide for their own nourishment. If I could get them on the other side of the river they would find food, and be safe as long as the boa remained buried in the rushes. My plan was to attach the animals together. Fritz, mounted on his onager, would direct of the procession, while I would see that the march was effected in good order.

I loaded all our arms; my sons were placed in the dovecot, with orders to observe the movements of the enemy, while Fritz and I arranged our beasts. But a little misunderstanding put an end to all my plans. My wife, who had charge of the door, did not wait for the signal, and opened it before the animals were attached together. The ass, who had grown very lively by his three days' rest, no sooner saw a ray of light than he shot out of the door like an arrow, and was away in the open plain before we could stop him. We tried to induce the poor animal to come back, called him by name, and by cowhorn, but all was useless—the unruly fellow advanced direct to the marsh. Suddenly, to our horror we saw the serpent emerging from the rushes. He elevated his head about ten feet from the ground, darted out his forked tongue, and crawled swiftly on toward the ass. The poor fellow soon saw his danger, and began to run, braying with all his might. But nothing could save him from his terrible enemy, and in a moment he was seized, enveloped, and crushed in the monstrous rings that the serpent threw round him.

My wife and sons uttered a cry of terror, and we fled in haste to the grotto, from whence we could view the horrible combat between the boa and the ass. My children wanted to fire, and deliver the poor jackass, but I forbade them to do it.

The ass was dead; we had heard his last bray stifled by the pressure of the boa, who proceeded with horrible avidity to his repast.

When all had been swallowed he remained perfectly torpid and insensible.

The time had arrived. "Now, my children," I exclaimed, "now the serpent is in our power!"

I set out from the grotto, carrying my loaded gun in my hand, Fritz following close by my side. As we approached the reptile, it raised its head, and darted at me a look of powerless fury.

Fritz and I fired together, and both our shots entered the skull of the animal. But they did not produce death, and the eyes of the serpent sparkled with rage. We advanced nearer, and, firing our pistols directly through the eye, we saw its rings contract, a slight quiver ran through its body, and it lay dead upon the sand before us, stretched out like the mast of a ship.

22. DISCOVERY OF A CRYSTAL GROTTO

WE HAD nothing more to fear from the boa; yet I was afraid it might have either left its mate behind it, or a nest of little ones, which in time would spread terror through the land. I resolved, in consequence, to undertake two expeditions—the one through the marsh, the other toward Falcon's Nest, through the passage in the rock.

We set out with our hunting equipage, and easily recognized traces of the boa; the rushes bent down where it had passed through, and there were deep spiral impressions in the wet ground where it had rested its enormous rings. But we discovered no trace of another boa, nor a nest of little ones. Arrived at the end of the marsh, we made an interesting discovery. It was that of a new grotto, out of which flowed a little stream that passed on among the rushes of the marsh.

The grotto was hung with stalactites, which rose in immense columns on each side, and forming singular and beautiful designs.

The ground was composed of an extremely fine, white sort of earth, which I recognized as "fuller's clay." I immediately gathered some handfuls, and carefully placed them in my pocket handkerchief.

"Here," said I to my sons, "here is a discovery that will be very welcome to your mother. Here is natural soap. It is called 'fuller's clay,' because it is used to clean woolen goods."

We had approached the source of the spring. Fritz, a little in advance, cried out that the rock had a large opening on one side. We ran forward, and found ourselves in a new cavern. We fired off a pistol, and judged by the echo that the grotto extended to a great distance. We then lighted two candles from our knapsacks. Having left the others behind, Fritz and I continued to advance, when suddenly we saw our torches reflected from every side of the rock.

"Ah, Papa," cried Fritz, in a transport of joy, "see! See! A salt grotto! Look at the enormous blocks of salt lying at our feet."

"You are very much mistaken, indeed," I answered; "this is crystal."

"Better yet—a palace of crystal! What an immense treasure for us!"

"Yes," I laughed, "such a treasure as the gold mine was to Robinson Crusoe."

We soon left the grotto, rejoined the others, and returned home to Felsenheim, bearing the fuller's clay, which greatly pleased my wife.

I had as yet only half accomplished my design. I wished, if it were possible, by fortifying the passages in the rock, to keep out all such visitors as the boa. We set out, taking plenty of provisions, arms, vessels of all sorts, and torches to scare away all intruders on our night encampments.

We advanced along the avenue of Falcon's Nest, and discovered the marks of the boa's progress half effaced by the wind. We found everything in good order at the Nest. The harvest and the fruit trees gave promise to an abundant crop. The goat and sheep came up of their own accord to receive the salt we threw them in passing. But we did not stop, as we wished to arrive as soon as possible, in order to gather, before night, cotton enough to make some pillows and mattresses that might render our slumbers more agreeable.

As soon as we arrived, our good housekeeper set about procuring dinner, while we went to gather the cotton.

After dinner I announced that we would immediately commence our search, and we divided into three parties. Ernest and his mother were to guard the provisions and all the ripe blades in the rice field; to defend them we left our brave dog Billy. Fritz and Jack, accompanied by Turk and the jackal, took the right bank of the lake, while I followed the left with Francis, and his two young dogs. It was his first expedition. Proudly he marched along, burning with ardor to try his new weapon. But the noise of our steps among the dried rushes frightened the herons, who flew off so quickly it was impossible to shoot them. Francis began to despair.

Suddenly we found ourselves in presence of a great quantity of wild geese and black swans, covering the waters in all directions. Francis was just about to fire into the mass, when a sort of deep, prolonged bellow issued from the middle of the rushes. We stopped, astonished.

"I am sure," said Francis, "that it is the little onager."

"Impossible," said I; "he would not leave his mother."

I called the dogs to my side, and, setting them in the rushes, presently heard the report of Francis' gun. He had discharged his gun right into the thickest part of the rushes, but the birds flew away safe and sound.

"I have him! I have him!" cried he. "Look!"

So saying, he pulled out of the rushes an animal resembling an agouti.

I examined it with attention. It was about two feet in length, had incisor teeth like the rabbit, webbed feet, long snout, but no tail at all.

"You have killed a rare and curious beast," said I to my little boy, "an inhabitant of South America, of the same family as the agouti and peccaries, but much rarer. It is a cabiai, and of the largest size."

"I have never heard of him before."

"Oh, yes, you heard him bray just now, exactly like the braying of an ass."

It was now time to return home. Francis took up his cabiai, threw it over his shoulder, and although I saw that it was much too heavy for him, I let him have the merit of the whole affair.

We found on returning, Master Ernest tranquilly seated on the bank of the river, surrounded by a prodigious number of rats which he had killed. Fritz and Jack returned with a ruffled moor hen and a nest of eggs. We then all united around a savory mess of rice my good wife had prepared. The repast was a merry one; we were all delighted to have found no traces of the boa. The conversation naturally turned upon what we should do with our rat skins, and it was determined to make a carpet of them. But our first care was to clean them with sand and ashes, as we were accustomed to do.

Presently Jack and Francis ran to their knapsacks.

"Look here, sir!" said the youngest, as he threw some pine cones before the philosopher.

"Look here, sir!" said Jack, placing on the table some little shining apples, pale green, with a strong odor of cinnamon.

A general cry of admiration greeted them.

"Stop!" cried I. "Before tasting this fruit, Master Knips must undergo the customary trial, for I am afraid these are the manchineel apples that produce most terrible colic."

I then opened one of the fruit. The manchineel apple has a nut, and these had very small seeds, like the common apple. While I was showing this, the monkey snatched one from the table and commenced to eat it, smacking his lips. This determined the matter, and I distributed the fruit which were excellent.

"They are," said I, "cinnamon apples. I think you gathered them from a low shrub. Did you not, Jack?"

"Oh, yes, yes—shrub-cinnamon." Jack was falling asleep.

I then gave the signal for retiring. We took all necessary precautions for safety during the night, and sought repose on our mattresses of cotton.

Next day, we renewed our search. We explored the sugar canes, a natural retreat for the serpents. Happily, our investigation was without result. Suddenly our dogs began to bark; I ordered my sons to proceed toward the plain, and we soon found ourselves clear of the canes. At the same time there emerged from them a troop of pigs. I at first thought it was the young family of our old sow, but their number, their gray color, and the singular manner in which they walked, banished that idea. I fired both barrels of my gun and two of the animals fell. The rest of the troop trotted on as before, exactly in his place. On examining them closely, we found that there was but one footstep in the sand, so regularly did they march.

But Jack and Fritz could not let them pass, and two more animals bit the dust.

The reports of two other guns were heard in the distance. Ernest and Francis had overtaken the pigs, I thought, and Ernest soon confirmed my conjecture. Fritz thought that these were the Otaheitan pigs of which Captain Cook speaks, but Ernest maintained that they were peccaries, very common in Guiana and South America.

After cleaning our game, we set out for the tent, made our entrance chanting a song of victory, and my children offered their mother the sugar canes we had brought home. Fritz proposed to regale the family with an Otaheitan roast, but the preparation of our pigs precluded all thoughts of anything else.

The two smaller boys gathered a quantity of green branches and leaves, with which to smoke our pork, and we set to work. Ernest skinned the pigs. Fritz and I cut them up, my wife salted the pieces. I piled the hams together, so that the salt would penetrate every part, and we allowed them to remain in salted water while the hut for smoking was constructed.

The next morning, Fritz prepared to serve us for dinner an Otaheitan roast. He began by digging a deep trench. He then washed the pig and salted it, and filled it with a stuffing made of meat, potatoes, and different roots.

When the trench was full of combustibles, Fritz set it on fire. At his direction, the boys threw in a quantity of pebbles, which soon became red hot.

"Beautiful cookery you will make," said my wife incredulously; "pig, some ashes, and a hole in the ground—delicious eating I do not doubt!"

Our cook-in-chief enveloped his "roast" in leaves and pieces of bark; a hole in the burning cinders received it, it was covered with red-hot stones, and the whole filled up with earth.

After about two hours, Fritz, having taken off the triple layer of earth, cinders, and stones, the most delicious odor saluted us, and we had before us meat cooked to a nicety. Fritz triumphed, his good mother avowed that she was conquered, and everyone fell to without delay. The meat was delicious.

During the three days while our meat was being smoked, I, with my sons, explored the country. We still discovered no trace of the boa, but each excursion ended with some addition to our comforts and luxuries.

One day we returned from the wood of bamboo loaded with cups of all dimensions, formed from rushes some twenty inches across, which we sawed apart at every knot. We also discovered that each knot of the rushes distilled a sugary matter which crystallized in the sun, resembling candied sugar. These rushes also furnished strong thorns, to take the place of nails.

At Prospect Hill, we found the greatest disorder. The walls of the farmhouse were pulled down, and the cattle gone. The monkeys had left unequivocal traces of their passing.

We then surrounded the hut where our hams were suspended, with a rampart of earth, fortified it with branches and stones, to keep out intruders. And we made ready to set off on the morning of the fourth day, to explore beyond the barrier between the district we had inhabited for nearly three years, and an unknown land which we had but once entered, and then were nearly destroyed by a troop of buffaloes.

23. EXCURSIONS — THE OSTRICH HUNT — NARROW ESCAPE

WE BEGAN our march at daylight. After two hours, we halted, at what appeared to be a favorable spot for encampment, on an elevated point that commanded a widely extended view with a thick pine forest on one side. Investigation presented nothing but two wildcats, who fled.

We then dined; but the powerful heat obliged us to postpone our excursion until the morrow.

On the morrow, we were up at daylight, to explore the savanna. I took with me my three eldest sons, as I wished to be in force on entering unknown country. We packed some provisions, took leave, and passed through the defile.

At its extremity we had erected a palisade of bamboo and thorny palm. It had been torn down, and we traced on the sand the spiral imprints of the boa, clearly demonstrating that he had come from the savanna through this passage.

We had now ventured into a country we had entered but once before, and where we had taken the buffalo. The river dividing the plain was bordered by a rich line of vegetation, which we followed for some time, but soon the vegetation disappeared. The sun beat down on our heads, the sand burned our feet. It was now a desert—a desert without a single tree. On crossing the river, we had filled our gourds with fresh water, but we were obliged to throw it away.

After two hours of painful journeying a great rock in the middle of the desert afforded us a refuge against the sun. Too fatigued to climb the rock and reconnoiter the country, we seated ourselves and could see the river in the distance, like a silver thread, winding through its green banks.

We had scarcely been seated five minutes when Master Knips, who had accompanied us, suddenly disappeared over the rock, having probably scented some brother monkeys in the neighborhood; our dogs, also, and the jackal deserted us, but we were too tired to call them back.

Some sugar cane relieved our terrible thirst, restored our appetites, and a repast refreshed us excellently.

Suddenly Fritz cried out: "There are two horsemen galloping up toward us. There, a third has joined them—doubtless they are Arabs of the desert."

"Take my spyglass, Fritz," said I; "your news astonishes me."

"Oh, I see now a number of wagons loaded with hay; but they are so distant I can scarcely distinguish anything."

"Let me have the glass," cried Jack, impatiently. He declared he saw a crowd of cavaliers who carried little lances, with banners at the point.

"Come, give me the glass now," said I. After having looked for some time attentively, I said to Jack, "Well, your Arabs, your cavaliers with lances, your haycarts, what do you think they have been transformed into?"

"Camelopards, perhaps?"

"No. They are ostriches, and chance has thrown a splendid chase into our hands. Do not let them pass us."

The ostriches were rapidly approaching. The best way would be to wait until they came up, and then attack them by surprise.

The family was composed of three females and a male, easily recognized by the long white feathers of his tail. We crouched closer to the ground, and held our dogs close to our sides.

The ostriches were now aware of our presence—they appeared to hesitate in their march; but, as we remained immovable, they seemed reassured, and were advancing directly to us, when our dogs, whom we could not restrain, suddenly sprang out upon them. Away went the timid birds, like bundles of feathers driven before the wind. Fritz unhooded his eagle, and it lit upon the head of the male ostrich, and brought him to the ground. When we arrived the gigantic bird was just expiring.

We were greatly disappointed, but, as the evil was done, we contented ourselves with preserving the lifeless corpse. The sumptuous feathers fastened to our hats were an excellent protection against the sun.

Jack and Ernest waved to us to hurry on.

"A nest!" they cried. "An ostrich's nest! Quick—quick!"

The ostrich nest was a hole dug in the ground, in which were symmetrically arranged from twenty-five to thirty eggs, each as large as a child's head.

My sons wanted to hatch the ostrich eggs by exposing them in the daytime to the rays of the sun, and wrapping them up as warm as possible at night.

I observed that each of these eggs weighed about three pounds, and the whole number about one hundred pounds, and that it would be impossible to transport them across a desert. But the children agreed that each take one egg, to be carried in his pocket handkerchief. I advised them to cut some branches from a low sort of pine that grew about the rocks, and make a basket to carry their eggs, as the Dutch milk women carry their milk pots. My boys followed my plan, and began their march.

We then arrived at the borders of a swamp that seemed to be formed by the confluence of several springs that flowed from the rocks. We could perceive troops of buffaloes, monkeys, and antelopes, but too far from us to take notice of them. Nothing, however, indicated the presence of a boa. We halted to refresh ourselves with some provisions; we were filling our empty gourds with water, preparing to depart, when the jackal made a discovery. It was a round object which he had dug out of the sand with his paws. On examining it, I discovered it to be a turtle of the smallest kind, scarcely as large as an apple.

"How is this?" said Fritz. "I thought that turtles inhabited the sea only."

"There are land as well as sea turtles," said I. "They are not only found in swamps, but even in gardens, where they subsist on snails, caterpillars, and all sorts of insects."

"Well, then," said Ernest, "let us carry some home to Mamma for her garden, and for our cabinet of natural history."

From borders of the swamp we followed a little stream of water. It led us to the rock where we had reposed on our first excursion into the savanna. It was a delicious route. We found trees, grass—it was a little oasis in the desert, and we named it "Green Valley."

Suddenly we heard a cry of distress, followed by two terrible howls, mingled with the barking of the dogs. A moment after, Ernest reappeared; he was running at full speed, his face deadly pale, and he cried out in a voice stifled with fear: "Bears! Bears! They are following"; and the poor boy fell into my arms. I shivered as an enormous bear appeared, immediately followed by a second.

"Courage, children," was all I could say. I seized my gun, Fritz did the same and took his place by my side. Jack also took his gun, but remained in the rear, while Ernest, who had no arms—for in his fright he had let his gun fall—took to his heels and ran away.

Our dogs were already at the attack. We fired together, and although our shots did not bring down the bears, one had a jaw broken, the other a shoulder fractured. But they were only partially disabled. Our dogs fought desperately, rolling in the dust with their enemies. We were afraid to fire again lest we kill the dogs. Advancing nearer, we discharged our pistols directly at the heads of the huge animals. Both bears dropped to the sand.

We drew the two carcasses into a cave, and covered them with thornbushes, to keep off all carnivorous beasts and birds of prey. We also buried our ostrich eggs in the sand until the morrow.

The sun was set when we rejoined my dear companion and our little Francis. A good fire and a well-cooked supper refreshed us and my boys commenced a long narration of the exploits of the day, with Master Jack boasting and swaggering enough for all.

My wife and Francis had discovered on the banks of a stream a sort of greasy white earth, which appeared to me to be a fine pipe clay. They had amassed, also, at the entrance of the defile, a quantity of materials necessary for our fort.

We lighted a large fire to guard us through the night, and our dogs, whose wounds my wife had washed and dressed with fresh butter, lay down beside it. We then all retired to the tent and to sleep.

The next morning we breakfasted in haste, the beasts were harnessed to the cart, and, after a pleasant little ride, we arrived at the cavern of the bears.

After having skinned the bear, I cut off the hams, and then divided the rest of the meat into long strips, about an inch in thickness. We exposed the whole to a good current of smoke, as the ancient buccaneers used to do, and the grease was collected in bamboo canes for use in the kitchen, in lieu of butter. The skins, as usual, were curried to render them sufficiently soft for all purposes.

My restless, turbulent boys were tired and fretful, I could see. Thinking to diversify our work with some amusement, I proposed to them to make an excursion alone in the desert. My proposition was joyfully received and rallied their flagging spirits. Ernest preferred to remain at home with us. But Francis was so eager that I at last permitted him to go.

In a small cavern near the tent, I found several minerals, among others, a piece of amianthus, known as being incombustible, and also a superb block of talc, as transparent as glass, and which I resolved to fashion into windowpanes. Ernest and I soon detached a splendid piece, about two feet in length, and the same in thickness. My wife was overjoyed at our new discovery, especially when I informed her that this mineral could be divided into leaves no thicker than paper.

As evening approached, we gathered round our hearth to wait the return of our huntsmen. The galloping of their steeds was soon heard and in another moment they were at our sides.

Jack and Francis each carried a little kid on his back, with the feet tied together, and Fritz's gamebag appeared to be pretty full.

"A fine chase, Papa!" cried Jack. "Fritz has two magnificent Angora rabbits in his pouch, and also a cuckoo, who led us to one of the finest hives I have ever seen; we shall be able to get plenty of honey."

"In addition," said Fritz, "we have taken a whole troop of antelopes prisoners. We can hunt them and tame them just when we please."

Turning toward Jack, whose face seemed very much swollen, I said, "What is the matter with your cheeks? Have your adventures been dangerous in any way?"

It was Fritz who began the story.

"We took the direction of the valley and, finding a narrow place, crossed on fallen trees to the other side of the river. After some time we discovered, in the distance, two herds of small animals, either antelopes or gazelles. We kept the dogs close by our sides. I then divided my forces—Francis' position was the line of the river; Jack occupied the middle; while I, mounted on the onager, sustained the right wing, and we drove the animals to the center. One of the herds passed the river quietly. The other herd suddenly raised themselves from the grass where they had been lying, and, stretching out their long necks and little heads, set off at full speed. We gave chase and soon forced the entire troop over the river, and into the defile which separated us from the savanna. After we had secured them in our dominions, we stretched a long cord from one side of the defile to the other, and fastened to it every light thing we could find. The continual motion frightened the animals away whenever they approached it. The ostrich plumes in our hats, our handkerchiefs, etc., furnished us with materials."

"Admirable!" said I, as the boy stopped. "But about the rabbits," I added, "what do you intend to do with them?"

"I thought that one of our two islands would make a good home for them. For instance, Shark Island would make a magnificent warren, and furnish us many a good dish, and fine furs to make caps of."

"But how did you come to take them alive?"

"My eagle pounced down upon a troop of rabbits that were flying before us, and carried off two in his talons. I rescued them before he had injured them."

Jack was struggling to put in a word.

"My turn!" said he. "I galloped on with Francis while Fritz was chasing the rabbits. The dogs followed us, and suddenly ran after two little animals that fled with incredible rapidity. After a hot chase, we captured the two fugitives. There they are. I think they are fawns."

"And I think," I said, "that they are antelopes."

"Well," continued Jack, "that was nothing to what happened afterward. A sort of cuckoo began to fly before us, singing away. We rode on, when suddenly he stopped just over a bees' nest, artfully concealed in the ground. I advanced and tried to suffocate the bees by throwing lighted sulphur matches down the hole, when suddenly, with a rumbling noise, a swarm of bees emerged, attacking me on all sides, and it was with the greatest difficulty that I could mount my buffalo and ride away."

I recognized the strange bird as being the "cuckoo indicator" of naturalists. "But," thought I, "how, if this coast is uninhabited, could the bird have known that human beings liked honey, and would share the discovery with him? Is it not a sign that we are not the first men on this soil? May not the interior be inhabited?"

I was convinced that it would not be prudent to advance into the interior, without the greatest caution. I also resolved to build a fortress on Shark Island, as it appeared to me that a strong fortification that would command the coast of Felsenheim, and manned by our two cannons, would enable us to defend ourselves against all attack from the interior, if any ever took place.

24. OSTRICHES AGAIN — A HUNT AND A CAPTURE

AT THE break of day I was up, and awoke my sons. Our labors were almost done—our bears' meat was smoked, our fat all run out into bamboo vessels. The approaching rainy season warned us to return to our home in the grotto. Nevertheless, I wished to see whether a second visit to the nest of ostrich eggs would now succeed, and I likewise wanted to gather some of the gum of the euphorbia.

To accomplish this end as rapidly as possible, it was resolved to go on horseback. We took with us Turk and Billy, and following the Green Valley, traced over again all the places of our last excursion—the spot where we had encountered the bears, the turtle marsh, and, at last, the rock from which Fritz discovered the ostriches.

Jack and Francis galloped off at full speed. I retained Fritz to aid me in gathering the euphorbia which had congealed in the sun. I had provided myself with a vessel to put it in, and I soon filled it with the little drops of hardened gum.

This gum is one of the most violent and subtle poisons, and my son asked me why I took so much pains to collect it.

"I intend to use it," said I, "to destroy the monkeys—a cruel necessity. We can also employ the euphorbia in preparing the skins of birds and other animals; it will preserve them from corruption, and keep out all insects. However, the greatest precaution must be observed."

As we sighted the nest, four ostriches rose from the sand and advanced toward us. Fritz prepared his eagle for the conflict. And to prevent it from repeating the former scene, he fastened its beak so strongly that it was almost harmless. Our dogs were also muzzled, and we stood motionless. On they came, with half-extended wings, gliding over the ground with inconceivable rapidity, the three females and a male—the last a little in advance—with his beautiful tail feathers floating behind him.

The moment of attack was come. I seized my string with balls and launched it against the male ostrich. Unfortunately, however, instead of catching him around the legs, the balls of my string took a turn round his body, and I only fastened his wings to his sides. It diminished his speed somewhat, and the frightened bird turned round, and endeavored to escape. Away we dashed after him, I on the onager, and Fritz on the colt. We were nearly exhausted, when Jack and Francis rode up, and cut off his further retreat. Fritz then unhooded his eagle, and, pointing out the ostrich to him, he immediately pounced upon his prey. And now commenced an arduous chase. Jack and Francis on one side, and Fritz and I on the other, harassed the ostrich without ceasing, but the most useful combatant was the eagle. He felt him on his head, and heard the flapping of his wings. The eagle was so violent that, at a vigorous stroke of his wings, the ostrich fairly tottered. Jack then threw his string and balls so skillfully that the noble bird hit the sand of the desert. A cry burst from the huntsmen, the eagle was recalled and hoodwinked, and we hastened to our prize in order to prevent his breaking the bonds that confined him in his struggles.

In order to reduce his fury, I threw my hunting sack, my vest, and handkerchief, over his head. No sooner were his eyes covered than he quieted. I passed a large band of sea dog skin around his body, two other bands were attached as reins to each side, and his legs were fastened with strong cords, long enough to allow him to walk, but which confined him sufficiently to prevent his escape.

I then attached our two buffaloes before and behind the ostrich with strong cords. And when all was ready, my two cavaliers jumped into their saddles, and I pulled the covering from the head of the ostrich.

The bird remained immovable, as if astonished at the return of light. It soon made a start; but the ropes pulled it roughly back. Again it made the attempt, and again it was foiled. It tried to fly, but its wings were tightly fastened by the band I had passed around them. It threw itself from side to side, but the patient buffaloes paid not the least attention to the pulling and hauling. At last the bird submitted to its two companions, and set off with them at full gallop, until the buffalo and the bull, less accustomed to the sands of the savanna than the ostrich, forced it to a slower pace.

Meanwhile Fritz and I set out in search of the ostrich nest. The cross of willows which we had planted near it still remained. As we approached, a female bird rose up from the nest and fled rapidly away into the desert, but her presence assured us that the eggs still retained the principle of life. I had taken care to bring with me a sack and quantity of cotton. I now took out six of the eggs, and enveloping them as carefully as possible in the cotton, placed them in the sack, leaving the others in the nest.

We traversed the Green Valley and soon arrived at the tent, where Ernest and his mother received us with astonishment.

I fastened the ostrich securely between two trees, and prepared for our departure on the morrow, to collect our new riches. I wished to leave nothing behind us.

Early the next day, the ostrich took his place between the bull and the buffalo, and as before, threw himself in vain from right to left. His two conductors were like immovable masses, all resistance unavailing.

Fritz mounted the young colt Rapid, and I the onager, while Ernest directed the cart, in which my wife sat among the provisions.

At the entrance of the defile we erected a solid palisade of bamboo, high enough to keep out all animals that do not climb. We planted a row of thornbushes on each side, and sprinkled a layer of sand all round, so as to discover what animals might frequent it.

Our labors over, it was night when we arrived at the cabin at Waldegg. We found our smoking hut and our provision of peccary untouched. We lighted a fire, and, after a frugal repast, extended ourselves on our sacks of cotton, and slept.

The next day, we discovered a new treasure. Our henhouse had twenty young chicks—the product of the eggs Jack had brought home in his hat. We returned to our dear Felsenheim, and to all its comforts and luxuries, but we were so exhausted, we could scarcely give our animals their evening food, before seeking our repose.

The day after our arrival at Felsenheim, my wife and two younger boys commenced "cleaning house." Windows were opened, beds aired, and all swept and garnished. I, with the two elder, unpacked and distributed the riches we had brought home.

We had tied the ostrich, at first, under a tree, and securely fastened his feet; and now tied him to one of the strong bamboo columns that supported the gallery.

The eggs were submitted to the trial of warm water. Three or four moved slightly when immersed and these were carefully preserved. To try the experiment of hatching them by cotton and artificial heat, I constructed an oven to maintain that degree of heat which the thermometer marked as being the natural heat of the hen.

Our Angora rabbits were then installed on Shark Island. We constructed a burrow in the ground, as in Europe, and putting the rabbits in, we combed them and removed all the superfluous hair. We also fixed wooden combs over the entrance of each burrow; the rabbits, passing in or out, would be deprived of some part of their fine wool, which I intended to manufacture into hats.

I erected a hut in the middle of the island, to shelter the two antelopes from the dogs and beasts of prey, and we took good care to provide them with plenty of provisions.

Before the rains came on, we prepared a field to receive the seeds we had hitherto confided to the earth without any order or regularity. Our faithful animals were of much assistance to us, but we could work only four hours in the day, two in the morning and two in the evening. However, we prepared about two acres of land to furnish us an ample harvest of maize, potatoes, and manioc root.

During the intervals of labor, we began the education of the ostrich. I had read that it could be accomplished, and I was resolved to try it.

The ostrich struggled, and snapped at us with his beak. Several times we were forced to burn tobacco under his nose. This had the desired effect, and the majestic bird was rendered insensible. Little by little we relaxed the cord which fastened it to the bamboo post, and gave it room to wander about the doorway. A litter of rushes was provided for him; calabashes filled with sweet nuts, rice, maize, and guavas were placed every day before the animal.

During three days our choice dishes were disdained, the beautiful captive would not eat, and I was seriously afraid of the consequences. At last it occurred to my wife to poke down the throat of the bird, willy-nilly, balls of maize and butter. All trouble on that point was over, and food placed before it was quickly devoured.

The natural savageness of the bird disappeared more and more every day. At the end of the month its education was complete, and I wished it to associate with our domestic animals; to submit like them to direction and to march and stop as we wished.

The first thing that was to be thought of was a bit; but how could I contrive a bit for a beak? At last I achieved my task. The ostrich would stop short when blindfolded, and move only when its eyes were uncovered. I made a sort of hood with the skin of a sea dog, which covered the head, being fastened about the neck. I made two openings in the side of this hood, one opposite each eye, and covered each hole with one of our little turtle shells, attached to a whalebone spring, so that it would open and shut. Reins were fastened to these springs; by their action, we could admit the light or shut it out. When the two shells were open, the ostrich galloped straight on; when one was open, it went in a direction corresponding with the eye that received light, and when both shells were shut, it would stop short. The most fully trained horse could not have obeyed better than our ostrich did under his novel headdress.

My children thought that the education of our captive was now complete, but I differed. The ostrich is an animal of great endurance. I wished it to learn to carry burdens, to draw a carriage, and be adapted for horsemanship. We had a great deal of difficulty in making the ostrich submit to a rider. But at last we had the satisfaction of seeing our new courser galloping between Felsenheim and Falcon's Nest with one of our young cavaliers mounted on his back.

Three of the ostrich eggs enveloped in cotton, and placed in a stove, had hatched. The young ostriches looked like ducks, mounted on long legs, and they tottered awkwardly about on their slender stilts. One died the day after its birth, but we preserved the other two by taking all possible care. Maize, acorns, boiled rice, milk, and cassava, were set before them.

We had had nothing to drink but water since our arrival on the island, except for the barrel of Cape wine that we had saved from the shipwreck, but that was long ago exhausted. I now determined to make some sort of drink for the winter.

I had often heard of the hydromel of the Russians, made with honey. We boiled some honey in a sufficient quantity of water, and after having filled two barrels with the fluid, I threw in a large cake of sour corn bread, to make the liquor ferment. When that process was finished, we found it of a pleasant flavor, agreeably acid, and the two tuns in our cellar were a great resource for our long winter days. A choicer drink, made by adding to our honey and water nutmegs, ravensara and all the aromatic plants we could find, was reserved for extraordinary occasions, such as holiday banquets, anniversaries, etc.

When all our provisions were gathered in, and we could get through the winter without famine, we commenced our manufacture of hats—a labor as difficult as novel for us. The first question was the form of our hats. Our means of execution was extremely simple. I cut a wooden head, which divided into two parts, and on which we spread a thick layer of soft paste, composed of rat skin and the glue of fishes. Dried, it took the exact impress of the mold—a sort of cap.

Even this ill-looking affair cost us a great deal of trouble to produce, but our European hats were so dilapidated that replacement was a necessity.

Using the cochineal, I gave to our beaver a beautiful brilliant crimson tint. The hat looked better, adorned with ostrich plumes, and a ribbon round it, from my wife's enchanted sack, and disdain changed into requests for its possession.

But it belonged to Francis. He had lost his old hat a few days before.

Now we tried our hand at other things. We were in want of kitchen utensils, and I passed from the art of hatmaking to that of potter.

I did not understand much about pottery, nor the way in which the earth was to be prepared before using it; and I had very little hope of succeeding.

In one corner of the grotto I constructed a large stove, divided into compartments, to receive the different articles; earthen pipes were conducted all round, so as to equalize the heat as much as possible. These preparations occupied me a long time. With no idea how to proceed, I can safely say I invented rather than imitated a furnace for pottery.

From a quantity of the porcelain earth, which resembled fine white sand, I removed all foreign particles, such as bits of stone, etc., lest they cut our hands while working the porcelain. I mixed with it a quantity of the talc we had brought home for windowpanes, to render the mixture firmer. When all was well worked up together, I left it a little while to dry, while I set to work to invent a machine on which to turn our utensils. The wheel of one of our cannon carriages, fixed horizontally on a pivot and surmounted by another wheel, united to it by an axle and turning with it formed my machine. I first turned out some plates and dishes, cups and saucers, bowls, and other things. When baked at a very strong heat, they were perfectly transparent and of the most beautiful grain. Overwhelmed with joy, my wife promised us numberless good dainties which she had hitherto been unable to make.

25. A NEW WANT — THE CAJACK

THE RAINY season, now rapidly approaching, soon obliged us to give up our excursions. The winds and the rain commenced, the sky became dark with storm clouds, terrible tempests announced the approach of winter, and we closed the door of our grotto, happy over our comfortable shelter.

The turning wheel was continually in motion. Our work greatly improved, and we manufactured utensils that we were proud to possess.

We divided the shells of the ostrich eggs by means of a string steeped in vinegar, thus converting the halves into elegant vases. I turned some wooden pedestals for bases, and we obtained drinking cups and vases for flowers in summer.

But these labors were much more interesting to me than to my young family. Ernest found occupation enough in his books, but for his brothers some active occupation was urgent. Fritz came to my assistance.

"We have," said he, "our ostrich, a splendid post horse, with which to travel our kingdom. We have carts to transport our provisions; a pinnace, and a canoe, which are riding at anchor in Safety Bay; but we have need of an equipage that will glide over the surface of the water, as the ostrich does over the sand. I have read that the Greenlanders have a sort of vessel which they call 'cajack.' Why cannot we construct one?"

I joyfully agreed. The cajack, the only vessel of the Greenlander, is a sort of canoe in the form of a shell; and a piece of walrus skin, with three or four strips of whalebone, are almost the only requisites for its construction. It is extremely light, and the navigator can easily carry it on his shoulder when on land.

The strips of whalebone, bamboo cane, and Spanish rushes, with some sea dog skin, were the materials that we employed in making our cajack. Two arched strips of whalebone fastened at each end, and separated in the middle by a piece of bamboo fixed transversely across, formed the two sides of our canoe; other pieces of whalebone, woven in with rushes and moss, well covered with pitch, formed the skeleton.

When the skeleton was finished, and the interior covered with a coat of gum and moss, we commenced the construction of an envelope. For this I took the two entire skins of sea calves, fastened one at each end of the canoe, and then drew them down under it, where they were strongly sewed together, and covered with a gum-elastic coat, to render them impervious to water. I also cut out oars of bamboo, and fastened bladders to one end, so that they might be useful in case of accident. I constructed, in the bow, a place to receive a sail, in case we should decide later to put one there.

There was yet an important thing wanting in the completion of our Greenland boat; it was the equipment of him who was to manage it. I had often heard of a sort of apparel well known to those who dwell near the sea, and which consisted in enveloping a person in an airtight costume, lighter than the volume of liquid his body displaced. I described this apparel and told how the head of the swimmer was covered with a hood, furnished with a pipe to let in air when it was necessary to breathe under water. The boys persuaded their mother to construct such a suit for them.

My good Elizabeth, in a few days, had made a complete swimming costume for Fritz.

A jacket of the skin of the whale's entrails, hermetically sealed and sewed round the borders, so that the air could not possibly escape, was furnished with a flexible pipe, closed with a valve, so that it could be inflated or exhausted at need by its wearer.

The winter had glided away. Reading, the study of languages and other literary pursuits had mingled with our domestic avocations, and helped to pass agreeably the days we spent in the grotto. But the wind calmed, the sea resumed its wonted placidity, the grass sprang up under our feet, and we revisited Falcon's Nest, with its giant trees and its rich harvest of springing grain.

Fritz was anxious to try the swimming costume. Consequently, one fine afternoon he put on his jacket, which was drawn close round his neck; then his hood, with its pipe for air, was fitted to the jacket, and two pieces of talc inserted to enable him to see.

On seeing him, we all burst into a fit of

laughter. But Fritz plunged gravely into the water, and struck out for Shark Island. We followed him in the canoe, arriving about the same time. We unfastened his hood, and found that not a particle of water had penetrated it. Everyone was rejoiced at the success of the experiment, and we persuaded our kind mother to make us one each.

We then explored the island, and the condition of the colony there. The antelopes fled at our approach, but they had devoured all their provisions. We strewed some rushes in their little hut, renewed the stock of provisions, and left the spot to the timid animals. We gathered coral and shells for our museum, and found the different plantations most successful, with some young trees already well grown. Our rabbits had also prospered, and increased enormously.

On Whale Island our plantations had also succeeded—all was prosperity around us. Our maritime possessions and those on terra firma afforded a most agreeable spectacle. Abundance, richness, and a luxuriant vegetation gave promise of an excellent harvest.

One day, when I was occupied in the interior of the grotto, three of my sons disappeared without saying anything; they carried with them their arms, provisions, and a number of rattraps. They had gone for rat skins for some new hats. I thought nothing more of the matter.

Ernest, always fond of home, had remained reading in the library. My wife was occupied in the kitchen, and I resolved to attempt an excursion alone. I needed some large blocks of wood with which to grind the grain we had gathered, but I would not cut down a tree near our habitation for fear of disfiguring our residence. I fastened the buffalo to the sledge, and set off in the direction of Jackal's River, taking with me the dogs Folb and Braun.

I chose the river road so that in passing I might take a look at our plantations of manioc and potatoes along its bank. I had not seen this land for four months, and I expected to find an abundant harvest preparing for us. To my surprise, I found the whole plantation a scene of ruin, and utter desolation. The prints in the moist earth revealed the authors of this devastation—the wild pigs, the family of our old sow.

Folb and Braun, off in search of the despoilers now returned driving before them a whole herd of pigs, headed by our old sow. I was so irritated that I raised my gun, and brought down two young porkers. The others took to flight. I placed the bodies on the sledge, marked with a hatchet the trees wanted, and set off for Felsenheim, with a saddened heart at the devastation seen.

Toward evening we began to grow anxious about the boys, when suddenly Jack appeared in the distance. He arrived at full gallop on his ostrich, Fritz and Francis following, and each carried before him a sack full of game. They had brought back with them four of those we had called "beasts with a bill," twenty ondatras, one monkey, a kangaroo, and two varieties of the muskrat, which they had found in the swamp.

During supper, each one recounted his adventures, Fritz describing their passage through the valley, the attack of the ondatras and the beavers. "We also," said he, "then saw those 'beasts with a bill' coming out of the swamp to partake of a repast not intended for them. We then caught a fish or two in the lake, and added to our dinner a plate of ginseng cooked in the ashes."

"Pooh, pooh!" cried Jack the boaster. "Rats and fishes! It is to my courser and me that you owe this royal prize, this noble kangaroo."

"Oh, yes," added Francis, "an easy prize. It remained quiet until you came up and shot it."

"I have brought home nothing but a plant," continued Fritz, "but it is of more value than the kangaroo. See the hard, sharp points of these thistles. Will they not be excellent to card the hair in manufacturing our hats?"

The thistles I recognized as the "carding thistle"—a precious discovery—one more instrument added to our resources. My sons had also brought home some cuttings of sweet potatoes and cinnamon. Their good mother carefully planted them in the garden the next morning.

The grain that we had sown before the rainy season had now come to maturity, and our hands were full. The herrings would soon arrive, then the sea dogs. My dear Elizabeth enumerated all the labors yet to come; the manioc to dig up, the potatoes to gather and sow, a thousand labors to undertake, that would occupy more time than the year has days.

I tranquilized my good companion, assuring her that the manioc and the potatoes would keep a great while in the earth.

I decided that our labors should commence with the grain, the first of our resources. But wishing to effect the harvest in the shortest time, and with the least expenditure of strength, I adopted the Italian method rather than the Swiss.

I leveled a large space before the grotto, to serve as a threshing floor. After having well watered it, we beat the earth for a long time with clubs. When the sun dried it up, the operation was repeated, until we obtained a solid, flat surface, without a crack in it, and almost as impenetrable to water as to the sun's rays.

My wife asked me what to use to tie up the blades into sheaves.

"Nothing," said I. "The Italians never use sheaves."

"How, then," asked Fritz, "do they carry their harvest home?"

"You will soon see," I said.

At the same time I gathered up in my left hand all the stalks it could contain, and taking a long knife in my right hand, I cut off the stalks about six inches below the head. I then threw the handful into a basket. "There," I said, laughing, to Fritz, "there is the first act of Italian harvest."

In a short time the plain bristled with decapitated stalks, and we hastened with the grains to the grotto. The blades were sprinkled over the threshing floor, while my three cavaliers stood by their coursers' sides, laughing at our way of threshing grain.

When everything was prepared, I cried, "To the saddle! To the saddle!" My sons had only to display their horsemanship among the grain. My wife, Ernest, and I, each armed with a pitchfork, followed after them, throwing the grain under the feet of the animals.

When the grain was all threshed, we set to work to clear it of the straws and dirt mixed with it. This was the most difficult and painful part. We laid the grain on close hurdles, and with wooden flails endeavored to disengage the dirt. We all coughed terribly, and were obliged to desist every few moments to clear our throats.

After several days in this work, we found ourselves enriched by sixty bushels of barley, eighty of wheat, and more than a hundred of maize. We had not prepared the maize as we had the other grains. But after having dried the stalks, we detached the grains by beating them with long, flexible whips. We took this care because we wanted its soft and elastic leaves to stuff our mattresses.

To obtain a second harvest before the end of the season, we now set to work to clear our fields of the straw. As we commenced, a swarm of quails and partridges started up from the dried stalks, enticed by the few blades of grain left behind. We were unprepared, and they all escaped, but we could anticipate the superb chase of quails and partridges we should have after our harvests.

With the land cleared I sowed it anew, but not to exhaust the soil, I varied the operation and sowed wheat and oats for the second crop.

We were scarcely finished when the bank of herrings appeared off Safety Bay. Our winter provisions being so abundant, we prepared just two barrels, one of salted and one of smoked herrings. We also preserved some of the fish alive, kept in Jackal's River, to be obtained at any time.

26. TRIAL OF THE CAJACK

THE TRIAL of the cajack was a grand holiday fete. When Fritz appeared, clad in his maritime costume, he was formally invited to take his place in his boat of skin. The cajack was furnished with two little wheels of copper, so that it could be used as well on land as on sea. Proud Fritz was installed upon his bench. I untied the canoe and held myself ready to start at a moment's notice, if danger should threaten our Greenland sailor. When all precautions were taken, "To the sea!" cried I to Fritz. "To the sea!" "Good-by!" repeated his brothers, and the cajack glided rapidly into the water, and the Greenland danced gaily over the waves. Then, like a skillful actor, he began executing a series of evolutions, each more adroit than the other.

This audacity provoked loud and frequent applause on our part. He then turned his frail bark toward Jackal's River, to mount the current. But this proved too strong for him, and threw him back so violently that he disappeared from sight. I jumped into the canoe to fly to his assistance, Jack and Ernest with me. While I exerted all my force at the wheel, my two sons each took an oar. We scarcely touched the surface of the water, yet we could perceive nothing of Fritz. Our cries had no echo but the rocks, and our sight was lost in the foaming waves that boiled up around us. I felt my heart beating violently, when suddenly, in the direction of a rock just visible through the foam, I saw a light cloud of smoke issue forth, followed by a report.

"He is saved!" I cried. "He is saved! Fritz is there in the direction of the smoke."

I then fired my pistol, which was instantly answered by another report in the same direction. After a hard row we perceived Fritz, and soon reached him.

We found our young hero established on the rocks. Before him lay a walrus, or sea cow, which he had killed with his harpoon. I reproved my son for his imprudence.

"My dear father," answered he, "it was the current that swept me away in spite of myself. My oars were like straws before the force of Jackal's River, and I felt myself thrown back into the sea. But I had no time for fear. A company of sea cows passed along, almost under my nose. I threw my harpoon and struck one of these animals, and at the wound I had inflicted, he dived down; but the traces of blood he left behind, and the bladder of air fastened to the end of the rope, served as guides to follow him. I launched a second harpoon direct in his side, and, after some struggles, the monster extended himself on this rock. Remembering the boa, I fired two pistols at his head. Those were the reports you heard."

"You were truly heroic, and the combat was perilous. The walrus is a redoubtable monster. But, God be praised, you are safe. However, I do not know what use this will be to us."

"Well, then, if it is good for nothing," Fritz answered, "I will prepare the head, and fasten it to the bow of my cajack. Its long, white teeth will have a fine effect, and I can call my cajack 'The Walrus.' "

"The teeth of the walrus, white and hard as ivory," said I, "are the only things worth preserving. But make haste, for the sky gives sure token of a storm."

I wished to take Fritz and his cajack into our canoe, but he refused, and dashed on, saying he would announce our return to his mother.

The storm came on quicker than I had anticipated. Thick, black clouds burst forth in torrents of rain. The wind, the lightning, the waves, were confounded in horrible confusion, and I repented of not having taken Fritz in the boat with us. Jack and Ernest put on their swimming corsets and lashed themselves fast to the ropes of the canoe, not to be carried away by the waves that occasionally broke over us.

The tempest increased, and my anxiety with it. The waves were like mountains. At one moment we would be high in the air, and at another at the bottom of an abyss. But the violent tempest spent itself quickly. The waves subsided, the wind fell, and the storm for a time was over, although black and angry clouds rolled over our heads.

Redoubling our efforts at the oars and the

wheel, we soon arrived at Safety Bay. As we entered the harbor, we saw Fritz, Francis, and their mother, kneeling on the beach, praying for our preservation. The heart of my poor Elizabeth was almost broken with anxiety.

We leaped from our canoe amid cries of joy and the embraces of the dear ones who rushed into our arms. My wife had not strength to articulate a single word; her only thought was of thankfulness to our Almighty Preserver. After uniting in prayer, we retired to the grotto to change into dry garments.

Fritz spoke up. "We are again united. I had given up all hope of ever seeing you again when the huge wave swept over my little bark; but I held my breath and the wave passed on, and I found myself still alive. It was the hand of God that saved me," added the young man, "and to Him have I rendered homage."

Jackal's River had overflowed its banks. The damage to our constructions demanded instant restoration. During our labors, we captured a number of superb salmon, which were salted and smoked, and we preserved some alive by passing a strong cord through the gills and fastening them to stakes.

One clear moonlight night, I was suddenly awakened by barks and cries, as if all the jackals, bears, and tigers had invaded our domain.

We ran out and found that our dogs had captured three large hogs.

I attributed this invasion to negligence and thought we had forgotten to take up the planks from Family Bridge. But they had been removed; the audacious pigs had come across on the beams of the bridge.

Family Bridge was therefore not sufficient for our security. It was a means of entering our domain, not a barrier. Now appeared to be the proper time for constructing the drawbridge I had long contemplated.

A drawbridge was not a little thing to undertake; but after having constructed two vessels, we could not recoil from the idea of constructing a drawbridge.

I understood the turning bridges; but as I had neither vise nor windlass, I was obliged to adopt the simplest kind of drawbridge. I constructed, between two high stakes, a sweep that could be easily moved, and by the means of two ropes, a lever, and a counterpoise, we had a bridge which could be easily raised and lowered. Thus our domains were enriched with a new masterpiece, and my young people engaged in a thousand gymnastic exercises about the stakes of the drawbridge. It was lowered, and raised, and for a few days it was a great source of amusement for them.

27. THE FORT ON SHARK ISLAND

OUR NEXT labor was a fort at the defile. Fritz had read of a Kamschatdale fort which consists of four high stones, upon which are laid planks and boards, forming a platform upon which a hut of bark or branches is constructed.

Instead of four stones for the foundation, we chose out four trees to answer the same purpose. We left the branches as rests for the beams of our platform. We surrounded our platform with a high and strong network of rushes and branches, with an opening for entrance, and we covered the roof with the waterproof leaves of the talipot palm—leaves so large that ten men can be covered by one of them. Our fort bore a strong resemblance to Falcon's Nest, and did not look much like a military construction.

To ascend to the platform, we employed one of the simplest means I could imagine. It was by a beam which descended perpendicularly to the ground, notched deeply into steps, and arranged so that it could be raised and lowered at pleasure.

Our new fort overlooked the savanna for a great distance, and we could see the river running like a silver thread through the immense plain. With spyglasses we could discern troops of buffaloes and other animals feeding around the brink.

Our labors at the fort were diversified by some important discoveries. From the rich vegetation of the river of the savanna, Fritz brought me some specimens to examine. I recognized them as two of the most precious productions of the tropics. The cacao bean, of which chocolate is made, and the banana, an article of food of several countries in America.

We did not find these fruits much to our taste. The beans of the cacao are filled with a sort of thick cream, with an odor like that of an overripe pear.

My wife sought in vain for some seeds of the banana to plant in her kitchen garden at home. I told her that the banana was always propagated from cuttings, which grow easily in rich, wet earth; and unless the seeds of the cacao were put in when the fruit was gathered they would be useless.

In consequence, Fritz set out the next day

in his cajack, in search of the necessary elements for reproduction of these two precious plants.

Fearing that his cajack would not be large enough to hold the intended cargo, Fritz fastened a raft of rushes behind it. He was ashamed, he said, to go for banana cuttings only, and he intended to bring home something else.

We occupied ourselves during the day in preparing to set out for Felsenheim, and it was late in the evening when we saw Fritz coming toward us, the cajack and the raft loaded down to the water's edge.

The cargo was soon unloaded by his brothers, and dragged up to the hut with much contentment.

Fritz now came up, holding in his hand a superb bird, the feet and wings of which he had fastened, as the principal booty of the day.

It was the Sultan Cock of Buffon, the king of water fowls. I recognized its long red legs, and its beautiful green and violet plumage, with a red spot in the forehead. My wife wished to add it to the inhabitants of the farmyard, and as it was very gentle, it soon became as tame as the rest of our domestic fowls.

Fritz informed us that, ascending the river

for a great distance, he had been astonished at the majestic forests which bordered it. He had encountered several families of turkeys, pintados, and peacocks, whose cries and screams gave life to the somber river. Farther on there were enormous elephants feeding along the bank, in troops of twenty or thirty. Some were in the water, squirting the cool fluid over their companions. Tigers and panthers, too, lay sleeping in the sun, their magnificent fur contrasting strangely with the green bank upon which they reclined. None of these animals paid the least attention to the young navigator.

"Suddenly," said Fritz, "on finding myself face to face with these terrible enemies, I felt the uselessness of my gun and my skill. I attempted to turn my cajack around, when, at about the distance of two gunshots before me, I saw a long and large mouth, armed with rows of formidable teeth, and the whole moving directly toward me. I cannot say how I found strength enough to escape, I felt so frightened at the apparition."

"What animal was it," asked Francis, "the mouth and teeth of which Fritz saw coming out of the water?"

"An alligator, probably," said Ernest.

We set off at daybreak next morning for

Felsenheim. Fritz asked permission to make the journey in his cajack, doubling by Cape Disappointment. I consented, reassured by his easy management of his little boat, and I was anxious to know more about the Cape.

We both set out at the same time, and both arrived home safely. In doubling the Cape, Fritz had made two new discoveries. On the rock he remarked two shrubs; one covered, with very highly scented, rose-colored flowers, and long, narrow leaves, the other with numerous small white flowers. One of the specimens Fritz brought home my wife recognized as the caper plant, used in pickling; the other was a sort of Chinese tea plant, which was received with marked appreciation.

When we were a little rested, my wife called to mind Falcon's Nest, which she suggested we occupy at once.

"It is wrong," said she, "to let that beautiful habitation go to ruin. Although Felsenheim offers us sure protection in winter, yet Falcon's Nest, with its gigantic branches and pleasant verdure, is the most agreeable habitation we could possess."

My wife spoke reasonably. We left Felsenheim and took up residence in our old habitation. The roof was now plastered with gum and resin, the staircase repaired; we substituted a bark roof for the old linen one over our chamber in the tree, we made a balcony all around it, and repaired everything, so that it was a clean, agreeable habitation.

But this was just a prelude. Fritz had conceived the idea of fortifying Shark Island, in case of danger. It was impossible to resist his plans and projects, and the work was at length begun.

Great were the obstacles that a man and four boys had to contend with, in order to convey two cannons to the island, and level them on a platform more than fifty feet in height. It cost us immense labor.

I placed on the platform we had built a large capstan, and to shorten the time and reduce the labor in passing around the rock, I let down a rope, made into loops, so that we could easily ascend and descend. The cannons were attached by strong ropes, and then hauled up by the capstan. The work cost us a whole day of hard labor. But at last the cannons were on the platform, and established with their mouths toward the sea. We placed a long pole in the rock, with a string and pulley, so that we could hoist up a flag at any time. How glad we felt when our work was done, and how proud we were of our ingenuity! The crowning of this military construction with a flag raised a cry of joy, and, as economical as I felt we must be in powder, six times we fired our cannons, and the rocks repeated the echo over a vast extent of ocean.

28. OUR COLONY AFTER TEN YEARS

TEN YEARS have passed away since we were thrown on this coast, each year resembling the one preceding. Our fields to sow, our harvests to gather, and our domestic cares to attend to formed the almost unbroken circle of our existence. My end in writing this journal will be fulfilled if any who read, learn how, with God's blessing, to provide for their necessities when thrown, as we have been, entirely on their own resources.

The land of our exile is one of the most favored quarters of the globe, and every day we offered up our thanks to Him for His goodness and beneficent kindness toward us.

In ten years we constructed three habitations, built a solid wall across the defile to secure us against invasion from the wild beasts which infested the savanna. Our part of the country was defended by high mountains on one side and the ocean on the other. We had traversed the whole extent, and rested in perfect surety that no enemy lurked within it. Our principal habitations were beautiful, commodious, and very healthy. Felsenheim was a safe retreat for us during the storms of winter, while Falcon's Nest was our summer residence and country villa; Waldegg, Prospect Hill, and even the establishment at the defile, were like the quiet farmhouses in the mountains of our own dear Switzerland.

Our native land is never forgotten. The love of one's birthplace is a love that survives youth and exists in all its ardor in old age.

We finished the gallery which extended along the front of our grotto. A roof was made to the rock above it, and it rested on fourteen columns of light bamboo, which gave to it an elegant and picturesque appearance. Large pillars supported the gallery, round which twined the aromatic vines of the vanilla and the pepper, and each end of the gallery was terminated by a little cabinet with elevated roofs, giving the appearance of Chinese pavilions, surrounded by flowers and foliage. A flight of steps led up into the gallery, which we had paved with the same stone as the grotto, soft when dug out, but hardening rapidly in the sun.

Our surroundings were rich and agreeable, our plantations had perfectly succeeded. And between the grotto and the bay a grove of trees and shrubs gave the spot the aspect of an English garden.

On Shark Island palm and pineapple trees had been planted everywhere, and the earth was a carpet of vivid green. While far above the trees towered a staff from which the Swiss flag floated gaily in the breeze.

Our European trees had grown with strength and rapidity, but their fruits had lost their flavor and withered away. But the indigenous fruits multiplied a hundredfold; the bananas, the figs, the guavas, the oranges, and the citron made our corner of the island a paradise. But the abundance of fruit brought on a plague of birds that flocked to the spot. We kept our bird snares already ready, and it sometimes happened that an unknown animal would be taken in the trap. For example, the great squirrel of Canada, remarkable for its beautiful tufted tail and lustrous red skin, was attracted hither probably by our almonds and chestnuts.

Our beautiful flowers also attracted the hummingbirds. It was one of our greatest amusements to watch these little birds flying around us, sparkling like precious stones, and hardly perceptible by the quickness of their motions. It was amusing to see these passionate, choleric little fellows attack others twice their size, and at other times tear to pieces the unlucky flower that had not yielded a rich feast. We induced the birds to remain by fixing little pots of honey on the branches, and planting the flowers they preferred. Our cares were recompensed; several couples suspended their little nests, lined with soft cotton, to the branches of the vanilla which wound round the columns of the gallery, or on the vines of the pepper, the perfume of which is very enticing to the hummingbird.

We gradually improved our manufacture of sugar and obtained a very satisfactory result, aided, of course, by the sugar press and great kettles we had saved from the wreck of the ship.

We embellished Whale Island with trees and shrubs; but here we performed our less cleanly avocations—the preparation of fish, the melting of fat, the tannery, and the candlemaking. The materials for these works were kept under an overhanging rock, which protected them from the sun and storm.

Those cares that were most distant from us we called our colonies. At Waldegg we transformed the swamp into a superb rice field, which repaid our labor by plentiful harvests. We also planted cinnamon, which yielded us an ample return. On Prospect Hill, when the capers ripened each year, we gathered a large quantity, which my wife preserved in spice and vinegar. And when the tea plant began to put forth its leaves, we gathered enough to take home to my wife, who, with Francis, occupied herself in rolling, drying, and preparing it for use.

From time to time, we made an excursion to the defile of the savanna, to see whether any elephants or other hurtful beasts had penetrated into our plantations. Fritz then took his cajack up the river of the savanna, and brought back a rich cargo of ginseng, cacao, and bananas.

We retained one new member of our canine family, which we called *Coco*, "because," said Jack, "the vowel *o* is the most sonorous, and will sound so fine in the forests."

The female buffalo and the cow had each

year produced us a scion from their race, but we had raised only one heifer, *Blanche*, and a second bull, *Thunder*. We also possessed two more asses, which we named *Arrow* and *Alert* on account of the swiftness of their course.

Our pigs were as wild as ever. The old sow had been dead many years. But she had bequeathed to her posterity a spirit of savage independence that all our exertions could not modify. Our other beasts had multiplied in the same proportion.

Such was the state of the colony ten years after our arrival on the coast. Our resources had multiplied as our industry increased, abundance reigned round us. It was a perfect paradise, but there was one great void—oh! if we could but have looked upon men, our brothers!

For ten years we had watched in vain both by sea and land for some traces of man's existence. Yet we hoped on and still gathered up all our treasures of cotton and spices, and ostrich plumes, etc., against the day when we might see the blessed face of man.

My sons were no longer children. Fritz had become a strong and vigorous man. Although not tall, his limbs had been developed by exercise. He was twenty-four years of age.

Ernest was twenty-three, of a good constitution, though not so strong as his brother. His reflective mind had ripened, reason now aided his studious disposition. He had conquered his habit of idleness and was a well-informed young man of sound judgment, unquestionably the light of the family.

Jack had but little changed. He was as headlong at twenty as at ten, but he excelled in physical exercise.

Francis was eighteen. He was stout and tall, his character, without any predominant trait, was estimable. He was reflective, without being as deep as Ernest; agile and skillful, but without surpassing Jack or Fritz. My sons were good and honest men, with sound principles, and a deep sense of religion.

My dear Elizabeth had not grown very old, but my hair had become whitened with age and but a few scattering locks were left, although I still felt young and vigorous.

There was one bitter, sad thought that always haunted my mind. Turning my eyes to Heaven, I often prayed: "My God, Who didst save us from shipwreck, and hast surrounded us with so many blessings, still watch over us, and do not let those perish in solitude whom Thy hand hast saved."

29. FRITZ'S EXCURSION — MESSAGE ON THE ALBATROSS

ONE CAN easily imagine that my young family was not so easy to govern now as it was during the first few years of our stay.

My children would often absent themselves whole days, hunting in the forest or clambering over the rocks. When they returned fatigued, at evening, they had much to tell of the rare and curious things they had seen.

Fritz one day went off in this manner, to our great disquietude. He had taken with him some provisions and also his cajack, and gone out to sea. He had set off before daylight, and night was approaching, but nothing could be seen of him. To alleviate my wife's distress, I launched the canoe, and we set out for Shark Island. There, from the top of the flagstaff, we displayed our flag and fired an alarm cannon. A few moments after, we saw a black spot in the far distance, and, by the aid of a spyglass, we discovered our beloved Fritz. He advanced slowly toward us, beating the sea with his oars, as if his canoe were charged with a double load.

"Fire!" cried Ernest, as commander of the fort, "Fire!" and Jack touched off the cannon. We descended to the shore, to Fritz and his loaded boat. Something heavy and dark, which looked like the head of a large animal, was towing behind.

"It appears," said I, "my dear Fritz, that your day has been profitable, and blessed be God that He has returned you safe and sound."

"Yes," replied Fritz, "blessed be God, for, besides the booty which you see, I think I have made a discovery which is worth more to us than all the treasures of the earth."

These words, half whispered in my ear, excited my curiosity, but I said nothing. When we had brought on shore his sack, filled with large oysters, and the marine monster which served as counterpoise, we drew the little cajack, with its master seated in triumph in it, up to the grotto. The boys then returned for the remainder of the cargo, while we sat down quietly to listen to Fritz's narrative. He first begged our pardon for running away, but he had resolved to visit the eastern part of our country, of which we as yet knew nothing.

"I had long ago intended to make this expedition," he said. "This morning I arose and ran, as is my custom, to the borders of the sea. The weather was so beautiful, the waves so tranquil, that I was tempted. I called my eagle, and seizing a hatchet, jumped into the cajack, and falling into the current of Jackal's River, was hurried out toward the shoals where our vessel was wrecked. I sailed toward the eastern coast, among shoals and rocks covered by the nests of sea birds. Great marine monsters lay extended on the rocks, while others were playing and bellowing frightfully in the waters. These were sea lions, and elephants, and walruses of all sorts, who, holding onto the rocks by their long teeth, let their hinder parts rest in the water. It seemed that this was their general rendezvous; the shore was strewn with their bones and ivory teeth.

"After a row of an hour and a half, I came to a magnificent portico of rocks, like the arch of an immense bridge, under which the sea flowed in like a canal, while the rock on each side of the entrance advanced out into the sea like an immense promontory. As I entered this solemn vault, from the other extremity issued a feeble light, and a delicious coolness filled the cavern. A swarm of little coast swallows surrounded me, uttering piercing cries. I tied my skiff to an angular stone and began t examine the inhabitants. These birds were not swallows. They were about the size of wrens, their breast of a pure white, their wings light gray, and the backs of lustrous black. Their nests, made of feathers and dry leaves, were placed on a singular spoonlike support, of grayish, polished wax. Some of these nests were empty, and I discovered that they were made of a substance resembling fish glue. I disengaged a few of them to bring home for you to examine."

"My son, if we carried on commerce with China or India, we could sell these nests for their weight in gold. For they eat them by millions as one of the greatest delicacies."

At the general cry of disgust from my wife and children, I explained that the feathers and moss lining were not eaten, but only the covering, which is carefully cleaned and cooked with spices, making a transparent savory jelly.

"I advanced through the passage," said Fritz, "and came out into a magnificent bay, whose low and fertile shores stretched out into a vast savanna, varied by trees and shrubs. On the right a mass of rocks rose up, a prolongation of those I had passed through, and on the left rolled a calm and limpid river. And beyond this was a thick swamp, ending in a dense forest of cedars.

"Along the shores of the bay, the transparent waters revealed beds of shells resembling large oysters. 'These,' said I to myself, 'are much better than our little oysters at Felsenheim; if they taste good, I will take some home with me.' I detached some with my hook and threw them on the sand, without getting out of my canoe, and set to work to obtain more. When I returned with a new load, I found that the oysters I had first deposited on the sand were opened in the sun. I took up one or two. But instead of a nice fat oyster, I found hard, gritty meat. In trying to detach this from the shell, I felt some little round, hard stones, like peas, under my knife; I took them out, and found them so brilliant that I filled a little box with them. Do you think, my father," added Fritz, "that they are really pearls?"

I took the box in my hand. "They are really pearls," cried I, "oriental pearls of the greatest beauty. You have discovered a treasure, my son, which one day will be, I hope, of immense value to us. We will pay a visit to this rich bay as soon as possible. But continue."

"Along the coast," resumed Fritz, "I came up to the mouth of a river which floated on tranquilly toward the sea. I gave to this river the name of 'St. John,' as it put me in mind of the description I had read of a river of that name in Florida.

"Having renewed my provision of fresh water, I moved toward the other promontory, opposite the arch by which I had entered. The tide had risen so high that I was obliged to await its ebb. I stepped on shore. On all sides, popping up out of the water, were the calf-sized heads of marine animals that plunged and frisked about. I was afraid that I would upset my cajack, so I secured it to a point in the rock, and, taking my eagle in my hand, stood ready to attack the first game that came near me. I wished to procure one of the animals, which resembled a stuffed valise, as I thought its thick skin might be of use to me. A company of them came, plunging and diving, close to the shore. I cast off my eagle, who seized on the largest and best, and soon blinded him. I jumped on a projecting rock, and, catching hold of the animal with my boat hook, drew it to the shore. All the others fled.

"I removed the entrails of the animal, to lighten the weight for my skiff, but a prodigious number of sea birds clustered around me—gulls, sea swallows, frigates, and others. I whirled my staff around to keep them off, and in doing so, knocked down a very large bird, an albatross, I think. At last I fastened my sea otter to the stern of my boat, and, taking a sackful of oysters, prepared to return. I soon passed through the arch, and sailed quietly along, until I saw your flag and heard the report of the cannon."

After this narrative, and while my wife and the younger boys had gone to the cajack, my son drew me aside.

"A very singular circumstance," said he, "happened on my voyage. In examining the albatross which I had knocked down, I saw a piece of linen around one of its feet. I untied it, and read the following words written upon it in good English: *'Save the poor shipwrecked sailor on the smoking rock.'*

"I cannot express to you, my father, what I felt on seeing this linen. I read and reread the line to assure myself that it was not an optical illusion. I cried aloud to the Almighty that it might be true. I shall search the coast in quest of the smoking rock, to save the sufferer—my brother—my friend. Oh! Once more perhaps I may see a human being!

"I attached the linen again to the foot of the albatross, and wrote upon a second piece, the following sentence in English, *'Have confidence in God. Succor is near.'* If the bird returns to the place from whence it came, thought I, the person can read the answer. At all events there will be no harm done.

"The albatross had been stunned, and I poured some hydromel down its throat to reanimate it. I attached my note to its foot, and let it go, earnestly praying that its mission be successful. The bird flew up, hesitated for a moment, and then darted rapidly away in an easterly direction, which decided me to take that route in my search.

"And now, my father," continued Fritz with emotion, "what do you think? If we could find a new friend, a new brother—what joy! What happiness! But alas! What despair if we should not succeed! I did not communicate this to my brothers and my mother, to spare them a hope that might never be realized."

My son pronounced these last words with deep sadness.

"You have acted very prudently," I said. "I am glad that you have sufficient strength of mind to resist the temptation of immediately flying to the assistance of the sufferer. As for an expedition, I cannot say much. The albatross is a traveler bird and flies swiftly. The linen might have been put on its foot thousands of miles from here. And even if near, perhaps years ago, and now succor may be too late. But keep the secret, and I will try to devise some way to save the poor unfortunate, if in our vicinity."

The pearls were too important to be forgotten, and my sons importuned me to start immediately for the newly discovered fishery.

"Softly," said I; "before riding, you must saddle your horse. To succeed, you must take necessary implements. Let each one invent something useful for our purpose, and then we will start."

Each member of the party set to work. I forged two large iron rakes, with wooden handles with iron rings attached, and two small metal hooks. I could fasten the rakes to the boat and drag them over the banks of oysters; with the hooks I intended to loosen the oysters not detached by the rakes. Ernest made a sort of butterfly net with scissors attached, intended to receive the birds' nests. Jack constructed a kind of ladder, made by piercing a long bamboo at regular distances, and fixing in sticks crosswise. The machine looked like the stick of a parrot's cage. To the top the young man fixed a hook of iron, and a spike at the bottom, so that it should rest firmly in the rocks. Francis made several strong nets to hold our oysters.

During this time, Fritz worked in silence at

his cajack, constructing a second seat in it. I alone knew his intention.

We next prepared our provisions. Two hams were cooked, cassava cakes, barley bread, rice, nuts, almonds, and other dry fruits; and for drink we took a barrel of water, and one of hydromel. These, with our tools and fishing implements, loaded down the boat.

30. ENCOUNTER WITH A LION

WE SPENT a day in preparing our cargo, and then embarked in a favorable breeze on a slightly ruffled sea. Francis and his mother were left to guard the shore, and we gaily put off, amid their prayers for our safe return. We took with us some of our domestics; young Knips, the successor of our good old monkey, Jack's jackal, Flora, Braun and Folb. Jack and Fritz were in the cajack; Ernest and I in the canoe loaded with our provisions and animals.

We followed the cajack, steering our course through the shoals and rocks with great difficulty. The rocks were covered with the whitened bones of walruses and sea horses, and Ernest made us stop to collect some of these for our museum.

We attained the promontory behind which, Fritz said, was the Bay of Pearls. Arch rose above arch, column above column. It resembled the front of an old Gothic cathedral, with the blue sea, instead of a marble pavement, and with columns washed by the waves. We penetrated into the vault; it was somber and gloomy, lighted only by a few appertures in the rock.

The noise of our oars frightened the peaceable salanganes, and they flew about in great numbers. But when our eyes became habituated to the darkness, we saw with pleasure that every niche and corner was filled with their nests. These nests resembled white cups, transparent as horn, and filled with feathers, and dry sticks of some sort of perfumed wood.

I resolved to gather a considerable number of these nests, only taking care to leave those which contained eggs or young ones. Fritz and Jack climbed like cats along the rocks and detached the nests, which Ernest and I placed in a large sack we had brought. I was glad it was soon filled, as the boys were tired and I could not bear to see them suspended on the ladder above the water.

Fritz had assured me that the canal which flowed through the vault was navigable. The flood tide carried us rapidly forward toward the other extremity of the cavern, through the magnificent passage, its roof covered with stalactites in a thousand forms. At length we issued into a beautiful bay. We were struck with surprise, and remained resting on our oars in silent admiration. The water was so calm and pure that we could see the fish far below us. I recognized the white fish, the shining scales of which are used as false pearls. My sons could not understand how a little stone could be worth so much more than the fish scales, fully as brilliant.

"It is not the object itself," said I, "but the difficulty in procuring it which costs so much."

We appeased our hungry stomachs with ham, fried potatoes, and some cassava cakes. And after having lighted fires along the coast, to keep off wild beasts, we left the dogs on shore, boarded the canoe—with Knips on the mast as vedette—drew the sail over our heads, wrapped ourselves in our bearskins, and sank to rest.

At daylight, after a frugal breakfast, we commenced our labors in the pearl fishery. With the aid of the rakes, hooks, nets, and poles, we brought in a large quantity of the precious oysters. We heaped them all up in a pile on the shore, so that the heat of the sun would cause them to open.

Toward evening the coast was so beautiful that we made an excursion to a little wood where we had heard turkeys gobbling all day. We separated, each taking one of our animals. Ernest, with Folb, entered the wood first. Jack followed him, while Fritz and I remained a moment to fix our guns. A few moments after, we heard a report, then a scream from Jack, followed by another report. Fritz unhooded his eagle, I snatched up my gun, and we ran in the direction of Jack, who was screaming, "Papa! Papa! Quick! I am killed! Quick! Come!"

The poor boy lay face to face with an enormous boar with formidable tusks, who had knocked him down, and he thought himself lost.

His brothers ran up quickly; two shots well fired freed him from his terrible enemy. Ernest acquainted me with the affair.

"I had entered into the little wood," said he, "with Folb, when suddenly the dog set off in pursuit of a wild boar, who was sharpening his tusks against a tree with a terrible noise. At that moment Jack came up; Coco sprang furiously upon the boar, while Folb attacked him on the other side. I approached cautiously, passing from one tree to another, until I was near enough to fire. Coco, however, had received such a terrible blow that he lay senseless.

"Jack then fired, but missed, and the boar, turning round, set off in pursuit of him. Jack would have escaped if a projecting root had not tripped him up. Down he fell. I fired, but missed, and the boar began to butt poor Jack with his head. However, Braun and Flora rushed in, and, seizing the animal by his ears, held him so firmly he could not stir. Then Fritz's eagle flew to the head of the boar, and began picking at his eyes. Fritz now fired, and hit the animal directly in the throat. It fell right across Jack's body. He could not disengage himself, and I ran up to help him. He groaned dreadfully, and I thought he was wounded, but he took Fritz's arm and walked away, while I remained by the boar. It was not without some surprise that I then saw Master Knips with some large black tubercles, with which the ground was covered. I gathered two or three which I put in my gamebag. Look at them."

The young naturalist presented six tubercles resembling potatoes, but with penetrating odor. I opened one, tasted it, and discovered that they were excellent truffles, of a perfumed, delicate flesh, marbled with white. I congratulated my son on his discovery.

Night had come on; we lighted our watch fires, swallowed a morsel of meat, and retired to our canoe. The dogs were again left on shore. We were soon asleep, and dreaming of the absent ones at our beloved Felsenheim.

On rising the next morning, accompanied by the dogs, we set out to look at the dead boar. He was enormous—between a boar and a buffalo in size, and his head was indeed frightfully large.

"My advice is," said I, "instead of dragging the immense carcass away, we cut off what we want and let the rest alone."

My sons agreed, and we cut off the hams and head of the wild boar. Some branches of trees furnished us with sleds to carry the pieces, and the dogs drew them to the shore.

Chance brought us an important discovery. Ernest found on the branches we had cut for our sleds a sort of nut. He opened one. Instead of a kernel, it contained a beautiful fine cotton, of a deep yellow, which I recognized as being the real Nanking cotton. This cotton owes its name to a province in China, where it is cultivated with much care. We made a large provision of these nuts, and dug up two young trees to carry to Felsenheim.

Having heard that boar's head was very fine eating, we cooked it with truffles, in the Otaheitan manner. Fritz and Ernest dug a deep ditch, while I cleaned the head and heated some stones. When these preparations were finished, we placed the head, stuffed with truffles, and seasoned with salt, pepper, and nutmeg, in a ditch, covered it with red-hot stones and a thick layer of earth. While our supper was cooking, we suspended the hams over the smoke of the fire, and tranquilly sat down to talk over the events of the day. Suddenly a deep, prolonged cry rang from the forest. It was the first time we had ever heard such unearthly tones. The rocks echoed it, and we felt seized with sudden terror; the animals commenced howling horribly.

"Build the fire!" cried Fritz, jumping up and seizing his gun. "While I discover the danger in my cajack, you retire the canoe."

We threw on the fire all the wood at hand, and without loss of time, regained the canoe. Fritz jumped into the cajack, and was soon lost in the obscurity.

During all this time the roaring continued, nearer and nearer. Our dogs gathered round the fire, uttering plaintive moans. I imagined that it was a leopard or a panther, but doubts did not last long.

We soon discovered by the pale light of our fires a terrible lion, considerably larger and stronger than those I had seen in the royal menageries of Europe. In two or three leaps he bounded over the space which separated the wood from the shore. He stood immovable for a moment, and then, lashing his flanks with his tail, and roaring furiously, he crouched down as if to spring on us. This frightful pantomime did not last long; every moment he would run to the stream, lap up some water, and then return. I remarked with mortal anguish that the animal came nearer and nearer to the shore. At length he lay crouched down, his flaming eyes fixed directly on us. Half in fear, half in despair, I raised my gun, and was about to fire, when suddenly I heard a report, the animal bounded up, gave a tremendous yell, and fell lifeless on the earth.

" 'Tis Fritz," murmured my poor Ernest, pale with terror. "O God! Protect my brother!"

"Yes, it is he," I cried, "our brave Fritz has saved us, let us go to him." In two strokes of the oars we were on shore, but our dogs, with an admirable instinct, began to bark terribly. I did not neglect this indication; we threw more wood on the fire, and again jumped into the boat. It was just in time. A second enemy rushed from the forest. It was not so large as the first, but its roar was frightful. This time it was a lioness, the companion of the superb animal just killed. The lioness ran straight up to the corpse of her late partner, smelled it, and licked up the blood which had flowed from the wound. When she was convinced that he no longer lived, she set up a howl of rage, lashed her sides and opened her enormous mouth, as if she would devour us all.

Again Fritz fired, and the shot, less fortunate than the first, only broke the shoulder of the animal. The wounded lioness rolled on the sand, foaming with rage, but all three of our dogs rushed upon her. Braun and Folb seized the animal in the flanks, and Flora caught hold of the throat. Another shot would have put an end to the combat, but I was afraid of wounding the dogs. I jumped from the boat, and, running up to the animal, who was held fast by the dogs, I plunged my hunting knife direct to her heart. The blood spouted out, and the lioness fell. But the victory had cost us dear; our poor Flora lay dead under the terrible wounds she had received from the fangs of the monster.

Fritz now ran up and threw himself into my arms, as did Ernest and poor Jack, shaking with terror. We lighted our torches and found poor Flora, with her teeth still clutching the throat of her enemy, while the royal couple lay extended on the sand. Full of sorrow for the loss of our faithful Flora, we gazed on the terrible beasts.

"Let us thank God," I observed, "for the wisdom with which He had endowed men, that they may be able to conquer such fearful beasts."

"Poor Flora!" said Fritz, as he gently detached the dead body of our dear dog from that of the lioness. "She has done for us today what our old ass did with the boa. Ernest, see if you can fabricate an epitaph."

"I have been too terribly frightened to make any rhymes."

"Tush! Go and meditate while we dig the grave of our poor hunter, and be ready when we are done."

Flora's funeral was held by torchlight. We dug a grave, and silently placed in it the remains of the faithful animal, and a flat stone marked her resting place. Ernest composed the following legend, which he read to us, saying that he was too frightened for poetry, and Flora must be contented with prose.

HERE LIES:
FLORA, A DOG
REMARKABLE
FOR HER COURAGE AND DEVOTION
SHE DIED
UNDER THE CLAWS OF A LION,
ON WHOM
SHE ALSO INFLICTED DEATH.

"Ernest," said Fritz," "you write fully as good prose as poetry."

At sunrise next morning we deprived our noble prey of their superb furs. Jack wanted to make a mantle of a lion's skin, such as Hercules wore after his victory in the Nemaean forest. But I adjourned all such arrangements.

The following morning we set sail for Felsenheim. Fritz set off before us, serving as pilot. But when he had conducted us through the vault, and over the shoals, he rowed up to our canoe. Handing me a paper, he shot off again like an arrow.

I opened the paper quickly, and found that, far from having forgotten the albatross and the smoking rock, he was going in search of the unfortunate being! Fritz rowed so fast, I could barely halloo through the speaking trumpet, "Return soon, and be prudent," before he was out of sight.

We gave to the cape where he left us the name of the "Adieu Cape." I prayed that Fritz might return safe, and begged my rowers to redouble their endeavors to arrive early at Felsenheim. My good Elizabeth would be worried at our long absence of three days.

We finally arrived without accident, and the treasures were joyfully received. The truffles and the lionskins, the pearls, the Nanking, became the objects of a thousand questions, but they could not drive away the thought of Fritz.

I had not yet spoken to my wife of the reason for Fritz's absence, but now it was my duty to do so. I therefore confided to her the secret of the albatross, and the dear woman, to my surprise, was calm and resigned. She only prayed with me for his success.

Five days had thus passed away and still Fritz had not returned. His mother was so anxious that I launched the pinnace for a new excursion to the Bay of Pearls. Early the next day we bade adieu to Felsenheim, and soon were in sight of the promontory of the bay. Suddenly the vessel ran against a black mass, and was nearly thrown over by the shock. The boat soon righted, and I perceived that the obstacle was a marine monster of the family of blowers, for into the air spouted a column of water mingled with blood. I instantly pointed the cannons of the pinnace, and a discharge of artillery prevented the huge monster from overturning us. The waves carried the enormous body to a sandbank, and there it lay like a stranded ship.

Suddenly Ernest cried out, "A man! A savage!" said he. He pointed out to us in the distance a sort of canoe dancing over the waves. The person seemed to have perceived us, for he advanced and then made toward a projecting point, as if to communicate his discovery to his companions.

We had fallen in with a band of savages, and we began to fortify our boat against their arrows, by making a bulwark of the stalks of maize and corn we had brought with us. We loaded our cannons, guns, and pistols, and, everything arranged, we stood ready behind our rampart, resolved to defend ourselves as long as we were able. We dared not advance, for there was the savage.

On Ernest's advice, I took up the speaking trumpet and bellowed out with all my force some words of Malay, but still the canoe remained immovable, as if its master had not comprehended us.

"Instead of Malay," said Jack, "suppose we try English." So saying, he caught up the trumpet, and in his clear, loud tone pronounced some common sailor phrases, well known to all who have ever been on board ship. The device succeeded. The savage advanced toward us, holding a green branch in his hand. Nearer and nearer he came, and at last we recognized in the painted savage our own dear Fritz.

31. THE STRANGER ON SMOKING ROCK

WHEN we had freed Fritz from our oft-repeated embraces, we poured all manner of questions upon him. I demanded an answer on two points only—whether his excursion had been satisfactory, and why he had dressed himself like a savage, causing us such anxiety.

"As to the purpose," said he, with unconcealed joy, "I have attained it"; and the young man pressed my hand, which he held in his. "For the other, I mistook you for a tribe of Malays, and disguised myself by painting the upper part of my body with powder, soaked in water. The Malay words convinced me more and more that you were enemies, and you would still have been in fear of *me* if Jack had not bawled out those sailor phrases in his unmistakable voice."

We laughed over the farce, and Fritz, drawing me aside, said joyously, "I have succeeded, Papa; the hand of God conducted me to the dwelling place of the poor shipwrecked girl—for it was a woman who had written those lines. Three years she has lived on that smoking rock, all alone, destitute of everything! Can you believe it! But the poor girl has conjured me not to betray her sex, except to you and my mother. I have brought her with me. She is near by, on a little island just beyond the Bay of Pearls. Come and see her. Oh! Do not say anything to my brothers. I want to enjoy their surprise when they find that I have brought them back a sister, for I am sure she will allow them to call her so."

I ordered the family to make ready to depart. Fritz, who had changed his dress and washed off his disguise, flew about, hastening his brothers. Then, jumping into his cajack, he piloted us through the shoals and reefs along the coast. After an hour's sailing he turned off toward a shady island not far from the Bay of Pearls. We sailed close to the shore and fastened the pinnace to the trunk of a fallen tree.

Fritz, quicker than we, was on shore and had entered a little wood in the middle of the island before we had landed. We followed him into the wood, to a hut, built like those of the Hottentots, with a fire burning before it, on which some fish were cooking in a large shell. Fritz uttered a peculiar kind of halloo.

From a large tree descended a young and handsome sailor, who, turning his timid eyes on us, stood still, as if he dared not approach!

It was such a long time since we had seen a man—ten years—that we remained stupefied. Our hearts felt for the young stranger, but our tongues remained dumb.

The silence was broken by Fritz, who, taking the young sailor by the hand, advanced toward us. "My father, my mother, and you, my brothers," said he in a voice broken by emotion, "behold a friend—a brother—that I present you, a new companion in misfortune—Sir Edward Montrose, who, like ourselves, has been shipwrecked on the coast."

"He is welcome among us," was the general cry, and, approaching the young sailor, whom I easily recognized as being a woman, and taking her by the hand, I comforted and encouraged her. I assured the seeming man that among us he would always find food and sustenance. My wife and myself would be his parents, and my sons his brothers. My wife, moved by compassion, opened her arms, and the young sailor rushed into them, bursting into a flood of tears, as he thanked us for our kindness.

The most lively joy now reigned in our little circle, and his brothers poured question after question upon Fritz, who joyfully replied, "I will tell you all afterward. Let us attend now to our new brother." Supper was served, and my wife brought out a bottle of her spiced hydromel to add to the feast. Everybody spoke at once, and my sons addressed their new companion with such vivacity as to embarrass the timid stranger.

My wife saw his distress, and, as it was late, she gave the signal for retirement, taking the sailor with her on the pinnace where she said she intended to provide a bed for him that would amply console him for the uncomfortable nights he had hitherto passed. We then separated, my wife and the stranger retiring to the boat, while my sons and I stopped to light and arrange our watch fires.

The newcomer naturally became the subject of conversation, Fritz recounting to his brothers the whole history of the albatross. He spoke of his thoughts and actions; but in the excitement of his narration, he forgot himself and his secret. He called the young sailor "Emily."

"Emily! Emily!" repeated his brothers, who had begun to doubt the mystery. "Emily! Fritz has deceived us, and Sir Edward is a girl! Our adopted brother is a sister!"

The next morning it was comic to see the embarrassment and awkwardness with which my sons approached one whom they had the day before embraced as a brother. My poor boys appeared to great disadvantage by the side of the beautiful English girl. The name of sister was pronounced with reserve and embarrassment. Emily was much astonished at the discovery the young men had made, and retreated to the arms of my wife. But, recovering herself, she advanced, and extending her hand to each one of the boys, gracefully demanded for the sister the friendship they had extended to the brother.

Gaiety was re-established, and we sat down to a breakfast of fruits, cold meat, and chocolate of our own making, which was a great treat to my new daughter, recalling to her mind her native land.

After breakfast I weighed anchor to return to the Bay of Pearls and our cachalot stranded on the shore. Arrived there, we debated in what manner we could carry away the oily substance with which the head and dorsal bone of this animal is filled. Unfortunately we had no barrels in which we could gather the precious product.

Emily mentioned a process she had seen employed in India: that of putting the half-liquid substance in wet linen bags. We immediately put the excellent idea into practice. I gathered all the sacks I could find, and dipping them in the sea water, stretched them open with pieces of branches.

We took the canoe and the cajack and set off, leaving the two women under the safeguard of Turk, and taking with us Folb, Braun, and Coco. The monster lay extended like a huge wall. Our dogs ran up to it, and a moment later we heard dreadful howling. We hastened up and found our brave dogs valiantly contending with a troop of black wolves, who were devouring the whale.

Four wolves lay stretched upon the sand, but the dogs had paid dearly for their victory, and the ears of Folb especially were dreadfully torn. Jack dressed their wounds with some hydromel. Fritz, after having armed his feet with cramp irons, climbed like a cat up the back of the monster, and cut off the enormous head with a hatchet, and then with a ladle dipped the spermaceti out of the head, and emptied it into one of the sacks which I held ready, while Francis covered the outside with wet sand and mortar, forming a solid crust through which none of the grease could escape. Our sacks were soon full, for as fast as Fritz emptied the head the cavity was filled by a fresh supply from the backbone. We then cut a quantity of willows, and wove them into little pointed caps, with which we covered the sacks, in order to shield them from the sun and birds of prey, who were assembling in great numbers.

We now returned. The tide was high, but the load was too heavy for the boat; we therefore were obliged to leave it and return to the verdant little island, which we had named "Good Rencounter," because there we had first found Emily.

After having recounted our adventures, and shown our four fine black wolves, we were invited by our dear housekeepers to sit down to an excellent dinner. I was undecided as to what means I should adopt to transport the spermaceti to the island; for the pinnace could not approach the bank near enough, without risk of running aground, and our other boats were not large enough. Everyone gave his advice. When it came to Emily's turn, she observed in her soft voice, "If you are willing, my dear papa, while you and my brothers are engaged in that disgusting tannery, I will promise to bring over your sacks."

The next morning, before my sons were awake, Emily prepared for her expedition. She took a bladder of fresh water, a basket of provisions, and lightly descended the ladder of the pinnace, seated herself in Fritz's cajack, untied it, and rowed off with a grace and ease that surprised me.

I would have called her back, but the little vixen gaily kissed her hand, and soon was far on her way toward the bank of sand. She had chosen just the right time. The tide was rising, and had just commenced to wet the bottom of the sacks. The adventurous girl jumped on shore, fastened all the sacks by cords to a rope she had with her, and tied the rope to the cajack. Again embarking, she drew after her all the sacks, the contents of which, being light, floated like bladders on the water.

It was now full noon. We sat down to table, and, after dinner, began our preparations for setting out for Felsenheim. We packed up everything we had, including Emily's treasures, both those she had saved from shipwreck and those she had made herself. Fritz had made her a box which held them all, and they really were very curious, consisting of clothes, ornaments, domestic utensils, and all sorts of articles which she had made in her exile, out of the scanty materials she had at her disposal.

Emily now bade adieu to the island that had received her during her short sojourn. We called the bay in which we were anchored, "Happy Bay," for the joyful meeting we had had there. We now took the direction of the Bay of Pearls, where we were obliged to make a short stay before returning to Felsenheim, to which we were impatient to introduce our new companion.

32. THE LIMEKILN — FRITZ'S STORY

FRITZ, seated in his cajack, piloted us safely through the rocks and shoals into the bay. Everything was found just as we had left it. But the birds of prey had left bodies of the lions and the wild boar only heaps of whitened bones.

We wished to go direct to Felsenheim, but an unexpected discovery detained us longer. On the shore was a sort of rock which could be easily converted into lime. The discovery was precious, and I resolved to establish a limekiln without delay upon the beach. We quickly made one to suit our purpose, but the calcination of the stones occupied us much longer, and we were obliged to sit up a great part of the night. During this time we made some barrels of pieces of pine bark, circled with strong withes of willows, with a round piece of bark serving for the bottom, and another for the cover.

To enliven our labor, and to abridge the length of the evening, I persuaded Fritz to give us a more complete account of the manner in which he had found our new sister. The boys formed a circle about Fritz, who thus commenced his narration.

"You all remember," said he to his brothers, "the manner in which I left you, after having given my father a letter about my intended excursion. The sea was calm, but I had scarcely passed the Bay of Pearls, when suddenly a violent wind arose, gradually increasing to a perfect hurricane—rising waves, rain, thunder, and lightning. My little bark could not resist the tremendous sea, and I abandoned myself to the current.

"After several hours the wind fell and the air calmed, and my canoe again found its equilibrium. I was far from all the familiar places, on a coast entirely new in the conformation of the rocks, the gigantic cliffs, the vegetation, the animals, and the birds which flew about me. My first care was to look carefully around and see whether some light smoke rose behind the rocks. There was nothing as yet. But, full of hope, I rowed along the coast and passed the night in the cajack, after having made a miserable supper on pemmican.

"Continuing my journey the next morning, a changing coast showed majestic rivers, which flowed onto the sea.

"After seeking shelter from the heat in some shade under the trees, I sailed on a long time without being able to land; the rivers and shores were both defended by elephants, lions, panthers—all the ferocious animals of creation. After traveling several leagues farther, the shore appeared peaceable, but desolate. I felt reassured and resolved to land and procure a repast. Accordingly, I fastened my cajack as strongly as possible, and jumped lightly to the shore. Being hungry, I lighted my fire and prepared a juicy dinner from a fat goose which I had shot while landing, and a dozen oysters.

"The next day took me through country different from any I had ever yet seen. There were beautiful green plains, dotted over with clumps of towering palms. On I sailed.

"Suddenly there appeared before me a long throat, armed with rows of strong teeth, distended to its full capacity, to take in at one mouthful myself, the cajack, and the oars. Seizing one of the oars, I drove it with all my strength direct into the yawning mouth of the alligator, who disappeared in an instant, leaving a long trace of blood behind him. I had wounded him.

"I did not remain long on this river. But I had escaped from one danger only to fall into another. At a little distance from the River of Alligators, the trees were loaded with rare and beautiful birds, among which were lyrebirds, parakeets, hummingbirds, and birds of paradise. I landed, attached my cajack to the bank and walked up to the wood, holding my eagle unhooded in my hand. I cast him off, and he returned with a superb parakeet, whose flame-colored feathers sparkled in the sun. While I was examining him, I heard behind me a light rustling on the sand, and I turned carelessly round. Not twelve paces from me there was a splendid royal tiger with open mouth, crouched down as if about to spring upon me. Horror paralyzed me, when suddenly my brave eagle, comprehending my danger, flew boldly at the advancing tiger, and began to pick at his eyes. This timely succor enabled me to collect my senses, and leveling my gun, I discharged its contents into the right flank of my enemy! Then two pistol balls lodged in the throat completed my victory. The tiger lay dead, but my victory had cost me my poor eagle, who fell at the same time. The tiger had torn him in pieces. I picked him up, weeping bitterly over my loss, and carried him to the cajack, hoping someday to have him stuffed and placed in our museum.

"I quitted the shore in sorrow and prayed to my heavenly Father to give me strength to continue my voyage. I doubled a little cape and suddenly, from the summit of the gray rocks bordering the coast, I perceived a light cloud of smoke rising in the air. I turned my canoe in the direction of the long-sought-for signal. At last I landed, and, with infinite difficulty, scrambled up the rocks until I arrived at a platform on which I perceived a human creature. At the noise which I made in approaching, the individual, who was arranging the fire, rose, perceived me, uttered a cry of surprise and joy, then, joining his hands, stood still, as if waiting for me to speak. Notwithstanding the midshipman's dress she wore, her exclamation, and the delicate contour of her features, convinced me that I was in the presence of a female. I stepped about ten paces from her, and calling to my memory all I knew of English, I said in a subdued tone, 'I am the liberator whom God has sent you. I have received the message of the albatross.' I must have pronounced those words very badly, as Emily did not at first comprehend them. I repeated them, however, and after a few moments we understood each other well enough to make a mutual interchange of our feelings. Gestures, looks, accents all filled up the blank that words left vacant. I spoke to my new sister about the castle of Felsenheim, Falcon's Next, our shipwreck, and ten years' sojourn on the coast.

"She recounted to me the history of her childhood, her shipwreck, and existence on the Island of the Smoking Rock, making a fine story for my papa to write out in the long winter evenings. Emily graciously invited me to supper, after which we passed the remainder of the night—I in my cajack, she in the branches of a tree, where she always slept for fear of wild beasts. The next morning we again met and shared the breakfast Emily had prepared of fruit and broiled fish. By then the sea looked so calm I thought we had better start. After packing up all her curiosities, and putting them on board the cajack, we set off.

"We sailed a long time, but an accident happened to my little bark, and I was obliged to cut in at the little island which you have called 'Good Rencounter,' in memory of our meeting. It was there I left my new-found sister, who, doubtful of her reception, begged me to go on and ask permission of my father to bring her among them. I consented, and my canoe having been repaired, I took the well-known route home. It was then that I encountered you, feared that you were pirates, disguised myself, and played you such a trick."

"Oh! I am sorry it is done," cried Jack, as Fritz finished his story. "But you must now tell us the history of our sister."

Fritz was about to commence a new narration, but I stopped him, and advised him to take a little rest before he talked any more.

33. EMILY'S OWN STORY

FRITZ'S story had detained us until midnight. The audience was not at all sleepy, however, but our labors on the morrow would require strength and agility, and I deemed it necessary to cut short the narration. So each one sought his accustomed resting place, either on shore or on the pinnace.

The next morning, when all the family assembled for breakfast, Fritz's enterprise and courage became the subject of conversation, and brought on the story of last night, and that Emily's history was to open the day. I wanted the dear girl herself to tell it, but she was so lively and busied in her domestic occupations that I could do nothing with her. Fritz was therefore entreated to resume his recital.

"As soon as I was able to understand my new sister," he said, "I asked her by what course of events she had been thrown on the desert coast where I now found her.

"She told me that she was born in India, of

English parents, and that her father, having served as major in a British regiment, obtained the command of an important English colony. The commandant, Montrose, Emily's father, had the misfortune to lose his wife only three years after his marriage. All his affections centered in their only child. He took charge of her education, developing to the highest degree her fine qualities. In addition he endeavored to make her a strong, healthy woman, capable of facing and resisting danger. Such was Emily's education up to the age of sixteen. She managed a fowling piece as well as a needle, rode as gracefully and firmly as the best cavalry officer, and shone resplendent in her father's brilliant salons.

"Major Montrose, having been appointed colonel, was ordered to return with part of his regiment to England. He was forced to separate from his daughter, as naval discipline did not allow women on board a line-of-battle ship in time of war. It was arranged, however, that she should set sail the same day in another ship, in care of the captain, an old friend of her father's.

"The voyage at its commencement was prosperous and agreeable, but a terrible tempest arose. The ship was thrown off her course, and a furious wind drove her down upon our rocky coast. Two shallops were launched, one chance of safety to the shipwrecked. Emily found a place in the smaller, the captain in the other. The storm continued, the boats were separated and the smaller broken in pieces. The poor girl alone, of all the crew, escaped death. The waves carried her, half fainting, to the foot of the rock where I discovered her. She crawled under the shade of a projecting rock, and, sinking on the sand, slept for twenty-four hours. There she passed several days in dark despair, with no nourishment but some birds' eggs which she found on the rocks.

"At the end of that time, the sun reappeared and the sea grew calm. The poor castaway thought of the crew in the large shallop and, in the hope that they might see her, established signals of distress. As she wore a midshipman's uniform on board ship, by order of her father, she had a box in her pocket containing a flint, knife, and other articles. She carried wood to the summit of the rock, and there kindled a fire, which she never allowed to die. In the first dreary days of Emily's exile she had to contend against all the horrors of hunger and the desert. How thankful she felt for the semimasculine education that her father had given her; it endowed her with courage and resolution far beyond her sex. She comprehended the extent of her situation, placed her trust in God and hoped on. She built a hut, fished, hunted, tamed birds—among others a cormorant which she taught to catch fish. She lived alone, with no earthly succor, for three long dreary years."

Fritz stopped. His eyes fell upon the heroine of his story, who could hardly conceal her embarrassment.

"My child," I said, "you are but another proof that God never withholds His aid from those who desire it. That which you have done for three years a poor Swiss family has done for ten, and Heavenly aid has never been withheld from them."

After a little time for commentaries on Emily's history, I gave the signal for work. The manufacture of lime had proved successful, and we prepared to depart for Felsenheim.

Toward evening the pinnace was laden with all that we could carry away. The poetic description we had given concerning the salt grotto, and our aerial palace at Falcon's Nest, had rendered Emily exceedingly curious.

The next day we weighed anchor just as

dawn was breaking. The sail of the pinnace fluttered gaily in the fresh breeze, and Fritz's cajack, containing himself and Francis, went before us as pilots. When we hove in sight of Prospect Hill, I proposed to stop at the farm-house, but Fritz and his brother asked permission to go on home, to have all in readiness for us. I consented, and they set out.

From Prospect Hill we sailed to Shark Island, where we secured a fine quantity of the soft wool of the Angora rabbits. From Shark Island we turned toward Felsenheim, and soon a salute of ten guns greeted our ears. This produced a very good effect, Dr. Ernest only regretting that the salute was not composed of an odd number of guns. "An even number," he said, "is entirely contrary to general usage."

We returned the polite salute by a salvo of eleven guns, performed by Jack and Ernest in true cannoneer style. Fritz and Francis received us in the canoe at the entrance of the bay, and followed us to the shore. They landed before us, and the moment Emily's foot touched the sand, a hurrah sounded through the air. Fritz, springing forward, presented her his hand, like a gallant cavalier, and led her up to the portico of the grotto. There a new spectacle awaited us.

A table was spread in the middle of the gallery, loaded with all the fruits that the country produced. Bananas, figs, guavas, and oranges rose up in perfumed heaps upon flat calabashes. All the vases, coconut cups, and ostrich eggs mounted on turned wooden pedestals, urns of painted porcelain, all were filled with hydromel and milk; while a large dish of fried fish, and a huge roast turkey, stuffed with truffles, formed the solid part of the repast. A double festoon of flowers surrounded the canopy above the tables, sustaining a large medallion on which was inscribed, "Welcome, fair Emily Montrose!" It was as complete a reception as our means would allow. Emily sat down to table between my wife and myself, Ernest and Jack took their places, while the two caterers of the feast, each with a napkin on his arm, did the honors of the table.

We passed from the table to the interior of the grotto, and our young companion had the apartment next to ours for her use. She could not restrain her admiration at what our industry had accomplished. She was much astonished that a man and wife and four children could have effected so much.

The chateau in the tree at Falcon's Nest had fallen into decay, and we passed a whole week in fitting it up. We then set out for Waldegg to gather our rice and other grains, for the season was advancing, and violent showers already warned us of the coming winter. Emily gave proof of an intelligence and goodwill which rendered her assistance very valuable, and she inspired everybody with such zeal and industry that when the winter set in we were prepared for it. Ten years had accustomed us to the terrible winters, and we calmly listened to the wind and storm as it raged furiously without. We had each year reserved for the winter several sedentary occupations, in which our new companion proved her skill and industry. She excelled in weaving and plaiting straw, osiers, etc.; and, under her direction, we made some light straw hats for summer, some elegant baskets, and conveniently arranged gamebags. My wife was delighted with her adopted daughter, and Ernest found a companion whose fine education rendered her a conversable and intelligent woman. In fact, Emily had become to my wife and myself a fifth child, and a beloved sister for my sons.

34. CONCLUSION

IT IS with a thousand different sensations that I write the word *conclusion.* It recalls to my mind all that has passed. God is good! God is merciful, is the reigning sentiment in my heart. I have many reasons for heartfelt gratitude to a gracious providence.

It was toward the end of the rainy season, the wind had lost its violence, and a patch of blue sky could now and then be seen. Our pigeons had quitted the dovecot, and we ourselves ventured to open the door of the grotto and tasted the fresh air.

Our first care was to take account of the damage suffered by our gardens, and then set out for our more distant possessions. Fritz and Jack proposed to make an excursion to Shark Island, to inspect our fort and colony there, and they set off in the cajack.

My sons, on their arrival, examined the interior of the fort, and assured themselves that nothing of importance was damaged, then began to look around and see if there was anything on the horizon, but all was blank. Wishing to see whether the cannons were in good order, they began firing away, as if they had all the powder in the world. But to their astonishment and emotion, a moment after, they heard distinctly three reports of a cannon in the distance! They could not be mistaken, for a faint light toward the east preceded each report. After a short consultation, the two brothers hastened home to recount their adventure.

We had heard the reports of the cannons they had fired, and we could not imagine why they were hurrying back so soon. On they came, and, jumping on shore, fell into my arms articulating, "Oh, Papa, Papa, did you not hear them?"

"Hear what?" I said. "We have heard nothing but the noise your waste of powder made."

"You have not heard three other reports in the distance?"

"No."

"Why, we heard them plainly and distinctly."

"It was an echo," said Ernest.

This remark nettled Jack a little, and he replied rather sharply—

"No, Mr. Doctor, it wasn't the echo. I think I have fired cannons enough in my lifetime to know whether that was an echo or not. We distinctly heard three reports of a cannon, and we are certain that some ship is sailing in this part of the world."

"If there really is a ship on our coasts," I said, "who knows whether it is manned by Europeans or by Malay pirates? Instead of preparing for deliverance, should we not make preparations for defense?"

We organized a system of defense for our safety. We watched alternately under the gallery of the grotto to be ready in case of surprise. But the night passed quietly away, and in the morning the rain commenced, and continued so violently during two long days that it was impossible to go out.

On the third day the sun reappeared. Fritz and Jack, full of impatience, resolved to return to Shark Island and try a new signal. I consented, but instead of the cajack, we took the canoe, and I went with them. We hoisted our flag over the fort, while Jack, ever impatient, loaded a cannon and fired it, but scarcely had the report died away in the distance, when we distinctly heard a louder answering report in the direction of Cape Disappointment.

Jack could not contain himself for joy. "Men, men," cried he, dancing about us. "Men, Papa; are you sure of it now?" And his enthusiasm communicating itself to us, we hoisted another and larger flag on our flagstaff. Six other reports followed the first one we had heard.

Overpowered with emotion, we hastened to our boat, and were soon in the presence of the family. They had not heard the seven reports, but they had seen our two flags flying and they were eagerly waiting for news.

I ordered that everything in the grotto should be put in a place of safety. My three youngest sons, my wife, and Emily set off for Falcon's Nest with our cattle, and I embarked in the cajack with Fritz, to reconnoiter. It was near midday when we set out, we coasted along without discovering anything, and the illusion of the moment began to dissipate. On more calm reflection, however, the certainty that we had heard the seven reports of the cannon kept up our courage.

Suddenly, on doubling a little promontory which had hitherto concealed it from us, we beheld a fine European ship majestically reposing at anchor, with a longboat at the side, and an English flag floating at the masthead.

No words can express the sentiments which

filled our souls. We elevated our hands and eyes toward Heaven, and thus returned our thanks to God for His great beneficence. If I had permitted it, Fritz would have thrown himself into the sea and swum to the ship, but I was afraid, that, notwithstanding the English flag, the vessel before us might be a Malay corsair, which had assumed the false colors in order to deceive other vessels. We remained at a distance, but could see all that was passing on board the vessel. Two tents had been raised on the shore, tables were laid for dinner, quarters of meat were roasting before blazing fires, men were running to and fro, and the whole scene had the appearance of an organized encampment. Two sentinels were on the deck of the vessel, and when they perceived us they spoke to the officer on duty who stood near, and who turned his telescope toward us.

"They are Europeans," said Fritz. "You can easily judge from the face of the officer. Malays would certainly be more dusky than that."

Fritz's remark was true, but yet I did not wish him to venture nearer. We remained in the bay, maneuvering our canoe with all the dexterity of which we were capable. We sang a Swiss mountain song, and when we had finished I cried out through my speaking trumpet these three words, *"Englishmen, good men!"* But no answer was returned. Our song, our cajack, and more than all our costume, I expect, marked us for savages. The officer made signs for us to approach, holding up knives, scissors, and glass beads of which savages in the New World are generally so desirous. This mistake made us laugh, but we did not approach. We wished to present ourselves before them in better trim. We contented ourselves with exclaiming once more, *"Englishmen,"* and then darted off as fast as our boat could carry us.

We passed a whole day in preparing the pinnace, and loading it with presents for the captain, as we wished him to see that those whom he had taken for savages were beings far advanced in the arts of civilization. We set off at sunrise. The weather was magnificent, and we sailed gallantly along, Fritz preceding us as pilot.

When we could clearly distinguish the ship we were filled with joy. My sons were dumb with pleasure and eagerness.

"Hoist the English flag," I cried, and a second after, a flag similar to the one on the ship, fluttered from our masthead.

If we were filled with emotion on seeing a

European ship, the English were not less astonished to see a little boat with flowing sails coming toward them. Guns were now fired from the ship and answered from our pinnace, and joining Fritz in his cajack, we approached the English ship to welcome the captain to our shores.

The captain received us with that frankness and cordiality that always distinguishes sailors, and conducted us to the cabin, where a flask of Cape wine cemented the alliance between us.

I recounted to the captain, as briefly as possible, the history of our shipwreck, and our sojourn for ten years on this coast. I spoke to him of Emily, and asked him if he had ever heard of her father, Sir Edward Montrose.

The captain not only knew him, but it was part of his instructions to explore those latitudes where, three years before, the ship *Dorcas,* which had on board the daughter of Commander Montrose, was supposed to have been wrecked, and to try to discover whether any tidings of the vessel or the crew could be ascertained. He manifested the greatest desire to see her, and assure her that her father was alive.

He informed us that a tempest of four days'

duration had thrown him off the course which he followed for Sydney and New Holland, and thus he had been driven on this coast, where he had renewed his wood and water. "It was then," he added, "that we heard the reports of cannon, which we answered. On the third day new discharges convinced us that we were not alone on the coast. We resolved to wait until, by some means or other, we discovered who were our companions in misfortune. But we find an organized colony, and a maritime power, whose alliance I solicit in the name of the sovereign of Great Britain."

This last sally made us laugh, and we cordially pressed the hand which Captain Littleton extended to us.

The rest of the family were waiting some distance off in the pinnace. We took leave of the captain, who, ordering his gig to be manned, arrived on board our vessel almost as soon as we did. We received him with every demonstration of joy and friendship, and Emily was half wild with happiness at the sight of her fellow countryman, and one who brought intelligence of her father.

The captain brought with him an English family, fallen ill in passage. Mr. Wolston, a distinguished machinist, his wife, and two daughters. My wife offered Mrs. Wolston her assistance, promising that her family should find every comfort and convenience at Felsenheim if they would return with us. They gladly consented, and we set out with them, taking leave of the captain, who did not like to pass the night away from his ship.

My readers can form an idea of the astonishment of the Wolston family on seeing our establishments. We pointed out to them Felsenheim with its rocky vault, the giant tree of Falcon's Nest, Prospect Hill, and all the marvels which were comprised in our domains. A frugal repast in the evening united both families under the gallery of the grotto, and my wife prepared, in the interior, apartments and beds to receive the newcomers.

The next morning Mr. Wolston came up to me, and stretching out his hand, spoke as follows. "Sir," said he, "I cannot express all the admiration that I feel on regarding the wonders with which you are surrounded. The hand of God has been with you, and here you live happily, far away from the strife of the world, among the works of creation, alone with your family. I came from England to seek repose; where can I better find it than here? And I shall esteem myself the happiest of men if you will allow me to establish myself in a corner of your domains."

This proposition of Mr. Wolston filled me with joy, and I immediately assured him that I would willingly share with him the half of my patriarchal empire.

Mr. Wolston hastened to communicate to his wife the success of his application, and the morning was devoted to the joy and pleasure that this news caused. But considerations of a painful nature occupied my mind. The ship which now presented itself was only the second we had seen in ten years, and probably as long a period might elapse before another appeared. Should we let Captain Littleton and his ship leave us without any addition to his crew? These questions affected the dearest interests of our family. My wife did not wish to return to Europe. I was myself too much attached to my new life to leave it. We were both at an age when hazards and dangers have no attraction, and ambition had resolved itself into a desire for repose.

But our children were young, their life was just commencing, and I did not think it right to deprive them of the advantages which civilization and a contact with the world presented. And Emily, since she had heard that her father was in England, did not conceal her desire to return. Although we regretted losing this amiable girl, yet it was impossible to detain her. So at last I decided to call my children together. I spoke to them of civilized Europe, of the resources of every kind which society offered to its members, and I asked them if they would depart with Captain Littleton, or be content to pass the remainder of their lives upon this coast.

Jack and Ernest declared that they would rather remain. Ernest, the philosopher, had no need of the world to interrupt his studies; and Jack, the hunter, found the domain of Falcon's Nest large enough for his excursions. Fritz was silent, but I saw by his countenance that he had decided to go. I encouraged him to speak; he confessed that he had a great desire to return to Europe, and his younger brother, Francis, declared that he would willingly accompany him.

Mr. Wolston's family was also divided. One of his daughters remained and the other went on to New Holland. These family arrangements were very painful, and when they were finished I hastened to inform the captain of the *Unicorn*. He readily consented to take our four passengers.

The *Unicorn* remained eight days at anchor, and we employed them in preparing the cargo which was to be the fortune of our voyagers on arriving in Europe. All the riches that we had amassed—pearls, ivory, spices, furs, and all our rare productions, were carefully packed and put aboard the ship, which we also furnished with meat and fruits.

On the eve of my sons' departure, I exhausted myself in a last conversation, in which I advised them always to carry out the principles in which they had been instructed, and so to live in this world that we might be united in the next. I then gave Fritz this narration of our shipwreck and establishment on the desert coast, enjoining him expressly to have it published as soon after his arrival as possible. This desire on my part was exempt from all vanity of authorship, and had for its only object and hope that it might be useful to others as a lesson of morality, patience, courage, perseverance, and trust in God.

Perhaps someday a father may take courage from the manner in which we supported our tribulations; perhaps some young person will see, in the course of this narrative, the value of varied education and the importance of becoming acquainted with first principles.

I have not written this as a learned man would have done, and all my results may not have been arrived at according to the correct theory. But we were in an extraordinary position, and were obliged to depend on our own resources. We placed our entire trust in God, and He ever watched over and protected us.

We none of us slept much during the last night. At the dawn of day the cannon of the ship announced the order to go on board. We conducted our children to the shore. There they received our last embraces and benedictions.

The anchor has been weighed, the sails unfurled, the flag run up to the masthead, and a rapid wind promises speedily to separate us from our children.

I will not attempt to paint the grief of my dear Elizabeth—it is the grief of a mother, silent and profound. Jack and Ernest are weeping bitterly, and my own grief and heartfelt sorrow is, I confess, badly concealed.

I finish these few lines while the ship's boat is waiting. My sons will thus receive my last blessing. May God ever be with you. Adieu, Europe! Adieu, dear Switzerland! Never shall I see you again! May your inhabitants be always happy, pious, and free!